DANGEROUS HERITAGE

DANGEROUS HERITAGE

Past secrets are best left undisturbed…

Robert S Birch

Dedication

For all victims of genocide

Acknowledgement

I would like to thank my wife for producing the artwork and my whole family for their endless patience during editing.

CONTENTS

Prologue

August 1946

Harold Wintern's life may have been unremarkable, but his death was notable because it dispelled a popular myth. We are sometimes told that life ends with bright lights, beckoning loved ones, and an instantaneous review of our memories and achievements. That might be so when the transition between life and death is a little fuzzy, but when life is extinguished violently at the hand of an expert there is no opportunity for final introspection. And Harold Wintern's assassin was a grand master. He had crept up on his victim and severed the main artery in Harold's throat so precisely that the blood flow to the poor man's brain was cut instantly. Harold might have been struck with a hammer such was the speed that he died. There were no grand thoughts or recollections, and certainly no realization of what had transpired; just a brief sense that something was wrong and then darkness.

Harold's assailant had taken no pleasure in the act. He offered a specialized service that was difficult to find, and there were few who could match his high standards. He made an unlikely killer as he was physically slight, and he walked with a distinctive limp from an old knife wound. That fight had nearly cost him his own life, and it had been a painful way to learn that physical confrontation was inefficient and unpredictable. It was far better to prepare properly and ensure that a victim died unknowing and without a struggle. Less risky and less distressing.

Earlier, the assassin had hidden his motorcycle in a wooded glade across the road from the house and found a discreet vantage spot on a nearby tree stump. In the late afternoon, he watched a woman leave the front garden pushing a child in a pram, and he knew that her route would take thirty minutes to complete before she returned home as evening fell. As she stepped into the lane, the man had been surprised to see Harold emerge waving a piece of forgotten muslin. He had called out the woman's name which made the assassin's work seem unnecessarily personal. On the other hand, it confirmed that his victim was at home and sticking to a daily routine. It was reassuringly predictable. The woman would walk with the child in the Somerset countryside, and Harold would lay the table for the evening meal before settling down to listen to the news.

Once the pram had disappeared around the corner, the assassin crossed the road and walked alongside the building to the rear. He was certain that he was unobserved. The Winterns' neighbours lived on the other side of the semi-detached building, but he knew they were on holiday in Brighton. The back door had been left open, and he had crept into the kitchen noting the cutlery neatly arranged on the table. The clipped voice of a radio news presenter came from the parlour beyond, and the man was even able to note that certain food items would no longer be subject to wartime rationing. The newscaster was correct; things were looking up.

The parlour was adjacent to the kitchen and extended through the house to a hall and the front porch. The assassin was familiar with the layout, and he knew how the room was furnished. He found Harold sitting on the settee and facing away from him. Even better, his victim's head had drooped with the onset of a small evening nap; his breaths were steady and slow, and his awareness was at a low ebb. It had therefore been the simplest matter to creep up behind the sleeping man, yank his head back and bring the hours of careful planning to a messy culmination.

Harold's body slumped forward. A red stain spread

down the front of his chest and scarlet spots began to transform the cream-coloured cushions into a garish work of art deco. The man listened carefully but the birds' evening chant continued uninterrupted. He checked his watch and saw that he had nearly twenty-five minutes before the woman returned with the child. And he was certain how she would arrive because she was a creature of habit too. She would be hot and sweating. She would push the pram through the front garden and park it inside the porch before opening the inner door and switching on the hall light. It was always the same, and it was a routine he would exploit.

The assassin drew the front curtains and left the house through the back door before following a path that snaked between well-kept flower beds and a narrow lawn. At the end of the garden, a painted wooden gate provided access to a farmer's field where some scruffy sheep eyed him briefly before returning to the clover, heads down and jaws active. After a short distance, he arrived at a disused byre next to some trees and was pleased to find that a jerry can of petrol was still in its hiding place under some old feed sacks.

Back at the house, the assassin splashed petrol around the parlour and onto the stair carpet, making sure that Harold and the settee got a particularly good drenching. Leaving the empty can on the table, he went into the front hall and removed the electric light bulb from the ceiling fitting. He spotted a small bronze figurine on the mantelpiece and used it as a makeshift hammer to tap on the light bulb until the glass broke. The vacuum dissipated with a pop, and when he held up the stem to the light, the assassin could see that the precious filament was still intact. He carefully returned the glassless bulb to its fitting and then repeated the procedure in the kitchen. If either light was switched on, the thin wire would shine brightly for only an instant before it burnt through, but that would be long enough. Both entrances were now booby trapped.

The man's final task was also in the kitchen. The gas cooker was a new model, and it was spotlessly clean. He looked behind the appliance and pulled on the main supply pipe with both hands. Initially, the pipe was reluctant to part, but eventually it came away at the main union and invisible gas snaked slowly, hissing and unimpeded, into the room. Outside, the birdsong was starting to diminish, and it was time to leave. Gas was spreading through the house, and the assassin was careful not to cause a spark through inadvertent clumsiness. He closed the parlour curtains, collected the jerry can, and left through the back, door leaving Harold with the radio newscaster for company.

The shadows were lengthening as he stowed the empty can in the sidecar of his motorbike and sat on the tree stump to wait. Normally he would try to put distance between himself and the scene, but his employer had insisted that he should personally verify that the job had been successful. Whilst this added a small degree of risk, the man was confident that discovery was unlikely. The house was far enough away from the village to allow him time to leave before anyone came.

As he waited, the assassin's expectation rose. A tractor passed by, and he wondered whether he had been discovered. However, the engine noise receded uninterrupted, and a comforting silence returned. He mustn't jump at shadows; he only had to wait a further fifteen minutes before she arrived. However, on this occasion the man was mistaken because it was only a few moments later that a baby's cry pierced the silence, and it came from the rear of the cottage. The assassin didn't like surprises. The woman always entered the building at the front. Always. And yet, he reassured himself, it didn't really matter because his modifications to the kitchen light fitting at the rear of the building would take care of it.

Sure enough, when the explosion ripped through the house a few moments later, he was left in little doubt that the job was a success. Glass and splinters flew by in a tremendous roar, and smoke and flames billowed from the frameless front windows as the fire consumed possessions and spread quickly into the timbers. However, the assassin needed to be certain. He left the glade and picked his way through the rubble littering the side of the building. The heat from the spreading fire was becoming intense, and he was forced to cover his mouth with his jacket to avoid choking on the acrid fumes. The blast had been most destructive at the rear of the cottage. The back wall was demolished, leaving the kitchen roof hanging precariously at one end. He could see that it would collapse soon as the remaining timbers were already burning. He peered inside the ruined kitchen hoping to see human remains, but the smoke and flames obscured his view, and he contented himself with the thought that anybody inside would soon become fine ash. The job was over, and the sight of two twisted pram wheels protruding from some plasterwork confirmed his assessment.

Returning to his motorbike, the assassin kick-started the engine and sped down the twisting lane away from the village and the oncoming crowd. The following day, the local paper named two adults and a child who were missing and believed to be dead following a gas explosion and fire at a country cottage in Somerset. The article stated that the police were still trying to trace the two adults living in the adjoining property who were believed to be on holiday somewhere on the south coast. The article noted that the mains gas supply had been installed only that year, and the reporter reminded readers of the importance of having appliances checked regularly.

Close by, the assassin's employer finished reading the same report. He lowered the paper and looked out over the grounds of a large country house. Mature trees made a spectacular frame for the immaculate lawns and gardens, although on this occasion the beauty of the view went unnoticed as the employer's mind was elsewhere. The assassin's work had been excellent, he thought, and there were no loose ends. It had taken years to kill off the truth, but his agent had snuffed it out and then burnt all the evidence with a skill that was worth every penny. It was hugely satisfying and quite a relief. The man sat on a leather chair, put his feet up on an antique desk, and started humming a popular tune. His certainty felt good, and the matter required no further consideration.

Chapter 1

The Funeral

November 2000

A wintery draught swept through the small North Yorkshire crematorium, stiffening the backs of the congregation and causing Michael Calvert to shiver. He watched as his mother's coffin disappeared into the void behind the altar, and a tear welled up, trickled down his cheek and stained the lapel of his suit. Was the tear for his mother or himself? He wasn't sure. The vicar had told him that funeral services were meant to provide comfort for the living, but he didn't feel comforted whatsoever. It was the year 2000, and the next millennium had started with all the implied optimism of a new era. But for Michael the year was unimportant, and it felt merely like the beginning of another chapter chronicling his decline.

As the small curtains closed behind his mother's final journey, a potent blend of grief, guilt and regret accentuated his loneliness. Grief, for he had loved his mother. She had always supported him even though he had done little recently to deserve her loyalty. Regret, because he knew that she had died feeling disappointed in him. And guilt, because there was much that should have been discussed before the end but wasn't. And that was his fault. As his mother confronted terminal cancer, she had been dismayed to see anger and self-pity corrode her son's life. They had spoken regularly enough but only to exchange platitudes, and they had not really talked. Near the end, she had tried to broach the subject, but Michael had cut her off, and the matter of his tattered life went unexamined. How that must have hurt her, he thought, and how utterly selfish he had been. And for that Michael was truly sorry.

The vicar touched him on the arm, and Michael realized that the service was over and that everyone was waiting for him to leave. He wasn't looking forward to the next part of the proceedings. The minister had explained that they would stand at the back of the chapel to meet everyone as they filed out. Michael knew that he would exchange brief words with people he hadn't met for years. They would offer empty words of comfort and wrap their collective arms around him. But their concern would be temporary, and Michael would soon be forgotten once they returned to the safety of their own comfortable lives. He sighed at the depth of his own cynicism and turned to follow the vicar past the rows of expectant faces.

Many were indeed strangers but there was one face at the rear of the chapel that was as intensely familiar as it was unwelcome. He looked away quickly from his ex-wife, pretending to be deep in thought and tried to beat back his rising anger. So, she had made the journey up from London. He should have expected her to attend the funeral as his late father and mother had loved Isobel as though she was their own daughter. Isobel had kept in touch with them, and Michael knew his mother had seen plenty of her since Michael's divorce almost five years earlier. No doubt, his mother would have kept Isobel fully informed on the extent of his decline he thought wryly.

At the rear of the church, the throng seemed to go on forever and it passed by in a blur of small talk and regrets. While Michael shook hands and offered his cheek, his mind was on Isobel, and he was dreading the moment when she would arrive. Perhaps he could escape before she came out. As the crowd started to peter out, he saw her in the vestibule searching for her coat. With a curt thanks to the minister and a quick handshake, Michael turned and started to walk away. Isobel emerged, hurriedly greeted the confused vicar and called after him.

'Michael. Wait.' The sound of her high heels tapped rhythmically on the path as she rushed to catch up.

Damn, he thought. I was too slow. He turned to face her, mentally preparing himself. 'Hello, Isobel, I didn't know you were coming. Thanks for making the effort.'

She ignored his empty greeting. 'I'm very sorry about your mum, Michael. I know how close you were.'

Michael looked at her trying desperately to think of something polite to say. Isobel had just turned forty, she was slim and blond, and a highly attractive woman. The trouble was that she was now Patrick Godwin's attractive woman. And therein lay the problem. Michael wanted so much to set aside the hurt and anger, but when it came to his ex-wife the only detail that came to mind was *that* day five years earlier when their marriage became irreparably broken.

Michael and Isobel had been at university together. They married soon after graduation and had settled into domesticity. She had foregone a career in public relations in favour of a family life although they had produced only one child, their daughter, Sophie. Michael had become a highly successful reporter for a major national newspaper. His career had flourished, and everyone expected that he would soon be promoted to foreign editor. He loved his job, but the long weeks spent working overseas undermined his relationship with Isobel. He could never admit this to himself because when he considered his marriage, he could only ever recall the details of the culminating scene rather the underlying causes for its failure. The truth of the matter was that Michael had taken his wife for granted, and for Isobel, loneliness had transformed love into disappointment which became boredom and finally resentment.

Michael had been oblivious to the approaching crisis until one day, *that day*, he had come home early from an assignment to find his colleague, Patrick Godwin, doing something to Isobel that should have been the sole preserve of her husband. He had walked from the tube station to their house and was surprised to see a smart and seemingly familiar sports car parked in the drive. He entered quietly through the unlocked front door and realized that everything he held dear was finished. There were unmistakable noises from the living room. He had tiptoed to the door, and in an act of brutal self-harm he looked in knowing what lay beyond but nonetheless compelled to record the details. They had been naked and entwined, his wife perched on the edge of the settee and Patrick Godwin locked energetically between her legs whilst kneeling on the floor. But it wasn't the spectacle that had made the matter so unbearable, it was the noise. The rhythmical slap of vigorous contact had intermingled with Isobel's enthusiastic cries and created a soundtrack of betrayal that played over and over in his mind. Michael's sense of loss was excruciating; he just couldn't shed the memory, and it had poisoned his life ever since. He had turned silently to leave just as his wife's eyes opened wide as the shock of discovery intruded on her exertions.

Oblivious to Isobel's calls, Michael ran from the house and had entered an inexorable decline. He returned two weeks later to collect some belongings, and Isobel had tried to explain how weeks of solitude had eaten away at their marriage. She told him that it wasn't that he had treated her badly. It was just that he had taken her for granted and treated her like a favourite car or other treasured possession. However, her shrill explanations were drowned out by the slap, slap, slap of adultery playing endlessly in Michael's ears. He had quietly gathered up his meagre belongings and left without a word. Subsequent discourse had taken place through the expensive offices of their respective lawyers.

Isobel's presence at the funeral had now broken this enforced separation, and it was in danger of releasing a torrent of bitterness. Michael looked at her, determined to remain civil on this of all days. If nothing else, he would try to do it for his mother.

'I know you were close to mum,' he said calmly. 'And she would have been grateful that you have made the effort to come. But I have nothing to say to you, Isobel. Nothing at all.'

Isobel looked disappointed but not entirely surprised. 'Look, Michael. I know how you feel but…'

'How I feel?' he snapped. 'You have no idea. Really. No idea whatsoever. If you did, you wouldn't have come today.'

Her eyes moistened with regret and, Michael noted angrily, with something else - pity. 'Michael, I don't know what to say,' she said gently. 'We have never closed this have we? I'm truly sorry that I hurt you, but it's been five years now. You must let it go. It's time to move on, not for my sake but for your own and…and for Sophie's.'

Anger was joined by guilt. The birth of his daughter had been a wonderful moment, and they had been extremely close. Sophie was fifteen when the marriage had ended, and she had been devastated. Isobel had been granted legal custody which Michael had not contested. At first, he made the effort to see his daughter in carefully scripted meetings that ensured no inadvertent contact with Isobel or Patrick. He remembered Sophie's birthdays. A card, some cash. But the visits had become infrequent, and they had eventually stopped about three years earlier. It wasn't that he didn't love her, of course he did. It was just that Sophie was a tangible product of his failed union with Isobel, and he couldn't bear to be reminded of it.

'Oh, I see,' he said scathingly. 'Is that what this is about? You've come to save the errant father from himself, have you? Don't you think that's a bit rich coming from you, Isobel?'

She sighed as the inevitable confrontation loomed. 'No, it's not like that, Michael. Sophie is almost a grown woman now. She loved your mother and wanted to come today, but she wouldn't because…' Isobel tailed off, unsure of how to frame her words. 'Please call her, Michael. I know that it will be difficult for both of you because of the time that has gone by. But please try. You were always so close, and it would…well…it would be good for both of you.'

Michael stared silently at his ex-wife. This was not going well, and there was a danger that too many home truths were about to be brought out into the open. He wasn't ready for them. Not today.

'I'm sorry Isobel. I can't talk about what is *good* for me right now. I have to go to the pub and eat sandwiches with people I don't really know. As I said before, we have nothing to discuss.' He turned and started to make for the chapel gates.

'Michael!' Her voice was compelling as she approached for one final attempt. 'Whatever I did is over. Finished. I'm not here to judge you, and I know I won't get your forgiveness. But for the sake of your mother and daughter you need to go away, take a good look at what you've become, and then move on. You just can't go on like this. If nothing else, you have a responsibility to yourself.'

The old Michael might have recognized that she was right, but the years of brooding, hurt and anger were deeply entrenched, and he wasn't listening. The shrill urgency in her voice served only to remind him of her noisy enthusiasm on that other occasion, and the memory of it swamped any chance of reason. Michael didn't even look at Isobel, and for the second time in five years he walked off without uttering a word.

***

Four hours later, the funereal small talk was finally over, and the last of the mourners had left the pub leaving Michael alone. He was glad it was over, but before he could go home he needed to collect some personal effects from his parents' house. As he approached the building, the sight of his childhood home rekindled vivid memories and increased his sense of solitude. He entered the house and wandered through the downstairs rooms remembering the family events that they had once housed. It seemed that if he listened carefully, he could even hear snatches of conversations from years earlier. His father pronouncing on the local football results whilst trying to eat a piece of his wife's Victoria cake. His mother pretending to listen while gently scolding her husband for dropping crumbs onto the floor. It all seemed so recent and vivid, and yet with only the memory of his parents now inhabiting the place, the house seemed empty and soulless.

A neighbour had helped him to clear his mother's belongings, and all that was left was a box of personal effects sitting alone on the living room floor and some pieces of furniture that would eventually fall under the hammer at the local auction house. Michael studied the box and wondered how it was possible to pack a lifetime of personal experiences inside such a small container. It had been a long day, and he felt drained by the funeral and his unexpected encounter with Isobel. He knew the contents would release a flood of fresh memories and emotions, and he decided it would be better to leave the carton unopened until he felt less raw. He glanced at his watch. It was getting late, and he needed to drop off the keys at the estate agent. With a final look around the sitting room, he gathered up the box, locked the front door and went outside to his car. The light was starting to fade as he turned and looked for the last time at the smart frontage of his childhood home. So many memories he thought, and good ones too. Those were important, and he would hold on tightly to them, but what he really needed was to create some new memories that were worth keeping. However, that would require a change in his outlook and there lay the central problem. Michael recognized that he had lost his way, but he couldn't see how to break out from the endless cycle of introspection and bitterness that was blighting his life. Michael couldn't see it, but his mother had considered the matter carefully, and before she died she had left her son the means for personal repair. She knew it might not work, but she had left it for him, nonetheless. It was waiting for him inside the cardboard box on the rear seat of his car.

Chapter 2

The Search

November 2000

The day after the funeral, Michael rose late but well rested. He lived near the city centre of Leeds and, as usual, his apartment was a tip. Discarded clothes littered the bedroom, unwashed dishes were piled in the kitchen sink, and his desk was obscured by half-empty cups and loose paper. He would tidy up today he promised himself as he hurried out. But only after coffee and a pastry.

Michael's usual breakfast haunt was at Lucille's, a small café down the street. The middle-aged woman serving behind the counter smiled at his unshaven face and reached automatically for a large mug with one hand and a fruit Danish pastry with the other.

'Hello, Michael, you're looking your best again today. Have you been burning the candle at both ends?'

Michael stuck his tongue out at her. 'Thanks, Lucille, your help and kind support for my welfare are always deeply appreciated.' She laughed. Their exchange of banter was a daily event, and she regretted that it never progressed beyond a couple of friendly sentences. He was a tall, attractive man, although beyond the jocular exterior she sensed a brooding sadness. He had never shown any interest in her, though, and so their exchanges were superficial, and the details of his personal life remained a mystery.

Michael paid for his coffee and a sticky bun, smiled at the disappointed Lucille and took up his usual seat in the window. He placed a blank greetings card on the table, and he sipped his coffee thoughtfully as he searched for the necessary words. Stung by Isobel's remarks, he had decided to write a very short note to his daughter; something to try and break the ice, although he had no idea what he could say that might bridge the gap between them. Sophie had just started her second year at St Andrew's University in Scotland where she was studying the History of Art. Beyond that, he knew little of her life. He sighed, expecting that the card would probably be discarded or that he would be told to get lost. At least he would have tried, though.

With the card dispatched, Michael ignored his natural instincts and blitzed the untidy flat with energy fuelled by caffeine rather than enthusiasm. As his reluctant hands worked on the apartment, he noticed the carboard box laid on the floor in his small office. It made an excellent excuse to stop work. He opened the lid and had a quick rummage through an orderly stack of papers and old family photographs that lay at the top. Beneath these, he noticed a brightly coloured shortbread tin with his name on it. He prised open the lid clumsily and the contents fell out. A black and white photograph fell onto the floor face up, and he saw his mother and father smiling up at him from the carpet. He rescued the old print and looked at it carefully. It was taken at the seaside, probably Scarborough he guessed, knowing that the resort had been his parents' favourite haunt in the late fifties and early sixties. The couple were lying in the sand and laid in front of them on a towel was a baby dressed in light summer clothes and a white sun hat. It was Michael.

The baby Michael had been smiling at the moment of capture, and he imagined the sound of gurgling and chortling as the unseen photographer had completed his task. The couple looked carefree. His father proud and content, and his mother serene and graceful. They had possessed so many admirable properties, he thought. It was a shame that they hadn't passed on more of them to their son. But then again why should they? He was not related to his parents by blood as Michael had been adopted at birth so there was no reason to expect any genetic advantages. He picked up the remaining papers and realized that they were all about him. Old school reports mingled with early art projects. There was a story he had written in primary school, and a small craft project he had made of wire pipe cleaners as a present for his mother when he was aged seven. All these things, seemingly trivial, but kept treasured over the years. He glanced down. The last remaining item was an envelope that his mother had addressed to him. He worried it might contain something unbearably personal. It did, but what she had to say about it was entirely unexpected.

My dearest Michael,

It has been lovely to see you during these last precious weeks, but I feel that there are many things that have gone unsaid that should have been discussed. Your father and I always tried hard not to interfere in your life, and I certainly have no wish to start now from beyond the grave. That said, I do know that your life has lacked purpose and joy over the last few years and for that I am deeply saddened. I was fortunate that my own marriage lasted so long and that it was filled with happiness, so it is difficult for me to understand how you have felt since you parted with Isobel. What I did learn when your father died was that memories of love and happier days can make a huge difference to the grief that follows the physical loss of a loved one. In fact, as my own days draw to an end, it is those old moments of happiness that bring me enormous comfort and mental strength.

I know that the matter of your adoption has always seemed to be unimportant to you as we have been the only parents that you have known. For us, it was a momentous occasion. We had tried for so long to have our own children that it was truly wonderful when you arrived. We had to wait a further year until the court issued the adoption order and until then I couldn't quite believe that you were here to stay for good.

Some adoptive parents never tell their children about their background, or they leave it until a child becomes sixteen. In your case, we decided right from the start that it would always be an open subject that we would never conceal from you. We wanted you to grow up aware of your roots and secure in the knowledge that our love for you was undiminished by the lack of blood ties. We knew little about your natural parents other than they were both young, your father was a trainee estate agent, and your mother was a trainee schoolteacher. Your natural mother had named you Robin, but we wanted to change this and call you Michael after your grandfather. I'm afraid that the name Michael Calvert does not bear much resemblance to Robin Belton, but the baby Michael didn't seem to notice the change!

Looking back, I have often wondered what it must have been like for your natural mother to have given up her baby. Apparently, her own family background and life had been extremely difficult and full of adversity, and the social worker told us that this had influenced your mother's decision to have you adopted. I suspect that it would have been a traumatic ordeal for her, but in those days, there was little else a girl could do if she had an accident. With this in mind, we should not judge her harshly. Indeed, I expect she still does that herself, especially on your birthday.

Over the years, I have often wondered why you have made no effort to discover your natural parentage especially now that the law permits you to find out. Perhaps it was because when you were a child, we always discussed the matter openly, and you grew up almost believing that adoption was the natural way that children came into *the world. Or maybe you thought it would hurt our feelings in which case you couldn't have been more wrong. In either case, I do wonder if this is now the moment when you should consider the matter. I am not trying to persuade you to go out and find a new family now that your own has passed on. No, my understanding is that such searches rarely result in happy long-lost reunions and more often than not they end in frustration and disappointment. But that said, it would be a journey of self-discovery with an unknown destination and surely that rouses your professional interest. You could learn more about yourself and your hereditary roots, and perhaps in doing so you might come to terms with some of the demons in your present life. If nothing else, it would give you some fine material for one of your excellent magazine articles. Just choose the right magazine this time!*

Anyway, it is something for you to ponder, my son. I wanted to say for one last time that we have always loved you. Please don't be hard on yourself as I know that there is always a tendency for those left behind to blame themselves for all manner of nonsense. Indeed, I did it myself for a while after your father died until I learned to rely on those happy memories. And you gave me plenty of those.

With love as always,

Your affectionate mother

His mother's words reactivated Michael's grief, but he managed a thin smile. Did he blame himself for the barrier between them at the end? Yes, of course; his mother had always known him better than he knew himself. It was funny how she had remembered the magazine though. Since leaving his foreign affairs job in London, Michael had drifted from regional reporting for a local paper into freelance work and then finally short story writing for any magazine that would publish. And he wasn't fussy. He suspected that his mother had been disappointed with these changes, but the nearest she had come to criticism had been a jokey remark following the publication of one of his stories in a magazine for young women embarrassingly called *Hello Girlie.* Well done, she had said. *Hello Girlie,* today, and *Time Magazine* tomorrow. Beggars can't be choosers, he had responded, but only half in jest.

But Michael knew that this wasn't the main point of his mother's letter, and he stared at it thoughtfully. It was true that he had never regarded his adoption as anything worthy of deep consideration, and it had never crossed his mind to conduct any kind of research into his ancestry. His mother and father had always been exactly that: his parents. They didn't need replacing, and his biological parents would in any case be complete strangers. Moreover, such an intrusion into their lives would surely be unwelcome after all these years. His mother knew these risks, but the matter had nonetheless preyed on her mind. Was she right? Would such a search help him to address some of the issues in his own life? Michael didn't think so. But was his journalistic interest aroused? For sure. The recent decline in the quality of his professional work had coincided with a marked deterioration in his imagination and artistic flair. Material for short stories had been in short supply and his output was drying up. Was it possible that his mother had come up with a good idea for a new piece of work albeit for different reasons? It was certainly an intriguing prospect. He had never been told his birth name before, and his mother's revelation sparked his curiosity. Why was Robin Belton adopted? What sort of person had his natural mother been and what was so difficult about the life she had led? These were questions that could only be answered if they were posed directly. However, to ask his natural mother, he would first need to find her, and he didn't even know her name.

As a reporter, Michael had occasionally searched for reclusive individuals, but they were usually well-known public figures, and he often had a tip off to get him started. He certainly knew little about adoption or how to trace lost relatives without a recent lead. As he studied the internet for advice, he marvelled at the amount of information that was freely available, and he quickly realized that he didn't need any third-party assistance. He therefore ignored the adverts for private investigators with their exorbitant fees, and he reached into a drawer for a fresh notebook. It was the start of a new project.

As he scribbled furiously, Michael learned that UK adoption law changed in 1975 to allow adoptees over the age of eighteen to discover their original birth name and to gain access to their adoption records. Since then, individuals could apply to the Registrar General who would release the information but only after counselling. At that point, the adoptee would learn their birth name and be able to obtain a copy of their original birth certificate showing the name of their natural mother. The Registrar would also authorize an adoptee to make an application to the local authority for the release of the court adoption papers. These would provide intimate details on the circumstances of the adoption including the reasons for it. Michael also noted that in 1991 the law had changed again, and the Registrar was now required to maintain a system called the Adoption Contact Register. This allowed natural parents to lodge contact details which would be released to the adoptee if both sides indicated that they were willing.

Michael leaned back in his chair. The Registrar General was clearly a good starting point except that Michael already knew his original name was Robin Belton and this alone was sufficient information to obtain a copy of his original birth certificate. Perhaps he should just make a start with the information he already possessed. On the other hand, the court adoption papers could be useful, and the Contact Register would certainly be the easiest way to make progress but only if one of his natural parents had used the facility to lodge their details. Was this likely? He didn't think so. The old laws had tried to make adoption a final and irretrievable decision, with the details kept secret and known only to the state. The idea was that once a child was given up for adoption then nothing except chance could ever bring the two sides together. This was as much to protect the identity of the natural parents as it was for the child. Michael thought it would probably be a fruitless line of enquiry, but he was keen to make progress, and he scribbled a quick note to the Registrar explaining the situation and asking for the Contact Register to be checked and his adoption papers to be released without the usual formalities.

Michael knew that the Registrar was unlikely to reply quickly, and he was impatient to make progress. The name Robin Belton didn't suggest anything familiar or, for that matter, anybody famous or aristocratic, he noted with a tinge of disappointment. Perhaps it was just as well, he thought. Famous families wouldn't appreciate a stranger coming along and forcing open their cupboards to look for hidden skeletons. He rescued his notebook from underneath a growing pile of papers and returned to the screen with a list of websites he had noted earlier. In the old days, individuals had to visit the Public Records Office at Somerset House to search manually through the official indices of births, marriages and deaths. These days, a few companies offered internet access to the records, some for free. Individuals could search the index electronically by name and date, and once an item of interest was located, the viewer could then pay a small fee to the General Register Office for a copy of the certificate.

Michael chose one of the free websites and excitedly entered the name Robin Belton and his date of birth in 1960. There was a pause while the database was searched and then the details came up. There had been nobody else called Robin Belton born on that day and so his index entry was the only one displayed. It was fascinating to see the official record of his birth especially as the name Robin Belton ceased to have any legal purpose on the day that his adoption was finalized. Michael peered at the screen. The index showed his name, his mother's maiden name,

Belton, and that Michael had been born in the district of Holderness in East Yorkshire. There was also a reference number that he would need to obtain his original birth certificate. There was nothing in the record to show that he was later adopted and there were no other details. The entry just looked like millions of others. Humans are a prolific lot, he mused wryly, as he ordered a copy of his original birth certificate and paid the small fee electronically with a credit card.

By the time the certificate arrived a few days later, Michael found himself watching the door for the mail to be delivered. He tore open the envelope and looked down on the familiar red certificate with the crown embossed at the top. The Registrar had recorded his details with black ink and flowing handwriting that Michael supposed must be a prerequisite for the appointment. He looked closely at the detail. His birth had taken place at Seacroft Maternity Home in East Yorkshire. That made sense as Seacroft was quite close to Hull where his adoptive parents had lived at the time. The certificate showed that his name was Robin, a male. The name, occupation and address for his father had not been recorded, and the relevant boxes merely had a line drawn through them as though the details were unimportant. His natural mother's details were there though. She was called Jocelyn Faith Belton, a trainee schoolteacher with an address in the coastal resort of Bridlington, further up the coast from Seacroft and funnily enough, on the way to his parents' favourite holiday spot at Scarborough. Finally, there was a diagonal line drawn across the right-hand edge of the document and written in the middle was the word 'Adopted' and the signature of the Registrar. Michael was intrigued. This document had lain undisturbed for years. He tried to imagine the young Jocelyn stood in front of the Registrar declaring the details of her new son but knowing already that she would soon hand him over to strangers. He wondered what had gone through her mind. Would she have been sad, reluctant or relieved? It was hard to imagine, and only Jocelyn could provide the answers to such personal questions.

Despite his satisfaction at finding the official record of his existence, Michael knew that he would need more than his birth certificate to locate his mother. His mother's Bridlington address shown on the certificate was forty years old and the electoral roll confirmed that she was no longer living there. Michael wasn't surprised. Jocelyn would surely have moved in that time, and it was quite possible that she had since married and was living elsewhere under a different name. He knew Jocelyn was an unmarried mother in 1960, but she might well have married later. If he could find a marriage certificate, then he could check to see if she had produced any more children, his half siblings. He would then be able to search to see whether any of those children had grown up, married and had their own offspring too. Each time he added a piece to the family tree, he could order a birth or marriage certificate, and with every certificate there might be the possibility of finding a relative's address. The more recent the certificate, the more likely it would be that an address would be active. It sounded simple enough, but Michael suspected that it might not be so straightforward. People's lives were much more unpredictable than that. Rather like his own, he reflected bitterly as he returned to the computer.

It was then that Michael encountered a difficulty that would later play an important role in the sequence of events that his search had already triggered. It would explain the past, but one day it would also help to save a life. It concerned the registration of his mother's birth which he found difficult to find.

Michael had guessed that a young unmarried mother having an accidental first child in 1960 would probably have a date of birth occurring sometime between 1935 and 1945. He used this assumption to conduct an electronic search of the digital records, but after examining a long list of hopeful entries he had come up empty handed. Resorting to viewing actual photographic images of the pages from the original index, he had ploughed through hundreds of entries for Belton before he finally found an entry for the birth of a Jocelyn Faith Belton on 2nd August 1939 in Islington. However, the way that the entry had been entered in the index was strange and explained why his search of the digital records had failed. Instead of Jocelyn's name appearing as a typed line in the correct alphabetical point in the index, he found it entered in tiny handwriting at the bottom of the page. Why would the entry be handwritten? It was almost as though it had been entered later as an afterthought. He couldn't think of a reason for this, but her birth certificate might have more details, so Michael ordered it straight away.

Whilst Michael waited for Jocelyn's birth certificate to be returned, he continued to search for her within the official records but became disappointed and a little downhearted when he was unable to make further progress. There was no record of any marriage or of any further children, and after checking fruitlessly for a record of her death, Michael decided that it was as though Jocelyn Belton had disappeared off the official state radar.

Eventually her birth certificate arrived, however, and it gave Michael an opening that he could exploit. The certificate was much like his own, and even the Registrar's curly handwriting looked the same. It confirmed that Jocelyn had been born on 2nd August 1939 in Whittington Hospital in the London Borough of Islington. The details of her father were blank. Another single parent. Jocelyn's mother was recorded as being Flora Harriet Belton, also Wintern, now Wainwright. That was a lot of surnames which implied that his grandmother, Flora, had been married more than once. However, Michael was puzzled after noticing that Jocelyn's birth had only been registered in 1968 following an affidavit written by Flora Wainwright. That was nearly thirty years after Jocelyn had been born.

Why should that be he wondered? Had Flora forgotten to do it at the time of Jocelyn's birth or was there some other reason? It was a mystery, but Michael's instincts told him it was probably an important episode in Jocelyn's life and one that he needed to remember, so he highlighted it carefully in his notebook.

Chapter 3

Service

December 1938

Mildred Grieveson was unsurprised when she found Flora vomiting into a large washing bowl. Mildred was the cook at Barrington Hall. She was a kind woman who took a close interest in the welfare of the other staff, particularly the younger ones who she often took under her wing. The sight of Flora bent over the bowl reminded her of Mary, the previous parlour maid. Both girls had arrived as servants in their teens, both were without relatives, and both had spent too many hours up in the master's study. But Mildred had hoped that was the extent of any similarities. Mary had successfully hidden her condition for several months, but she was eventually caught out and the matter was referred to the master, Sir Roland Pendleton. Dismissal had been instant, and the young maid was quickly dispatched from the house but bearing some physical reminders to stay silent. Mr Denton, the butler, had observed her departure, and in a moment of uncharacteristic indiscretion he later described Mary's injuries to Mildred and some of the other kitchen staff.

'Battered and bruised beyond recognition she was. In all my years, I have never seen such a terrible sight, Mrs Grieveson,' he had whispered to Mildred while peering fearfully at the kitchen door in case he was overheard. 'What's more, I understand from Mrs Pearson in the village that Mary lost the child the following day and may never be able to have another. It's a bad business and make no mistake.' He had turned to a couple of the other young girls on the serving staff who were listening to his account. 'This is what happens when downstairs' folks start mixing too closely with upstairs' folks,' he had warned them. 'I've seen it happen before. Don't do it. Nothing good ever comes of it, and it always ends in tears.'

A shocked Mildred Grieveson had heard nothing like it either and her first instinct had been to seek employment elsewhere. However, since the end of the First World War the aristocracy had been selling up and leaving their large country estates, and opportunities for domestic service were becoming harder to find. Besides, Mildred's invalid husband needed her support at home, and she could ill afford to lose her job. She had therefore set aside her misgivings and kept silent on the matter, steadfastly refusing even the smallest comment when the other girls were gossiping about it in the kitchen and scullery. Since Mary's departure an uneasy peace seemed to have settled on the household, but Mildred knew all this would change when she discovered that Flora was following the same path as Mary. She confronted the girl who tearfully confirmed that her period was overdue. Mary put a comforting arm around Flora's shoulder.

'Listen dearie, you mustn't wait to be discovered. You'll have to run away without telling anyone where you're going. If you get caught out, you could end up like poor Mary.'

Flora winced. She knew the story about Mary's beating as well as anybody else on the staff. 'But where can I go,' she sobbed. 'Since Pa died, I have nobody who can help me.'

The death of Flora's father was a tragedy. Her mother had died in childbirth, and she had been brought up singlehandedly by her father in a small cottage in the nearby village of Ashill. He had been Sir Roland's horse trainer, and it was through this connection that Flora had managed to find employment at the house. However, disaster struck a few months after Flora started work. A stable hand had found her father lying dead amongst the muck and straw under the hooves of a horse that was well known to be dangerous. Nobody knew why such an experienced horseman would have gone into that stable alone but the doctor who examined his corpse was in no doubt that the terrible head wound was the result of the mare kicking out at the unfortunate man. Flora had been distraught, and Mildred was glad that the girl seemed to be unaware of staff whispers suggesting the tragedy was not as accidental as it seemed.

Flora's misfortune made Mildred think of her own daughters. The outbreak of Spanish Flu twenty years earlier had killed millions of people, and the epidemic had been no less ruthless in its treatment of Mildred's family. Mercifully, her beloved baby twins had died quickly and without too much suffering, leaving Mildred to tend the tattered remains of a husband irreparably damaged by the horrors of the trench warfare that had only just ended before the disease struck. Life can be terribly cruel, Mildred thought as she considered Flora's predicament and arrived at a decision.

'Now don't you fret about a thing, Flora. I'll speak to my sister, Margaret, and arrange for you to go and stay with her in London until the baby comes. You'll have to leave here suddenly, without any explanation, and it will remain our secret. Don't you worry about the Master.

Nobody else will know where you've gone so he will never find out.'

Flora turned pale at the idea of her employer's involvement but nodded her agreement. 'When should I go?' she whispered.

'I think the best time is on a Sunday afternoon after the family have eaten lunch. You normally get time off on that day so nobody will miss you for a few hours. There's an afternoon train from Taunton that arrives at Kings Cross at just before ten, and I'll make sure Margaret meets you at the other end. In the meantime, you must stop crying and try to act normally. The mistress has a nose for trouble and if she catches you blubbing or being sick into that bowl she will know straight away, and then I won't be able to help you.'

Flora nodded. 'Please promise you won't tell anyone where I've gone, Cook. Nobody. Not a soul. The master is a terrible man, and….and he has ways of finding out. I've seen what he's like.'

Mildred didn't really understand Flora's cryptic persistence on this point, but she smiled to reassure the girl. With the tears falling down her cheeks, Flora looked so young and vulnerable. Her crestfallen expression was childlike, and the pale skin of her face was enhanced by her blue eyes and the long dark hair pulled up under a white maid's hat. Despite the baby that was growing in her belly, Flora was still boyishly slim although her breasts had already started to swell making her features appear womanly. A child with a woman's body, Mildred thought. No wonder Flora was so popular with the seedier males of the household.

Flora was grateful for Mildred's help. She knew she had to leave and as soon as possible. Flora had been forced by events to grow up quickly, and her soft exterior concealed a growing resilience to adversity. She also possessed a slightly calculating streak. It wasn't selfishness, but with growing maturity Flora instinctively recognized when it was necessary to make changes to her life and this was one such moment. She was worried by Mary's treatment and had briefly considered seeking police protection before deciding that nobody would believe the word of a poor servant girl when it was pitched against her aristocratic employer. At least Mary had escaped with her life, but then her only offence had been to get pregnant whereas Flora had also meddled in the master's affairs, and in view of the secret she had discovered a beating might be the least of her problems. Perhaps the coming war could work to her advantage, she wondered. She had eavesdropped on Sir Roland discussing the prospects for peace with his brother, Maxwell, who had recently returned from a visit to their London auction house. He related a conversation with a government minister who said that despite all the talk of an international accommodation, politicians were gloomy. Flora had also overheard the same pessimism expressed by a German official from the embassy who occasionally visited Barrington Hall on unofficial business. It seemed that both sides could see what was coming.

Flora imagined that a war was likely to bring great upheaval, and she wondered whether she could use this to hide her tracks. London sounded ideal. She could live anonymously in the city, have her baby and blend in as just one more frightened soul amongst all the millions of others. So long as her whereabouts were kept secret it seemed there was little chance that Sir Roland would find her. Flora sniffed away her tears. She gripped Mildred's hand with gratitude, thanked her profusely, and told her she would be ready to leave on Sunday.

Chapter 4

Old Memories

November 2000

Michael was frustrated that following the birth of his mother, Jocelyn, she seemed to disappear from the official records. However, her birth certificate had at least revealed that his grandmother's name was Flora, and that Jocelyn had been born in Islington. Flora seemed especially intriguing, but Michael didn't want to switch the focus of his research until he had exhausted all avenues leading to Jocelyn. At least he knew her surname was Belton. Maybe it was time to take a speculative chance and start making some phone calls.

He turned to the computer, and searched directory enquiries and the electoral roll in Islington for the surname Belton. Three addresses and telephone numbers came up. The first two addresses had occupants under the age of thirty who confirmed that they were unrelated and unable to help Michael with his enquiries. The third entry in the electoral roll showed a single female occupant called Margaret Belton with an approximate age of seventy-five. Michael hesitated. She was quite old, and he didn't want to cause any distress. On the other hand, Margaret would have been in her early teens when Jocelyn was born and it was possible that she was related to Flora in some way, a younger sister perhaps. Promising that he would tread very gently, Michael picked up the phone and dialled her number.

When Margaret Belton answered, her voice was still reasonably firm despite her advanced years, and she had a marked London accent. Reassured, Michael told her his name and explained that he was researching his background and was trying to trace his grandmother and mother who were called Flora and Jocelyn Belton. He told her that he thought they had lived in the Islington area during the Second World War. He apologised for cold calling but wondered if Margaret was related to Flora in any way and asked her whether she could assist him with his search. The line was silent for a moment as the old woman tried to form the words. Then it all came rushing out in a confused jumble of disorderly memories.

'Flora Belton. Now there's a name I haven't heard for a very long time. There was always somebody looking for Flora, and fancy you turning up after all these years. Everyone still looking for her, are they? Last time it was the Salvation Army, must be thirty years ago. Flora was scared witless of something or somebody, and always told Ma not to tell anybody where she was. No good 'll come of it, she used to say. Mind you, Ma told the Sally Army anyway as they said it was something to do with the baby Jocelyn.' She paused as though the name Jocelyn was somehow painful. 'I suppose I shouldn't be telling you anything now really, but Flora died years ago, and Jocelyn was lost so I don't suppose it'd matter.'

She paused for another breath and a jubilant Michael jumped in quickly, a multitude of questions straining for release. 'So, you did know Flora and Jocelyn, Mrs Belton. How were you related?' he asked.

The old lady took a deep breath and continued in full flood. 'We weren't related. They were never married you know, Flora and Uncle Albert, and Jocelyn wasn't even his child. She lived with him and took his name, but Ma told me that they didn't marry. Still, plenty of folks didn't in those days. It was the war and the bombing, you see; you never knew just how long you'd get together. Mind you, it didn't make her any the less heartbroken when he was killed.' She broke off, her thoughts interrupted by the painful memory of Uncle Albert's death.

By now, Michael had realized that this was a conversation that would have to take place in person. Margaret Belton's memory seemed sound, but she was rambling and occasionally seemed to be having difficulty putting things in the correct order. Michael wondered if there was something else hanging in the background. Something like a half empty decanter of sweet sherry or an unfinished bottle of gin, perhaps. If so, it would be better to meet the old lady. It was going to take time to make sense of what she had to tell him and as this was his best lead so far it would be worth a trip down to London. The old lady agreed to meet him the following day and she asked him to visit in the afternoon, after her home help had left and in time for afternoon tea. So long as it was just tea, he smiled to himself.

***

The next day Michael was up early, impatient and full of purpose. For once, he abandoned Lucille's coffee, and instead took a taxi to the station where he caught a direct train to King's Cross. As the industrial north gave way to the rolling hills of the midlands, he thought about his muddled phone conversation with Margaret Belton. What had she meant when she said that people were always looking for Flora, and why had Flora tried to keep her location a secret? Who was she scared of? Then there were Margaret's remarks concerning the baby Jocelyn going missing. Did this explain the curious date of registration on Jocelyn's birth certificate? Michael peered at the notes he had made after their conversation but aside from further whetting his appetite for that afternoon's visit, he was no clearer.

After arriving at King's Cross, Michael took a tube train for one stop along the Northern Line and alighted at Angel Station in Islington. In Tudor times, much of the land around Islington was requisitioned from the monasteries and handed over to the Crown's friends in the aristocracy. It had been a prosperous rural area that specialized in farming but the gradual growth of urban London and the eventual arrival of the railway in the nineteenth century saw the fields give way to brick terraces, overdevelopment and social decline. Rich families and merchants escaped to outlying rural suburbs and for much of the next one hundred and fifty years the Islington area was well known for its slums and deprivation. The Blitz had seen many of the old terraces reduced to rubble, and the post-war reconstruction effort had acted as a catalyst for gradual regeneration. These days, Islington was a bustling and rather chic London suburb where the rich and pretentious mixed with the well to do middle classes in an uneasy cohabitation. It seemed a strange place for Margaret Belton to call home although it sounded as though she had outlasted most of the other residents.

As he left the station, Michael was struck by the familiarity of the place. The London roads were as busy as he remembered, and the cold winter air was a keen blade on his face after the mugginess and stale air of the underground. It was only a short distance to Margaret's place on Popham Street and he was glad of the opportunity to stretch his legs and gather his thoughts as he battled through the crowd of shoppers. Ten minutes later, he stood outside a plain block of flats in a quiet side street and pressed the buzzer for her ground floor flat. There was no reply from the adjacent loudspeaker, but a moment later a middle aged and slightly formidable woman came to the door. He guessed correctly that she was Margaret Belton's home help, and he felt uncomfortable as she stared at him with suspicion.

'I presume you are Mr Calvert?' she asked confrontationally. Michael nodded. 'Mrs Belton is expecting you and I'm just leaving. May I just say that I don't entirely approve of strangers making unsolicited visits. Mrs Belton is easily excited and all this talk about the past has made her more excitable than usual. What's more,' she lowered her voice slightly, 'when she gets over stimulated, she tends to drink a bit more sherry than she should and at her age that is something she can ill afford to do.'

She looked at Michael sternly to make sure that he understood that he was personally responsible for Mrs Belton's alcohol consumption for the next few hours and held open the door for him. 'Right then, in you go and I shouldn't take much of what she says as the gospel truth. The years are gradually getting the better of Marge's memory, and she is a bit inclined to invent things that she can't quite recall. Please bear that in mind and don't over tire her. I shall be back later,' she warned protectively, and without waiting for any response, the woman stepped out of the doorway and set off down the street at a remarkable pace. Michael was left open-mouthed on the doorstep wondering whether the home-help provided Margaret Belton with daily assistance or a daily ordeal.

Hoping that the old lady would prove a bit more amenable than her protector, Michael went through the open door and followed the corridor to the entrance of Margaret Belton's flat. He knocked and a moment later a slightly built old lady with white hair opened the door. She was dressed simply in a skirt and blouse with a string of pearls that seemed at odds with her bright pink slippers. She was twisted by old age and chronic arthritis, and she was cruelly bent over such that she had to crane her face up slightly sideways to see Michael's face. Physical difficulties aside, her rheumy eyes were nonetheless bright and intelligent, and Michael felt slightly unsettled by her scrutiny. There was a momentary silence as she absorbed his features, and then, apparently satisfied with what she saw, the old woman nodded to herself as though she had seen something familiar.

'Mrs Belton?' Michael enquired uncomfortably. The old woman smiled, finally breaking her gaze and held open the door for him.

'It's uncanny,' she said in a marked London accent. 'You have the same piercing blue eyes as Flora, Mr Calvert. You could be peas in a pod, but we will get to that in a moment when you tell me your story which, I have to say, I am very much looking forward to hearing. Do come in, and please call me Marge. My mother's name was also Margaret, so I was always called Marge to make sure there was no confusion.'

Michael thanked her and followed the shuffling Marge into a sparsely furnished but neatly kept living room.

'Please have a seat,' she said indicating a worn but comfortable sofa covered with a white lace throw. 'Would you like a cup of tea or perhaps a small glass of sweet sherry?' she asked with slightly too much enthusiasm. Mindful that he had recently been made personally responsible for Marge's welfare that afternoon, Michael told her that tea would be just fine and settled back as the lady slowly made her way through to a small kitchenette just off the living room.

As he waited, Michael absorbed his surroundings. There was a pair of small watercolours on the wall depicting mountainous scenes, perhaps in the Lake District or in Scotland. On the other side of a small table, a steeply backed armchair faced a small television. The chair looked as though it was designed for somebody who might struggle to leave a more comfortable version, and Marge's walking stick was propped up against one of the arms. A bookcase to his side was filled with Penguin paperbacks and seemed to contain a full set of Agatha Christie novels. As he read through the familiar titles, he noticed a framed photograph on top of the case, and he leaned across to get a better look. There were two ladies sat smiling on a bench in a park, and judging by the style of the clothes Michael guessed it had been taken about fifty years earlier. One of the ladies was clearly Marge before old age and arthritis had whitened her hair and twisted her back, and the other lady was older but similar looking. Michael wondered whether she was Marge's mother.

'I have some other photographs that I am certain will interest you, Michael,' a voice called from the kitchen. At that moment a rickety trolley laden with porcelain cups, plates and cakes emerged though the doorway, pushed slowly and rather erratically by Marge. The trolley made it to Michael's side, and with a gesture that made it clear that Michael was now in charge of the precious cargo, Marge sat heavily in the upright armchair, relieved to take the weight from her tired old legs.

'Before I start, Michael, I think you should go first. Why don't you pour us some tea and tell me how it is that you are sat in my dear old flat asking about somebody I haven't seen for over sixty years?' Michael reached for the teapot, and as he poured tea and proffered cakes he explained about his adoption and his recent decision to research his natural roots. He told Marge that he had discovered the identities of his mother and grandmother but was trying to find out a bit more information that might allow him eventually to track down his mother.

When he had finished Marge smiled at him. 'I would never have guessed that this day would come, Michael. It really is astonishing how stories come around in a circle. Our house used to be just around the corner from here before it got knocked down in the early seventies. Your grandmother, Flora, lived with me and Ma, off and on, for about five years during the war. I can still remember when she arrived. It was a few months before the war started.' Marge broke eye contact, and she smiled to herself as she remembered the night she gained an elder sister.

Chapter 5

Flight

December 1938

Mildred had made all the arrangements for Flora to escape from Barrington Hall on the following Sunday afternoon, but by Friday morning she knew something had gone very wrong because Flora was already a fugitive. The Pendletons' annual Christmas party had taken place on the previous evening, and it had gone on into the early hours. When the staff were eventually allowed to retire, they had first been addressed by the Master who was clearly furious. He told them that Flora had used the party to steal some important papers before she had run off. He told them it would soon be a police matter and warned them not to shelter the girl but to tell the family immediately if they came across her. Mildred instantly thought of her husband who was unable to work and their reliance on her job at the Hall. It was unusual for a household cook to live away from her place of employment, but the Mistress had allowed it in consideration of Mildred's domestic circumstances. This placed Mildred in a difficult situation when, as expected, Flora appeared at her house the following day.

The urgency of the knock announced that it was Flora who had arrived, but before she answered it Mildred first peeped out of a front window to check that nobody was following the forlorn figure on her doorstep. When she was certain that the girl was alone, she opened the door and was shocked at Flora's tired and bedraggled appearance which suggested a night spent outside. The girl was streaked in mud and her maid's uniform was torn and dishevelled. She was clutching a small suitcase to her chest protectively as though carrying her unborn baby, and her eyes were brimming with tears of desperation. She really did look like a fugitive. Flora suddenly sagged as exhaustion overwhelmed her, and she looked pleadingly at Mildred as the colour in her face drained away.

'Please, Cook. Don't let him find me.' With that, Flora swayed and collapsed onto the step.

Mildred managed to take the sting out of Flora's fall by half catching her, and they staggered together across the small parlour and collapsed onto an old sofa. Mildred was nervous of discovery, but her protective instincts were strong too. She sensed that there was more to Flora's plight than pregnancy, there was injustice too. So, ignoring her fear of retribution, Mildred took Flora into her home and set about modifying her plans.

Three days later, Mildred's bravery came to fruition when Flora stood in the London home of Mildred's sister looking at her new bedroom.

'I'm afraid it's not much, but it'll do until the baby arrives and then we'll have to see,' Margaret Belton told her. Flora looked around. The blackened brick terrace with four storeys and a basement actually housed two families. Margaret Belton lived on the third and fourth floors, and Flora's bedroom was right at the top in the roof space. She shivered slightly. It was spotlessly clean but cold and draughty, an impression reinforced by a small threadbare rug marooned on an ocean of bare floorboards. On one side, the roof sloped down steeply to a wall that was only three feet high. A bed sat awkwardly beneath and was made up with clean sheets and a rough blanket. Elsewhere, there was some rudimentary furniture which looked like it had been stood there for many years. Flora knew it was plain, but it was dry and most important of all, it was sanctuary.

'I can't tell you how grateful I am, Mrs Belton,' Flora declared. 'You could've given me a hole in the ground to live in and I would still be in your debt for the rest of my life.'

'That's alright, dear, and please call me Margaret. Us ladies are always left alone to cope with the consequences of our mistakes, me included,' she added cryptically heading for the door. 'It would be a tough world indeed if there was nobody there to help us through it.' Flora stared after her, recognising that Mrs Belton had a particular empathy with her own situation. Mildred had made no mention of a Mr Belton but Flora knew there was a daughter. As if reading her mind, Mrs Belton reached the door and called over her shoulder, 'I'll leave you to unpack for a while and then Marge will come and get you for some supper.'

Margaret Belton shut the door behind her and paused momentarily at the top of the narrow staircase as the sobbing started from the room behind her. She didn't know the full facts behind Flora's flight from Barrington Hall, but she was certain that it must have more to do than just a baby. She shrugged to herself as she started the steep descent to the floor below. It was not her business, and the girl would tell her story when she was good and ready. But it could be a hard life for the young, she reflected. And it will get harder still she added silently to herself as she remembered the leaflet on air raid precautions that had been posted through the letterbox that morning.

Inside the spartan room, Flora sat on the bed and allowed tears of relief to fall unimpeded onto the bed. She was grateful too. Mildred had hidden Flora in her home for three days while they waited for the Master's search to die down. Mildred was beside herself with worry that they might be discovered, and so Flora stayed entombed in the spare room for the whole period, hiding under the bed every time there was an innocent knock on the front door. She had few possessions except what she had managed to stuff into her small suitcase during her desperate escape, and she was grateful when Mildred kindly donated a few items of clothing and a little cash to bolster Flora's resources.

In the end, Mildred's plan had gone smoothly. Mildred had checked that nobody was around, and Flora left the house by the back door after hugging Mildred so tightly that her gratitude almost stopped Mildred's breathing. The yard was empty, and Flora was unobserved as she crossed to a small gate that led to a path through some trees. Five minutes later, she had reached the road where she was relieved to find Mr Denton waiting with a horse and trap that he had borrowed from an acquaintance in nearby Ashill. The five-mile journey to Taunton took forty-five minutes, and little was said as butler and maid looked at the passing fields and sank deep into their own private thoughts. At the station, a relieved Mr Denton helped her down and handed Flora her small suitcase.

'We seem to have got away with it,' he said. 'Good luck, girl. This really is for the best you know.' And unable to resist offering a last piece of advice he had added, 'and you take care in London, Flora. It's no place for a young girl from the countryside. There's plenty of bad folks there that'd soon as take advantage of you.' And with that parting advice, he had left Flora alone on the station forecourt waiting for the three-thirty train to London.

An exhausting eight hours later, Flora was relieved to

be in the safety of Margaret Belton's house. She felt a little disorientated, but her fear had dissipated, and her tears dried quickly. She turned to the suitcase and started to unpack. It didn't take long, and she was soon looking protectively at the final item lying in the bottom of the case. It was Flora's most precious personal possession. It was her journal.

With only one hard working parent, Flora had missed out on many of childhood's opportunities, and a meagre and intermittent education had left her unable to read or write. At the age of ten, financial pressures at home forced her to abandon school, and she ended up cleaning and keeping house for an eccentric old lady called Victoria Evans. Victoria was a childless widow who considered herself to be an amateur thespian. She quickly took to the young girl, and appalled by her lack of education, Victoria decided to make Flora her grand project. And so it was that over the next few years Flora cleaned in the mornings and studiously learned to read and write in the afternoons. Under Victoria's careful tutelage she achieved a remarkably high level of literacy and general knowledge. Her mentor expected nothing else.

'Without art and literature, we lose our humanity,' Victoria would declare, thrusting another book under Flora's nose. 'And without humanity, we are lost for all time,' she added rather dramatically and with a theatrical gesture of her hand for the benefit of an appreciative but imaginary audience.

Flora loved the dotty old lady, and over the years she came to regard Victoria's house as a second home. Flora's busy father didn't mind, and he was relieved to share some of the responsibility for his daughter. He was just happy to see the girl growing up so contentedly, and he was impressed that her academic studies were flourishing under Victoria's firm guidance. And for Flora, those years really were the happiest of her life. As soon as her father left for work, she would rush round excitedly to see Victoria. She would sit captivated as the old lady described great works of art and they discussed the finer points of English poetry. She had hundreds of books, and Flora spent hours browsing through the packed shelves in Victoria's study marvelling at the treasures she found there.

Unfortunately, time eventually caught up with Victoria Evans, and she died after a short illness. Two months later, just before Flora had started work at Barrington Hall, there was a knock at the door. An immaculately dressed and rather solemn gentleman stood on the doorstep looking as though he would rather be elsewhere. He declined to enter the house and told Flora he was from Mayhew and Mayhew, solicitors in Taunton and representing Victoria in the disposal of her will. He informed Flora that Victoria had left her a small amount of money. There was also a short letter and a leather-bound journal which he handed to her before taking his leave with a brief tip of his hat.

The letter was from Victoria and the expressions of love it contained had reopened Flora's grief. It was written in Victoria's characteristically flowing hand and was embellished throughout with theatrical prose. Amongst more general expressions of affection, Victoria told of the great joy that Flora had brought into her life and how pleased she was that Flora had 'grasped the beating heart of literature and brought it into her own breast.' She told Flora that a lifetime of reading, learning and knowledge awaited her and that she should record 'the experiences of her life' in the journal so that one day she could produce 'a great autobiographic work of literature' that she might have published.

The journal was beautifully made. The edge of the thick red leather was embossed with gilt scrolling, and there was a flap that came across the open end of the book. A brass fitting on the end of the flap fastened into a lock on the front preventing anyone from opening it unless they had the key. On the inside cover, Flora found an inscription in Victoria's flowing hand:

'To Flora, for your lifetime of trials and tribulations that you must face bravely if you are to triumph, and most of all for the love of art and literature, yours affectionately, Victoria.'

It had been a wonderful gift that Flora had treasured ever since. Her first entry explained to the reader how the journal had arisen and described the love and gratitude Flora felt for her mentor. Thereafter, she carefully added an entry covering the day's notable events, and it was developing into a masterpiece that in more fanciful moments she imagined might rival the works of the great diarist Samuel Pepys. She looked down at it lying at the bottom of the suitcase and felt for the key that dangled on the thin chain around her neck. Up until now, the diary had been a personal record of no real interest to anybody else. However, the journal and the envelope that was now tucked inside the rear cover had recently become inextricably tied to Flora's safety. In fact, her life depended on keeping it safe, and she knew the journal needed to be hidden carefully. She looked around the small room for a suitable place to conceal it but was interrupted by a sudden knock on the door which opened to reveal Margaret's teenage daughter.

'Umm, you must be Flora. Me mum's called Margaret, and I'm Marge. I've come to say hello and to tell you that supper's ready.' The girl advanced uninvited into the room and smiled at Flora. 'You're beautiful. Will you be my big sister?'

Flora laughed at the girl's directness, and she knew instinctively that they would get along just fine. 'Yes, of course I will.'

'Ma says you are going to have a baby. Can I help you when it comes?'

Flora's smile faded slightly as she was reminded of the souvenir she was carrying from Barrington Hall. 'Yes, of course you can, Marge, but there is something I must ask of you. You must never ever tell anyone about where I've come from or anything about the baby. Would you promise to do that for me?'

Marge nodded vigorously. 'Yes, Ma has told me about that already. It's our shared secret which means,' she added enthusiastically, 'we really must be sisters already!'

Flora laughed without answering and hugged the child. But Marge hadn't quite finished with her inquisition. 'Ooh what's that? Is it a bible?' she asked pointing excitedly at the leather-bound book on the bed.

'No, it's called a journal,' replied Flora protectively. 'It's like a diary. I record everything that happens to me, all my private thoughts and things like that.'

'Oh, you mean like secrets and love and stuff. Can I read it?'

Flora laughed at the girl and how close to the truth she was. 'No, I'm sorry, Marge. It's a private book, and I couldn't possibly show it to anyone.' And then, spotting the crestfallen look on the girl's face, she added, 'not even to my younger sister!' Marge giggled, disappointed that she was unable to extract further secrets from Flora but delighted that she had managed formally to cement her position with this beautiful stranger.

'I'll persuade you one day,' she laughed as they made their way down the steep stairs for supper.

Chapter 6

Photographs

November 2000

Marge took a thoughtful sip of tea and studied Michael's face.

'Before we go on, perhaps I should show you a picture of Flora. I just can't believe how similar you are to her. Here, I'll show you.' She leaned forward conspiratorially. 'Pass me that box just by you.' Michael looked down on the bottom shelf of the small bookcase at the side of the settee, picked up the box file lying there and carefully handed it over. Marge opened the lid and peered over the top of her glasses as she rummaged through a pile of old photographs. Near the top she found a black and white print and handed it over to Michael. Two girls were arm in arm in the street. The younger one was clearly Marge in her early teens, and she was laughing at the unseen photographer. The other was older, perhaps in her early twenties and pretty. She was slim with long dark hair, and although she was smiling enthusiastically there seemed to be a slight tinge of sadness behind her eyes.

'Lovely, wasn't she?' Marge remarked echoing his thoughts.

'She certainly was. When was this taken?'

'I think it was late on in 1940. That pile of rubble you can see in the background was on the corner of Raleigh Street and Packington Street after it was bombed. Flora and I went to have a look, and we met a press photographer from the local evening paper. He was a real flatterer, and I think he probably quite liked the look of Flora because he persuaded us to let him take our photograph. A couple of days later this print was posted through the door and Flora gave it to me.'

Michael looked at it again and then reluctantly handed the photograph back to Marge. Seeing an actual image of Flora really brought home the reality of his natural family. Until that moment, they had merely been names printed on official documents. Now they had started to become actual individuals with faces. He returned to Marge.

'Do you know where Flora came from, Marge? What was the big secret?'

Marge started polishing her glasses. 'Well, Flora really didn't like discussing her previous life, so I don't know much, but I do know that she had been a servant girl at a big house in Somerset and that she was running away from some kind of danger. To this day, I don't know what it was, but she seemed to be on the run. Sometimes she would disappear for weeks on end, and then come bouncing back to us as though nothing had happened.'

Michael's interest stirred. 'Do you know where this big house was, Marge?'

'No, I'm sorry, Michael. I don't recall the name, but here, look, there's this too.' She returned to the box and took out another photograph. It was rolled up with an elastic band. 'When Flora left us for the last time, I found this in the bin and kept it in case she decided she wanted it back. I'm sure it's where she worked. See if you can spot her.' Michael removed the band and unrolled the photograph. It was a long black and white print of an impressive country house with the whole household lined up in front of the building. The staff were in their working clothes and stood either side of the owners who were dressed formally for what looked like an annual household record. The maids were all in uniform and it was easy to pick out Flora. She stood in the middle, smiling, and looking terribly young. As Michael examined the old print he noticed that something had been scribbled on the back along one edge. It was extremely faint and easily missed. He peered at it more closely.

Marge spotted his interest. 'What is it, Michael? Is there something on it?'

'I think it says Barrington Hall 1937,' he told Marge.

'Well goodness me,' she said. 'I've never noticed that before although I mainly look at the other picture of me and Flora together when I want to remember her.'

'Well, we know where she came from now. That is very interesting,' Michael said, pleased with his discovery. 'But tell me about Jocelyn, Marge. Flora must have been pregnant when she arrived from Somerset?' Marge nodded, and suddenly looked so sad that Michael regretted asking his question.

"Yes, she was pregnant,' Marge sniffed as she dabbed at her eyes with a handkerchief that had appeared from up her sleeve. 'Your mother, Jocelyn, was born at the hospital just up the road. She was so tiny and wasn't with us very long.' She paused to compose herself. 'And all of that was my fault really.'

'Your fault?' Michael queried.

'Yes.' She looked away from him and her troubled expression deepened further. 'You see, Michael, it was me that lost Jocelyn in the first place.' Guilt clouded Marge's face. There was one terrible day that would always live with her. It was the day she broke a promise.

45

Chapter 7

Evacuation

September 1939

Eight months after Flora's arrival, she sat with Margaret and Marge Belton in their small parlour listening intently to the evening news on the radio. With the German Army poised to invade Poland a new war was depressingly inevitable, and the authorities had announced that they were initiating Operation Pied Piper, the mass evacuation of nearly three million children from the major cities. There were few who appreciated the scale of what was planned, and nobody listening could have imagined that a week later nearly a quarter of Britain's population would have a new address. Flora looked away from the radio and gazed down at her new baby daughter, Jocelyn.

'What should I do, Margaret? She's only a month old.' Margaret Belton was at a loss and looked at her sympathetically, unsure of what to say.

There was an uneasy silence for a moment as the two women absorbed the significance of the announcement, and then Marge blurted out, 'I know! Jocelyn can come with me. I may be only thirteen, but I can look after her. I can do baths and nappies, and I know how to prepare a bottle. You've seen me do it, Flora.'

The two women looked at each other. All the talk of another war had sent everyone into a panic which was not helped by the occasional practice air raid drill and the arrival on every street corner of piles of sandbags and officious air raid wardens. Such was the feverish atmosphere that it seemed that German bombers or para troopers could appear at any moment. Things must be bad, Flora thought, if the authorities had now decided that the children should be moved away from the cities. The radio presenter had announced that the mass exodus would occur over the next four days. The children were to assemble at their local school before catching trains to the countryside. At their rural destinations, they would be met by the local authorities and then matched up to their new families. Each child would get a stamped and addressed postcard for them to send home to notify their parents of their new address once they had arrived.

'I don't know, Marge,' Flora said reluctant to deflate the girl's enthusiasm. 'Jocelyn's so young. It's not that I don't trust you it's just…' She tailed off unable to finish.

'But if the German bombers come, Flora,' interjected Margaret. 'What would we do then? They're talking about building shelters at the back of the houses, but I can't see them stopping a bomb and it'll be no place for a baby. Are you sure there isn't someone back in Somerset who could put you up?'

Flora was startled by the idea. 'There's no way on earth that we could go back there, Margaret. It's not safe…for either of us.'

'I wish you would tell me what the danger is, Flora,' Margaret replied softly. 'Mildred told me only that you were going to have a child and that you needed somewhere to stay but there's more to it than that isn't there?'

Flora was resolute and shook her head, remaining silent while she considered what to do. She felt maternally protective towards her new daughter, but she recognized that the circumstances of Jocelyn's conception would always tarnish her feelings. She had never sought motherhood, and even though her hormones were demanding that she nurture the tiny child, Flora couldn't fend off the sense that her baby was more of an hinderance than a blessing. Perhaps evacuation was the best outcome. It would remove Jocelyn from wartime dangers and take her further away from Sir Roland. It would also free Flora temporarily from the responsibility of having to look after a new-born baby, making it easier for her to move quickly if she was discovered. She studied Marge's expectant face. The young girl was sensible, and from the moment Flora had returned from the hospital, she had fussed around helping Flora with feeding, bathing and tending the new arrival. Flora was certain Marge could look after Jocelyn full time so long as the two girls were kept together. She came to a decision: Evacuation to the countryside was for the best.

'Safety first,' she announced. When do they leave?'

Margaret Belton rose in resignation. It was placing a great responsibility on Marge's shoulders, but she could tell it was pointless to argue. 'I'll go and speak to Mr Bainbridge down the street,' she said. 'He teaches at Marge's school just up the road and he's sure to know what the arrangements are.'

Mr Bainbridge did indeed know about the evacuation plan, and fifteen minutes later, Margaret returned breathless.

'We'd better get packing. It's tomorrow, Flora. They're going tomorrow. We must have them at the school at eight in the morning. I mentioned about Jocelyn, and Mr Bainbridge said that she should go with Marge. He said that the two of them will be kept together and that they'll stay with the same family. Apparently, the children from

49

our district are going to South Yorkshire.'

Flora was shocked that everything was going to happen so soon and that the children were to be sent so far from home. 'South Yorkshire? That's miles away.'

'I know, Flora, but further away from us means they will be further away from the German bombs, so it'll be for the best. Come on my girl,' she said turning to Marge and trying to sound more light-hearted than she felt. 'We need to get your things together. You're going on an adventure.'

The next morning, Flora rose early, fed and bathed Jocelyn and went down to join Marge and her mother in the kitchen. Overnight, a rather solemn atmosphere had descended on the household as the occupants absorbed the full implications of what was to occur. Even Marge who was usually irrepressible was sitting in silence gazing into a half-drunk cup of cold tea. Flora looked at them both, noticing Marge's best Sunday clothes, the tear-streaked cheeks of the older lady and the damp hanky laid on the table in front of her.

'Is it time?' Flora asked gently.

'I'm afraid so,' Margaret sniffed.

Marge suddenly seemed to perk up. 'Come on you two. Cheer up and stop worrying. I've been thinking about this, and I reckon it'll be like going on a summer holiday to the countryside. They'll be loads of other kids all playing outside in the sunshine. They'll be cows and sheep and picnics, and we'll all have a wonderful time.'

Margaret smiled. Marge's sudden optimism was infectious although Margaret wasn't at all sure about her daughter's vision of country life as Marge had never been on a summer holiday and the closest she had been to the countryside was the occasional picnic on Hampstead Heath.

Conscious that the moment of parting had arrived, they gathered up their things and stepped outside. The street was already busy with people making the same journey, and the crowd got bigger still as tightly packed terrace doors opened and tearful mothers and excited children spilled out onto the pavement. They joined the throng, Margaret carrying her gas mask and the two small cases, and Flora pushing Jocelyn in a pram with a bag of bottles and nappies perched precariously on a wire shelf by the wheels.

They arrived at the school ten minutes later to find chaos. Shouting children raced excitedly around their distraught parents whilst the teachers tried their best to round up the flock. Eventually, Mr Crofton, the headmaster, called the children and parents into the school hall, and after some spluttering and a good deal of school masterly sarcasm he managed to restore a semblance of order. The children were split into their classes and a teacher issued each child with a blank postcard which the parents annotated with their home address. Mr Crofton was grave as he addressed the children.

'You must keep this card safe and hand it to the adults waiting for you at the other end. If you don't, then you may end up getting lost,' he warned them. 'In a moment we will form up in an orderly line and make our way to the station. When we get there, it's important that you stay together and don't board the train until directed. The whole of Islington will be watching you,' he declared, 'so let's show them how brave we are by singing as we march along. And do let's be on our best behaviour. That includes you, Crowther,' he added, spotting the fidgeting fourth form boy most likely to let the side down.

The children and their adult minders left the school hall and made their way out onto the road. The police had closed it to traffic so there was plenty of space to form up. At the front, Mr Crofton unfurled the school banner, and with an ostentatious wave he set off slowly for the station. As they followed behind him, the children started to sing, 'Doing the Lambeth Walk.' The sound attracted the crowds, and it seemed to Flora that the whole of Islington had come along to offer their best wishes and farewells. Householders, shopkeepers and customers spilled out onto the pavement to watch. Calls of 'good luck' and 'see you soon' echoed off the walls. One store holder even gathered up a huge bag of sweets and tried to give one to each child as they passed. In fact, all he managed to generate was a confused scrum that broke the continuity of the crocodile, and after a withering stare from Mr Crofton the well-intentioned man retreated to the safety of his doorway.

At the station there was further confusion. Council workers and railway staff tried unsuccessfully to retain control, but they were overwhelmed by the huge number of children and parents from several schools who rushed forward through the unmanned ticket booths and were now milling around on the platform. Mr Crofton submitted the list of children from Queen's Head Street School to a flustered official who was doing his best to instil some order into the proceedings. The besieged man was sitting at a makeshift desk on the platform, shuffling reams of paper and seemingly oblivious to the mayhem surrounding him.

'Thank you, Mr Crofton,' he said. 'The plan is that children from each school class will embark in the same carriage. The train will make its way north and at each stop along the way one carriage will be unloaded. That way, children that know each other will be hosted in the same community. Please ask your teachers to ensure the loading plan works along these lines.' Mr Crofton nodded his understanding and turned to search for the rest of his school.

It was a good plan that would have worked very well given more time and better planning. However, it was never going to be successful once the procession had lost its integrity, and although Mr Crofton did his best to round up everyone, it soon became obvious that it was a lost cause. Schools had intermingled, classes became mixed and confused railway officials were already allowing some children to board randomly. Even worse, some distraught parents had followed their offspring onboard to say their final farewells in the carriages. This ensured that not only was the platform a confused mass of heaving humanity, but the carriage aisles were also blocked with noisy children and their clinging parents.

Outside on the platform, Flora was seemingly unaware of the confusion around her, and she ignored Mr Crofton as he passed by vainly calling out for his school to form up again at the ticket booth. Despite the shadows hanging over Flora's relationship with her daughter, the moment of separation proved to be unexpectedly painful. With tears streaming down her face, Flora quietly leaned over and took Jocelyn out of the pram. She glanced at the sleeping baby for one last time, ensured that she was well wrapped in the blanket and handed her to Marge. Stood amongst the crowd, Marge suddenly looked much younger and more vulnerable than her thirteen years suggested. But she put on a brave face and smiled reassuringly as she received the baby into her arms. Temporarily overcome with grief, Flora could barely speak but managed to blurt out a few last words.

'Promise me you'll take good care of her, Marge. I'm relying on you.' She hugged the nodding girl tightly, desperately trying to stifle a sob and stepped back to allow Margaret to say her own farewells. Margaret stepped forward stoically and put her own arms around her daughter.

'Off you go then, Marge. You look after that baby and make sure you write as soon as you get to your new home.' Her daughter forced a thin smile and bravely turned to mount the steps into the nearest carriage. As she did, a passing guard stopped, helped her onboard with her bags and kindly offered to take the pram to the guard's van. This left the two women on the platform to follow Marge as she slowly made her way down the busy aisle to a vacant seat in a compartment further down the carriage.

Twenty minutes later, the doors started to close. The platform was now occupied only by adults who were pressed up hard against the train and calling out their last farewells through the glass windows. Further back, a whistle sounded, a green flag was waved, and the driver pulled a lever to set the train in motion. The locomotive belched smoke, and with a reluctant groan it moved forward as pressurised steam took up the strain. Along the platform desperate mothers tried to follow the train's progress but they were quickly outpaced as the train left the confines of the platform. Soon, there was a nothing left but a mournful silence and a cloud of sulphurous fumes swirling amongst the steel girders. On the platform, waving hankies fell to their owners' sides and tearful parents turned to make the lonely walk home.

On board, Marge was relieved that the seat next to her was vacant. It seemed that nobody wanted to sit next to a baby for a journey that would last several hours, and so Marge had a convenient space on which to lay Jocelyn. None of the other occupants in her compartment was from Queen's Head Street School but they were of a similar age. Their faces had dropped when Marge had struggled through the sliding door laden with a baby and two cases, but they had allowed her in and had shuffled up to give her some room. There was silence initially, but curiosity and excitement soon overcame the reticence of her travelling companions and before long they were all gossiping away, exchanging experiences and speculating on what lay ahead.

And what did lie ahead was further confusion, loneliness and for Marge, an utter disaster. It was seven hours, one nappy change and two bottles of milk later, before the train began to make occasional stops. Rolling countryside had given way to green hills covered in bracken and gorse, and dry-stone walls surrounded fields of brooding cattle and sheep. The train had forked away from the main line, and the stations they now passed through had become progressively smaller. Earlier, a guard had popped into the compartment and explained that he would come and tell the children which stop was theirs. The conversation had previously dwindled as fatigue caught up with the tired children. However, the prospect of imminent arrival rejuvenated them, and with eyes expectedly searching for the guard, they chattered excitely each time the train pulled into a station. Finally, as the train started to slow for a fifth time, the guard opened the sliding door and smiled at them.

'Right then, everybody. Get your things together. This is your stop coming up. And don't you worry about the pram, Miss, I haven't forgotten.'

As she queued to leave the carriage, Marge looked down at Jocelyn. The baby had been extremely well behaved and had cried only twice during the journey. Otherwise, the gentle motion of the train had lulled the child into a deep sleep. Now as Marge struggled through the carriage to the door, the baby awoke, turned bright red as she filled her nappy for a second time and started to complain.

'Not now Jocelyn, we're nearly there', Marge cooed to the child. 'I'll sort you out in a minute.'

Outside on the platform, the guard kept his word and was waiting with the pram. Marge placed Jocelyn into it and tried desperately to calm the crying baby. As they emerged from the carriage, the children had assembled with their bags on the platform unsure of what to do next. It was quite a large group, and Marge supposed that there must have been around twenty of them. Aside from one boy who was in the year ahead of her at Queen's Head Street School, the rest of the children were strangers from other parts of Islington. As the doors slammed and the guard's whistle echoed off the walls, a thin gentleman with a cleric's collar suddenly appeared wraith-like through the steam.

'Goodness me, goodness me,' he puffed sounding rather like the departing locomotive. 'How many of you are there? We were told there would be ten or so. Oh, my Lord, a baby too.' The vicar stared at the screaming Jocelyn and looked incredulously at Marge. 'How old are you, child?' he asked.

'Thirteen, Sir,' replied Marge, and then added lamely, 'she just needs her nappy changing.'

'I see" said the vicar, not seeing at all and looking around in the forlorn hope that the baby's mother might suddenly appear and rescue the situation. 'I'm afraid the child's nappy will have to wait for a little while longer. We really must get to the church. The adults have been waiting hours as it is.' He turned to the other children and cleared his throat. 'Welcome to Upper Padley, children. I'm the Reverend Saddler but you can call me vicar. In a moment we'll walk to the church hall, and you'll meet your new families. But please stay together. You've come too far to get lost now.'

He turned for the exit and gently led the nervous children out of the station and up the road to where Marge could see the church spire poking up from behind some tall trees. The village seemed to be deserted, although as she walked by the rows of tidy front gardens Marge got the distinct impression that the eyes of the whole community were on them. The church hall was situated just next to the rectory and as they filed in Marge could see a line of people waiting for them across one side of the room. There were hushed gasps from the assembled adults as they absorbed the number of children that needed homes.

'Now children,' the Reverend Saddler said kindly, 'these people are going to look after you until it is safe to return home. However, it seems that we have been sent rather more of you than we were led to expect so before we start matching you up, I need to speak to the adults to see what can be done.' He walked over to the men and women stood against the opposite wall and gathered them around him. He spoke to them in hushed terms that Marge couldn't hear but whatever was said seemed to cause a good deal of consternation.

'Well, there's no way I can take more than two,' remonstrated a severe looking lady wearing a red headscarf. 'Even if they have got ration cards. What would my Bill say if I came home with a handful of bairns? Anyway, we just haven't got the space for more than one.'

'What were they thinking of sending all of these? And look, there's a baby over there that can't be more than two months old,' another woman exclaimed amid murmurs of angry agreement. The children looked at each other helplessly. Some had tears in their eyes and Marge had to blink back her own as an overpowering feeling of homesickness and rejection fell across the assembled refugees.

'Now, now,' said the vicar. 'Show some charity, please. Look, you're upsetting them.' He lowered his voice again and addressed the adults in hushed tones that the children couldn't hear. There was some muttering and shaking of heads, but he eventually turned to face the children. Evidently, some kind of accommodation had been struck as the adults reluctantly formed a line opposite the children and started to scrutinize them. Marge felt like an item in a salesroom, and she wouldn't have been at all surprised if the vicar had started to auction them off. Even so, she wanted to make a good impression and so she stood up straight and tried to look as sweet and engaging as she could. There was silence for a moment and then a tall man with a pretty wife stepped forward and took the hands of a boy and the girl next to him. He smiled reassuringly at them and gestured across to his wife. The two children gathered up their bags and followed him over to the other side of the room where the woman stood waiting. There was a brief conversation that Marge couldn't hear, and then the man smiled at the vicar and all four of them trooped out of the hall together.

The selection of the first children then caused a bit of a stampede. Encouraged by the vicar to take home two or three children, the other men and women rushed forward anxious to get the best-looking prospects, and before long there was only Marge, Jocelyn and two ladies left looking at each other. The younger lady looked at the Reverend Saddler and stuck out a resolute jaw.

'I'm sorry, vicar. I can't take a baby home, but I'll take the girl if you want.'

The other, older, lady nodded. 'We haven't got space for two, but I suppose I could take the baby. Lord knows what my Archie will say when I come home with that bundle of joy, though,' she laughed pointing at Jocelyn who promptly started a renewed bout of disapproval. 'He thinks we stopped all of that nonsense years ago.'

Marge gripped the handles of the pram as tightly as she could, horrified at what seemed to be unfolding. 'Excuse me, vicar,' she said shyly but as politely as she could manage. 'I made a promise to look after Jocelyn. We can't possibly be split up.'

The vicar looked at her sympathetically. 'What's your name child?' he asked.

'Marge, Sir.'

'Well Marge. I'm sure your mother explained about the coming war and the sacrifices that will have to be made. Well, it's not just the men that will make those sacrifices; it's everybody, women and children too. Now Mrs Timmerson here has kindly offered you a home and you mustn't be ungrateful and cause a fuss. This other lady, Mrs Hindmarsh, will look after your baby sister, and when it's time to go back to London you will both be reunited with your family. Until that time, though, we all must make the best of a bad job. I can promise you that Mrs Hindmarsh will look after Jocelyn very well. I recall that she has four children of her own although they have all grown up and left home now.'

The courage that had sustained Marge throughout that

long, uncertain, day finally deserted her, and she started to sob. 'You can't split us up, Sir. Please. I promised Ma and Flora. I promised.'

'Now Marge, come along,' Mrs Timmerson said reaching forward and grasping Marge's hand firmly. 'Mrs Hindmarsh lives a little way out at Grange Farm, but I am sure we can find a way for you to visit your baby sister, can't we Mrs Hindmarsh?' The other lady nodded her agreement and gently prised the pram handles out of Marge's other hand.

'You will look after her?' wept Marge as the moment of defeat became evident.

'Of course, dear, I know all about babies,' Mrs Hindmarsh replied airily. 'Now, have we got all the bottles and nappies and everything else that I need?'

Marge nodded and gestured helplessly at the bag underneath the pram. Mrs Timmerson was moved by the weeping girl's distress and gently pulled her away from the pram to give her a hug.

'You've been very brave, Marge, and you've done nothing wrong. None of this is your fault. It'll all turn out fine just you wait and see.'

But matters did not turn out fine at all. As they left the church, Marge saw Mrs Hindmarsh push Jocelyn over to a car and remove the crying baby from the pram for the journey ahead. The sun was already starting to settle behind the trees and the lengthening shadows seemed to add a funereal dimension to the scene. A fresh sob rose in Marge's throat. She had broken her promise to Flora and her mother, and she was not at all reassured by what she had been told in the church hall by Mrs Timmerson. As she watched, Mrs Hindmarsh got into the rear of the black car with the baby, the doors slammed shut and the vehicle left the church hall in a cloud of dust and disappeared up the lane.

Chapter 8

Recollections

November 2000

Sixty years later, Marge paused momentarily, and her head drooped. For a moment Michael thought the old lady had fallen asleep, but she was merely adrift in the sad memory of Jocelyn's loss. He allowed her a moment of reflection and then gently cleared his throat. The sudden noise brought Marge back to the present and she looked up with glassy eyes.

'You know, I never saw Jocelyn ever again, Michael,' she sighed. 'I tried to visit her, but the Hindmarsh's farm was too far away, and Mrs Timmerson always found a reason for why we couldn't go. The other problem was that nobody returned Jocelyn's postcard, so Flora and Ma didn't know where she was living. I only stayed in Yorkshire for a short while and then Ma brought me home. You see, they ordered the evacuation too early really because the bombing didn't start properly for nearly another year. In the meantime, Ma got fed up with waiting and decided I was better off at home. When I returned, Jocelyn was still in Yorkshire.'

'You mustn't blame yourself,' Michael said gently. 'You were only a child yourself, and I know that many other children were temporarily mislaid in the confusion of the evacuation. But it shouldn't have been difficult to find Jocelyn as everyone knew the name of the village where she was staying. Didn't Flora make further enquiries?'

The old lady looked sad. 'I've asked myself the same question for many years. But you know, I don't think Flora tried very hard. I remember Ma going on at her about it after the Blitz had ended. Flora told her that she had made some enquiries, but she said that the authorities couldn't find Jocelyn. Ma and I didn't believe a word of it, though.' Marge paused for a moment, uncomfortable and seemingly reluctant to continue. 'I don't know how to tell you this, Michael, but Flora was a bright spark, and we all loved her, but she was what some people might call a free spirit. She lived with us in the sense that her possessions were stored in our top room, but she would disappear for months on end living goodness knows where or with whom. Then she would return to stay and usually because she was in trouble, pregnant again and needing Ma's help.'

'Pregnant?' Michael asked, surprised at Marge's description of Flora's love life but excited at the prospect that Jocelyn might have siblings.

'Yes, it was always the same with Flora. She loved the men, and they loved her. She even took up with my Uncle Albert for a while before he was killed in an air raid. I suppose it was the war that did it. It had a strange effect on everyone and affected their view of life. You see, people living in and around London were under the constant fear of death, and they had ideas about love and sex that would shock us now. Flora was no different, but she was more careless than most, and during the war she must have had another two or three children in our house.

She didn't keep any of them either. She always told Ma that she could never be a good mother to the children and that they were better off elsewhere. The fathers were never around for one reason or another, so Flora usually put them up for adoption. It became almost a routine. Ma didn't approve one jot, but she cared so much for Flora that she just put up with it.'

Michael was staggered. During Marge's initial account he had formed an image of Flora as a victim of circumstances, but that picture seemed very much at odds with this latest information. The old lady looked upset, and Michael wondered if she was about to cry. He tried to distract her.

'Tell me about Jocelyn and the Salvation Army, Marge. Why were they looking for Flora in the late sixties?'

'I'm not sure,' Marge replied. 'At the end of the war, Flora left us for the final time to get married, and we heard that she had been killed in a gas explosion. It was a real shock when nearly thirty years later the Salvation Army came around asking if we knew Flora, much like you've done today. It seems that after the war Jocelyn was brought up in local authority care believing that her mother had been killed in the Blitz. Jocelyn had eventually met somebody who lived abroad. She wanted to marry him and leave the country except she couldn't because Flora had never registered her birth, and without a birth certificate she couldn't get a passport. That's when the Salvation Army got involved. Apparently, quite a few children were lost in this way. The woman who came around told me that they knew of many cases where young evacuees were told incorrectly that their parents were dead and had ended up being fostered or put into orphanages.'

'Hmm, that's fair enough for lost children except Jocelyn was abandoned rather than mislaid,' Michael replied dryly. He was not only feeling a tinge of disappointment in Flora, but his heart had sunk on hearing that Jocelyn had been trying to move abroad. This might explain why he had been unable to find any further trace of her in the records, and if she was living in another country, it would make his search for her even more difficult. Maybe even impossible, he thought.

He studied the old lady wondering if her memory was still reliable. 'There's one thing I don't understand, Marge. Jocelyn's birth certificate shows that Flora made an affidavit in 1968 to register the birth retrospectively. That means she couldn't have died in the forties in either the Blitz or in a gas explosion. What was it that made you think that she had?'

'Well, a year or two after she left us, we had a visit from a man who said he was responsible for Flora's estate following her accidental death in a gas explosion. He told us that his law firm had been appointed to clear up the legal matters. He said they had discovered that Flora had lived with us for a while, and he was calling to find out if she had left any belongings behind. He walked with a bad limp I seem to remember. I thought he seemed to be a nice man, and he gave me some chocolate.'

'And were there any of Flora's belongings?'

'No, she took everything with her when she left for Somerset.'

Flora's death and her apparent resurrection were a mystery that couldn't be explained at that moment, so Michael parked the matter. However, there was one piece of the puzzle which would be really useful to discover if Marge's memory was up to it.

'Marge, do you know what Flora's real surname was?' he asked. 'It seems that whenever I find out anything about her, she is using the surname Belton.'

The old lady fought to dredge up an answer to this unexpected request. 'Umm, yes, it'll come back to me in a moment. I was told it, but a very long time ago.' She tailed off deep in thought. After a long silence she turned back to him. 'I'm sorry, Michael, it's not there anymore,' she said tapping the side of her head. 'Let me have a good long think about it. I'm sure it'll come back to me eventually. Flora became almost like one of the family and it seemed quite natural that she used the name Belton. It suited her as well and she told Ma it was safer.'

'Safer? Marge, do you believe that Flora was really running away from something or was it just an elaborate story?' Michael asked dubiously.

The old lady gave him a sharp look. 'No, Michael. I'm sure she was telling the truth. After I returned from the evacuation in Yorkshire, we had a visitor. I remember it was just before Christmas in 1939. We were all sat round the radio: Ma, Flora, Uncle Albert and me when the doorbell rang. The lights were out because of the black out and the curtains were drawn. Ma went to the front window and looked down at the front door and told us there was a man standing there. I remember she remarked that she didn't like the look of him. Flora rushed over to have a look and turned absolutely pale with fear. She pleaded with Ma and Uncle Albert not to tell the man anything about her and then raced down the stairs and out of the back door into the street at the rear. Uncle Albert went down to see the man and there was an altercation. The man was looking for Flora and he didn't believe Uncle Albert when he denied all knowledge of her. He kept going on about some stolen papers, and after he tried to barge his way in there was a scuffle and an exchange of blows. Poor Uncle Albert ended up with a terrible black eye and the man only went away when Ma threatened to tell the police. Flora didn't come back home for a week, and not long after she moved out to live with Uncle Albert a few streets away. She was never the same after that night. Whenever she was at our place, she would have one eye on the door and was off like a shot whenever a stranger rang the bell.'

Michael's interest twitched. 'Stolen papers? Do you think it was something to do with this Barrington Hall place?'

'I don't know for sure. She wouldn't tell us anything

about it, but right from when she first arrived, Flora seemed to be frightened of something or somebody. And she arrived so secretly it wouldn't surprise me if Barrington Hall had something to do with it. I tell you what, though, it would all be in her journal if you could ever find it. She was always writing in it, and she treated it like it was a precious treasure or something.'

'A journal?' Michaels asked excitedly. "Did she keep a journal? What happened to it, Marge, do you know?'

'Yes, it was a beautiful leather-bound book with a lock, and Flora guarded it as though her life depended on it. She used to hide it under a loose floorboard in her room because I found it once when she was away on one of her trips. The book was locked though so I couldn't read its contents. It was probably for the best really as I shouldn't have been looking for it.' Marge shuffled in her chair, embarrassed by the memory of her childhood snooping. 'The strange thing is that Flora knew that someone had removed it from its hiding place. I think she must have had some system for detecting that someone had interfered with it. Anyway, she gave me a frightful telling off and I never touched it again. It disappeared with her when she went back to the West Country after the war.'

Marge fell silent. Outside, the shadows were lengthening, and Michael sensed that the old lady was tiring and that he should leave. 'It would be really helpful if I could discover Flora's proper surname, Marge,' he said gently. 'I think I have found out as much as possible about her using the name Belton, but there might well be further records of births or marriages registered under her proper name. If there were, I could use them to locate more of Flora's children and they might know something about Jocelyn's whereabouts. If you remember her name, would you call me?' he asked, passing over a card with his details.

The old lady nodded and put the card carefully on the table. 'What will you do next, Michael?'

He paused before replying. 'Well, Marge, without

Flora's surname I don't think I'll get very far searching the official records so I think a trip to Barrington Hall might be in order. I'm not sure whether the same family still live there, but if they do, it's possible that they might have some knowledge or records of Flora.'

Marge looked away. 'You know, Michael. I'm just a simple old woman, but one thing I have learned in my life is that things are never as straightforward as they seem. I do understand why you want to find Jocelyn, but if you go poking around in the past you may well discover things that are best left well alone. I'm pretty sure that something bad happened to Flora at Barrington Hall and I can't see the family having much interest in helping you to uncover it. Are you sure there isn't another way?'

Michael smiled to allay her concerns. 'You forget that I'm a journalist, Marge. I'm used to dealing with people on sensitive matters. Besides, whatever threatened Flora all the years ago is interesting but not my main concern. I just want to find Jocelyn and I'm sure that if I stay focussed on that then everything will work out just fine.'

The old lady looked unconvinced but saw that Michael couldn't be dissuaded. 'I'll think about Flora's name, Michael. Will you let me know what you discover. I still feel …. well … in some way responsible for losing Jocelyn, and I would like to find out what happened to her in the end. To find out if it all worked out well for her if you see what I mean.'

Michael nodded his understanding and rose to leave. He liked Marge and admired the way that she still felt responsible for Jocelyn even after all these years. Loyalty and genuine concern seemed to be so rare these days, he reflected as he pushed the rickety trolley back into the kitchenette. His mother had been very similar. Perhaps it was a generational thing. The spirit of the Blitz perhaps. He left the trolley waiting by the sink and with a final farewell to Marge, he let himself out into the hallway. He looked at his watch as he left the outer door. He had learned much from Marge, but without Flora's surname he would make no further progress. However, he had gained a useful lead and there was still time to catch a train to Somerset if he got a move on.

Chapter 9

First Visit

November 2000

The following morning, Michael awoke in a comfortable but slightly faded coaching inn in the middle of Taunton. Before leaving London, he had found Barrington Hall on the map and then spoken on the phone to a pleasant and well-spoken lady calling herself Emily Pendleton who had agreed to see him the following day. Michael had been deliberately vague about the reason for his visit and had merely mentioned that he was trying to trace a lost relative who he believed had worked at the house during the war. The woman didn't think that they would be able to help but she was nonetheless interested to hear his story.

At the hotel, Michael had charmed the evening receptionist who had granted him the use of her computer for half an hour. He had used the time to search the official records for more information about Flora Belton.

He was unable to find a record of any marriages, but he did discover a further three births in the Islington area that were registered by a Flora Belton over a period of several years during the War. He ordered the certificates for completeness, but he was not really expecting them to reveal much additional information as he already knew from Marge that the children were likely to have been fathered by unnamed men and then adopted. Smiling his thanks to the receptionist he had retired early.

After breakfast, Michael set off in a small hire car to find Barrington Hall. The main road soon gave way to narrow countryside lanes lined by tall hedges that reached up and overhung the road. As he approached the hall, Michael was forced to slow down as he passed a telecommunications van that was parked in a small passing place. The workmen had set up a triangle of cones and seemed to be digging a small hole next to a telegraph pole. As Michael went by, one of the men in overalls stopped work and stared at him as though it was Michael's fault that the peaceful countryside reverie had been disturbed. Ignoring the man's scrutiny, Michael saw that the road turned sharply to the right and away from a weathered brick wall that stood either side of an imposing set of wrought iron gates. An inscribed stone slab was set into the wall and informed Michael that he had arrived. Michael turned in and made his way up a gravelled drive surrounded on both sides by mature Yew trees. The house appeared beyond a sprawling patch of Rhododendron bushes and Michael parked on a large area of gravel in front of a set of steps leading up to the front door. It was a spectacular Georgian building that looked exactly like it did in the household photograph that he had seen at Marge's. He could even locate the exact place that Flora had stood smiling at the camera.

At the top of the stone steps, Michael pulled on a rope and heard a distant bell. A moment later, a polite lady wearing a white pinafore appeared, invited him inside and announced that Mrs Emily would be along to see him shortly. As he waited alone, Michael admired his surroundings. The hall was lined with panelling punctuated by a magnificent collection of oil paintings. One row contained the family portraits, with quite a few of the subjects wearing military uniforms. Below the portraits, there were more traditional paintings of country landscapes. All were framed with heavy gilt and the antique collection looked extremely valuable. As he glanced at the walls, Michael remembered an internet article he had found the previous evening. It had been about the Pendleton's family business, a large firm called Pendleton International Art. The fine arts and auctioneering company had been celebrating ninety years of successful enterprise since it was founded by Sir Thomas Pendleton in 1910. Judging by the paintings on display in the hall, the company's owners had possessed a fine eye for quality and had reserved some of their better acquisitions for the walls of the family home. As he waited, Michael noticed that there were two rooms to one side of the hall. Both were guarded by closed oak doors, but one was slightly ajar and as he glanced in through the narrow gap, Michael could see a wall that looked as though it might be one side of a gallery. A large horizontal picture with overhanging wall lights made a striking centrepiece. The composition was a surreal representation of a woman holding something he couldn't make out whilst overlooking what seemed to be a golden altar adorned with some kind of sculptured face. Michael was more literary minded than artistic, but even with his limited knowledge, the unmistakeable art nouveau period and the artist's unusual use of colour made the painting seem familiar. He was just moving to step inside the room to take a closer look when he was interrupted by a commanding voice that cut through the silence of the hall.

'Mr Calvert? I'm Francis Pendleton. I believe Mrs Barrow showed you into the hall to wait. I'm not sure that her invitation extended to a full tour of the house and its contents.' Michael turned and was met by a man with fair hair of similar age to himself. He recognized him immediately from one of the more recent portraits hanging in the hall. The subject had been wearing an army general's uniform and as Michael coolly appraised the man, he decided that the artist had captured his features brilliantly. General Francis Pendleton was of medium height and build, with cold and unsmiling grey eyes that were firmly fixed on Michael with a mixture of contempt and mistrust. At first sight, the man's youthful complexion gave the impression of a life untouched by troubles but a pale scar just above his right eye betrayed an earlier strife and added a menacing dimension to his disapproving scowl. The General had walked into the hall so silently that Michael had only been aware of his presence when Pendleton had broken the silence with his barking introduction. There could be no mistaking his air of authority, and Michael instinctively knew that he was a man used to getting his own way. Pendleton was clearly irritated by Michael's curiosity, and without offering a hand in greeting, he stepped past Michael to close the heavy door and locked it with a large iron key. Michael flushed with sudden embarrassment and shame.

'I'm terribly sorry. I didn't mean to intrude but the door was open, and I was fascinated by your collection.'

The man ignored Michael's feeble apology and indicated that they should both move further along the passage. Francis Pendleton clearly had no time for excuses or further pleasantries, and as they walked silently past the line of disapproving family portraits, Michael got the overpowering impression that he was marching under close escort. He followed Francis into the last room leading from the hall and was blinded by the bright sunshine that flooded in through a series of huge, south facing sash windows. The wall was covered with more paintings and tapestries, and the room was furnished with plush antiques. As they entered, an elegant woman stood up from a chaise longue and extended a slender hand.

'Hello Mr Calvert, I am Francis' mother, Emily Pendleton.'

Michael smiled. Emily Pendleton was immaculately dressed in a tweed suit. She wore a pearl necklace, and her hands were covered in several jewelled gold rings. She looked to be every inch the lady of the manor, and even walked in an upright and effortless way that seemed to emphasize her fine breeding. He took her hand and tried to use a little levity to ease the tension from his encounter with Francis Pendleton.

'Hello, Mrs Pendleton, please call me Michael. I would like to thank you for seeing me at such short notice. I'm sorry to say that your son has just caught me admiring some of the fabulous pieces of art that you have hanging in this house.' The old lady glanced at her son who raised his eyebrows at her noncommittally before glaring at Michael.

'Yes, we do have a marvellous collection,' she said returning her gaze to the visitor. 'The Pendleton family has had an interest in fine art for many years, and since my late husband's uncle founded the family firm, we have gradually built up more pieces than we know what to do with.' She patted the chaise next to her. 'Enough of that, though. Come and sit here and tell us about this search of yours. I have to say, I am very interested to know how we might be able to help you.'

Michael sat carefully on the plush red velvet. Across the room, Francis Pendleton walked over to one of the large windows and stared out at the well-kept grounds. While he gazed with apparent disinterest, there was something rather too intent about his stare, and Michael was certain that he was listening carefully to every detail. Ignoring Francis' feigned boredom, Michael told Emily about his adoption and his recent decision to research his family tree. He explained how his efforts to find his natural mother had so far been unsuccessful and that he had instead transferred his investigations to his natural grandmother, Flora.

'The main problem is that there is some confusion about Flora's surname,' he explained. 'Unless I can discover that then I have little hope of finding my natural mother. But I have found a lady in Islington who knew Flora during the war and although she couldn't remember her surname, she was certain that Flora used to work as a domestic servant in this house during the late thirties. In fact, she seemed to think that Flora might have left this household under a bit of a cloud. I know it's a bit of a long shot, but I wondered if you had any knowledge of the household from that period. Perhaps there are some old staff records? The main thing I need is Flora's surname.'

'Well, no, I'm very sorry but I don't think we'll be able to help you at all,' Emily said carefully, glancing across the room to her son. 'You see, I'm a Pendleton only by marriage, and I wasn't here then. Barrington Hall was originally owned by Francis' great uncle, Sir Roland Pendleton. He had no children, and so when he died in 1978 the estate passed over to his younger brother, Maxwell who was my father-in-law. So, though I did eventually inherit the estate, it was much later, I'm afraid.'

'Who is this lady in Islington?' interjected Francis breaking his silence at the window. 'Is she reliable? I must say this so-called connection to the Pendleton family sounds a bit tenuous.'

Michael paused briefly, wondering how much he should reveal. Deciding that honesty was probably the best approach, he continued. 'Well, she's called Margaret Belton. Her aunt was the cook in this house in the late thirties and during the war. Apparently, Flora went to live with the Beltons after she left here in late 1938. She was treated almost like another daughter; she gave birth to my mother there and even adopted the Belton surname as her own. Margaret was able to show me an old household photograph taken in 1937 just outside here with all the staff lined up. She is clearly stood with the other maids.'

'I see,' said Emily Pendleton. 'How fascinating, but as I said this is well before our time here and I don't think we can add anything further to your story.'

Francis Pendleton shifted from his position next to the window and advanced across the room to where Michael sat next to Emily. His movements were purposeful but conducted with the minimum expenditure of energy. His eyes seemed to grow darker, and their intensity made Michael feel uncomfortable. The man seemed almost feline or reptilian perhaps.

'No, I don't believe we can help further,' he fired at Michael. 'As you said earlier, Mr Calvert, it was always going to be a long shot and I'm afraid it's one that has missed the target.' He stared down at Michael wearing an expression that was rather too satisfied for Michael's liking. 'It seems that you have had a wasted visit.' His tone softened slightly. 'I'm sorry if I was rude earlier but we are very particular about security at the hall. Perhaps it's my military background and all the time I spent in Northern Ireland. I'm sure you will understand that many of the pictures in the family collection are worth a great deal and we tend to be a bit careful about strangers.'

Michael stood up, recognising that he was being dismissed. Despite his instinctive dislike of General Francis Pendleton, he feigned pleasantries and took the General's hand. The man's grip was firm, not to the point of rudeness but it was unmistakably designed to leave the recipient in no doubt about the strength of character and determination of the man behind it. When Michael had been a young foreign correspondent, he had once spent several weeks in the desert with the British Army covering the first Gulf War. He had mixed freely with the men and had the opportunity to observe them closely and listen to their views about the commanders who led them. In Michael's experience most army officers were tough individuals who possessed a real sense of humility. However, the soldiers he lived amongst also described a small number of their leaders for whom arrogance and blind ambition were the key attributes for progress. It seemed that these officers were fiercely intellectual but lacked the confidence to succeed on their own merits, and so they sought promotion through patronage, by plagiarizing others' work and by standing on the shoulders of their colleagues. Michael had been shocked at the soldiers' description but faced with Francis Pendleton he now wondered whether the General was a commander who the soldiers would recognise and try to avoid.

Michael was determined to avoid any sign that the General's intimidation had been successful, and so he released Francis' grip with a smile. He was unsurprised that the Pendletons had no knowledge of a young servant girl from nearly sixty years earlier, but he was disappointed that his search appeared to have reached a dead end. He placed his card on a silver tray by the chaise and asked them to contact him if anything new came to light. Emily Pendleton smiled reassurance, and then rang a small bell to summon Mrs Barrow to show Michael out.

As he left the front door and descended the steps, Michael glanced at the window where Francis had stood. There was something very unpleasant about General Pendleton, Michael thought as he drove out of the gate and headed back to Taunton, and he sincerely hoped that he would never have to meet the man again.

As Michael's car disappeared up the drive, Emily Pendleton studied Francis with similar misgivings, but they were overlaid with maternal guilt. Emily was the daughter of a wealthy landowner whose estate had neighboured the Pendletons'. Her father had been a regular visitor to Barrington Hall where he was made welcome by Sir Roland. The two men became close friends, and nobody was surprised when Emily eventually married into the Pendleton family. Sir Roland had no children, but he had a younger brother, Maxwell, whose amiable son was called Thomas. Emily's father thought that Thomas made an ideal match for his daughter, and Maxwell and Sir Roland both agreed. It was the British aristocracy's version of an arranged wedding, but it wouldn't last long. Emily and Thomas were only in their early twenties when they married in 1948 and there was only just enough time to conceive their son, Francis, before Thomas was killed in a shooting accident. And that was when matters had started to go awry.

When Francis was born a few months after his father died, he fell under the influence of his Great Uncle Roland rather than Maxwell his grandfather, and this arose through hereditary custom rather than planning. The two brothers ran Pendleton International Art from Barrington Hall. As the older brother, Sir Roland was entitled to live as the permanent occupant of the house, and so Maxwell lived in a similarly impressive but smaller property a few miles away. After Emily was widowed, Sir Roland offered her living accommodation in one of the wings at Barrington Hall which she had accepted gratefully. It became her side of the house, an island of independence which allowed her to remain distant from the dull routine of the art business taking place elsewhere in the building. But the living arrangements also meant that Francis gravitated to his great uncle who he saw daily. At first, Emily was happy with this arrangement because it released her to become the de facto lady of the manor and to pursue her passion for horse-riding and country pursuits. Meanwhile, Francis seemed to thrive under Sir Roland's influence, and Emily was pleased to observe the boy's happiness despite the absence of his father. However, Emily's view changed as she gradually became aware that beneath Sir Roland's genial exterior there lurked a more ruthless, calculating and selfish man. Worse still, she could see that her son was assuming many of Sir Roland's worst character traits, and that he was gradually becoming his surrogate father's clone. But by then it was too late for Emily to intervene, and so when Francis left Barrington Hall for the Army, he was the mirror image of his mentor. He had been groomed to take over Sir Roland's legacy and to run it in the same ruthless manner once he had completed his military service.

However, it would be a few years before Francis would take control of Pendleton International Art. After Sir Roland died, the reins passed to Maxwell, but he was increasingly frail, and the business suffered through neglect. Eventually he died and Emily asked her son to retire from the Army and return home to run the company. Francis was initially reluctant because he had just been promoted to General, but he acquiesced when Emily told him that she would activate her controlling interest in the company and find someone else to run it if he refused. Her son's immediate capitulation surprised her at the time, and she wondered if he knew something about the business that he didn't want to share with an outsider. However, she was delighted when he returned, and she didn't press him on the matter. Despite his flaws, her son was an effective steward, and the business seemed to recover quickly following his return, so she stopped interfering and let her son get on with it.

As she reflected on her son's life, Emily hoped Francis wouldn't overreact to Michael Calvert's intrusion but in her heart, she knew he probably would. He was staring at Michael's retreating car and was clearly considering what to do next. She knew a little about the servant girl and why she was dismissed. It was a matter that would cause only passing embarrassment to the Pendletons, but it wouldn't threaten their livelihood. She would mention it to Francis only if it became absolutely necessary.

Chapter 10

The Locals

November 2000

Michael was not normally impulsive, but a short distance from Barrington Hall he spotted a signpost to the local village called Ashill and turned off the lane to take a look. He was aware that the owners of many large country houses had often employed domestic staff locally, and he wondered if Flora had come from somewhere close by. His visit to Barrington Hall had been disappointing, and although a visit to the local village was a bit speculative, it would do no harm to ask a few questions of the locals.

Ashill could have featured on the front of any number of countryside magazines. Thatched cottages with immaculate gardens lined a single narrow lane and containers of flowers stood guard on each gateway. In the middle of the village, the buildings opened out, and the road skirted by the edge of a tidy green encompassing a well-populated duck pond. A church overlooked the area, standing opposite a small pub with blackened timbers set against freshly painted white render. Michael glanced at his watch as he parked the car by the edge of the grass. It was lunchtime and his empty stomach was grumbling. The pub would be the best place to start his enquiries, and it wouldn't harm to pop in and try a small glass of the local cider.

As Michael entered the pub, the conversation temporarily dimmed as the regulars turned to look at the stranger who had appeared in their midst. The ceiling was low, and Michael had to stoop slightly to avoid a low wooden beam. As he did so, he stumbled slightly and was aware of a laugh from somewhere further along the small lounge. Muttering a curse, he lurched to the bar and was met by a smiling landlord with a set of spectacular sideburns straight out of Victorian England. The man's accent was thick, and his voice was gravelly from the unlit pipe that hung from the corner of his mouth.

'Most folks trip on the way out rather than the way in,' he observed dryly and then smiled a toothy welcome. 'What can I get you, Sir?' Michael asked for a glass of the local cider and a sandwich and perched on a stool that stood vacant at the end of the bar. His neighbour shuffled up to give Michael more room, and then turned away to continue the conversation with his drinking companion. The landlord returned with Michael's drink and food.

'We don't often get visitors in Ashill,' he remarked and peered at Michael waiting for an explanation. With the glass held to his lips, Michael nodded both to acknowledge the fine quality of the local brew and to indicate that he would comply with his interrogator's silent question once his thirst had been partially slaked. He placed the glass down on the bar.

'Yes, I'm researching my family tree. I believe my grandmother may be from around this area, and I wondered if somebody might know of her.'

'Family tree? I see. Well, if you're looking for a lost lady then you need to speak to old Archie. He's lived here for years and always used to be the local stud in the old days,' he laughed lecherously. He turned to look at a group of old men sitting in the corner playing dominos. 'Oi Archie!' he shouted. There's a gentleman here who's looking for his grandmother. You knew all the girls from around these parts you old ram. Come over here and help.' The rest of the pub laughed and then went silent as curious faces turned to listen. Archie was as old as many of the fixtures in the pub, and it was clear that he had been a regular for most of his long life. Michael immediately recognized the type. Archie would always sit in the same seat – a chair that would be left vacant by those in the know. He would be recognized by everyone in the village and would be regarded as somewhat of an oracle when it came to village folklore. 'Ask Archie' would be the cry whenever a matter of local history or practice was in dispute. 'Good old Archie, he will know.'

However, as the overweight old man made his extensive preparations to stand up, Michael noted that it must have been many years since he had been the ladies' man of the village. At the landlord's bidding, Archie carefully put down his dominos, placed his large hands on the table and rose to his feet, swaying slightly. There was a slight pause as he confirmed to himself that his legs were not about to give way, and then he waddled, wheezing and puffing, over to the bar. Michael guessed that he was well into his eighties with a face lined from tobacco and sunshine and a nose glistening red from too much cider.

'Never you mind him,' he said jabbing a finger at the smiling landlord. 'He don't know nothing about rams or tupping. He's forgotten what to do with his anyway!' Archie laughed at his own crudity and then started to cough. After a few moments of unproductive spluttering, he recovered from the consequences of his great hilarity and turned to Michael. 'Well now, young man who's this grandmother of yours?' Michael suddenly felt self-conscious and started to regret his candour.

'Erm, well I know her name was Flora and that she used to work at Barrington Hall as a domestic servant some sixty years or more ago. I've been up there and spoken to the Pendletons who can't seem to help. Beyond that, there's little else I know about her.'

The old man looked into the distance as he fired up his creaking memory and searched it for the necessary records. 'Flora, you say. Now let's see.' He paused, wiping his nose with the back of his hand. 'Yes, there was a girl called Flora in Ashill. She used to live at the other end of the village, and she worked round at Mrs Evans' place for a while. I don't know much else about her though as she was a bit older than me, and I was only a young boy.'

'Can you remember her surname?' Michael asked excitedly.

Behind the bar, the landlord was consulting his unlit pipe as though he expected it to combust spontaneously into life. 'How come you don't know your own grandmother's name?' he interjected.

'It's a long story,' Michael replied, reluctant to go into detail with strangers.

Archie screwed up his eyes in concentration. 'Flora's name? No, I'm afraid it's gone, but I do remember her father died in an accident up at the Hall.'

'What sort of accident?' Michael asked, hoping there was more.

'I can't rightly remember I'm afraid, something to do with a riding accident I think, but I do remember it being the talk of the village for a while.' At this, the man next to Michael snapped round and glared at Archie.

'You old fool,' he sneered menacingly. 'Always the village gossip, aren't you, Archie? Always have been, always will be.' He turned his threatening scowl to Michael. 'You don't want to listen to much of what he has to say. Most of it is made-up rubbish. Besides, there isn't much good going to come from you poking your nose around here or up at Barrington Hall. We don't like strangers asking questions around these parts. You're not wanted and you're not welcome.'

Archie backed away looking slightly alarmed at this unwarranted intervention. Michael mentally joined him. He had not really noticed his neighbour when he had first sat down at the end of the bar, but now Michael could see that his adversary was middle-aged and powerfully built with rough features that perfectly matched the man's aggressive demeanour. Michael was astonished at the man's outburst, and he was about to remonstrate at his rudeness when he became aware that a further two men had joined the spat. They looked so alike that Michael was sure they must be father and son or perhaps elder and younger brothers. The older man seemed to have a surprising lack of lines on his face and his smooth complexion gave him an air of youthfulness that was at odds with his years. The younger man's features were very similar, but he was certainly younger at around sixty or so Michael guessed. The pair had arrived at Michael's side silently and had timed their arrival to perfection.

'You've never had any manners, Ron Stanton,' the older of the two men observed quietly. 'What's the harm? This gentleman's only looking for a relative. Or are you that scared of his lordship up at the hall? That would be typical of your family, wouldn't it?' He glanced at Michael. 'His lot have always been in the pocket of the Pendletons. From grandfather to father to son. You all end up with your hands dirty at Barrington Hall don't you Ron? What've they paid you to do now?'

Ron flushed and stood up to confront the two men, his hands clenching and unclenching into fists as he fought to control his anger. He was very tall, with broad shoulders and judging by the odd angle of his nose Michael guessed that he was quite accustomed to settling disputes in the traditional way. However, next to Michael, the older man stood his ground, and for a moment Michael thought they were going to come to blows. Thankfully, the moment passed, and Ron settled for an invasion of the older man's personal space. He leaned forward so that his face was inches away from his opponent.

'Well, Arthur,' he said in a low voice full of bilious hatred. 'I would have thought that you of all people would know exactly what happens to folks that start poking around in Pendleton business. Haven't you learned anything from the past or perhaps you need teaching the same lesson again?'

'Now please gentlemen,' Michael said, confused at how the situation had inexplicably spiralled out of control but anxious to avoid a brawl. 'I don't quite know what this is all about, but I don't want to cause any trouble.' He looked at the landlord. 'I'm very sorry about this. Look, I'll be getting along now. I'm sorry that I seem to have caused a fuss.' The landlord nodded his approval but continued to stand guard over the two men who were standing eye to eye and exchanging unspoken insults through malevolent stares. Michael quickly drained his glass and headed for the door to escape the oppressive atmosphere that had pervaded the small bar.

Outside, he sucked in the cool air and tried to make sense of the exchange. He was pleased that there was at least some recollection of Flora in the village, but he couldn't understand how an innocent question about Barrington Hall could have triggered such a vitriolic exchange between the two men inside. It was clear that the pair had previous history between them and that the matter related in some way to the Pendletons. But beyond that, their exchange was mystifying. Inwardly attributing the matter to alcohol and village politics, Michael was about to set off to the car when a hand gripped his elbow. It was Arthur and the younger man. They had rushed out after him and Arthur was slightly out of breath. The old man glanced behind him to see if he had been followed and lowered his voice.

'You'll not get anything but trouble asking questions of Ron Stanton, but you might try his grandfather, Frederick Smithieson. He was a stable hand at Barrington Hall before the war and would have known all the servants at the time. Watch out though, that family have all worked up at the Hall at one time or another and they're as bad as each other.'

'I see,' Michael said interested to know more. 'Look, if you don't mind me asking, what was all that fuss about in the pub?'

'It's an old story and nothing to concern you,' the older man replied, releasing Michael's arm. 'My name is Arthur Blackford, and this is my son, David. Our family have lived near here for years and we know the Pendletons only too well. If my father was still here, he would tell you a thing or two about Barrington Hall and the old days. But it's history that's best left well alone as none of it will help you find out about your grandmother.'

'Did you know Flora?' Michael asked.

A fleeting shadow passed across the old man's face, and he broke Michael's gaze whilst shaking his head.

'Can't say I rightly do. But it was a long time ago and you forget things easily at my age,' he added lamely. 'Anyhow, it's time we were going,' he announced as a commotion in the entrance to the pub indicated that the landlord had called time on the lunchtime's proceedings. 'I've nothing more to add. But speak to Smithieson. He lives in the last cottage on the right as you leave the village, and he'll probably remember if he's prepared to speak to you.' The old man walked away with his son and then looked back. 'Don't tell him I sent you or you'll get nothing,' he added before walking off. Michael watched the pair make their way slowly towards an old car parked on the edge of the green. The old man had been helpful, but Michael was sure that he knew more than he had revealed. And that knowledge included more about Flora too. It was the strange look that had crossed his face when

Michael had mentioned Flora's name that gave it away. Was it guilt or loss? Michael couldn't tell but he would find out one way or another, and as the occupants of the pub began spilling out of the building, he set off briskly in the direction that Arthur had indicated.

It was only a short walk to the end of the village, but it was far enough for Michael's mobile telephone to regain the signal it had lost inside the pub. Now connected, the small device announced shrilly that he had missed a call and had voicemail waiting. Without breaking step, Michael checked his messages and was surprised to hear Francis Pendleton's voice. The man's tone was curt but a bit more polite than it had been during Michael's earlier visit to Barrington Hall. He explained that after Michael had left the house, Emily had remembered a set of old accounts books found in a drawer in one of the downstairs rooms when she had taken possession of the house. They had checked the records dating from the pre-war period and had found reference to an unnamed parlour maid who was dismissed in January nineteen thirty-nine for gross misconduct. Pendleton said that there were no other details other than the girl had been sent on her way without serving notice and that she had received no back pay. Before ending the message, the retired general promised to contact him again if they discovered anything else.

Michael snapped the phone lid closed to end the call, surprised that the tetchy general had bothered to call him. It was disappointing that the household records had not included the maid's name, but the date was about right and if the accounts book was referring to his grandmother, then it seemed to confirm Marge's story that Flora had left Barrington Hall under a cloud. He replaced the phone in his pocket and looked ahead to the last house on the street. As he did so, he saw a young athletic man with closely cropped hair come out of the front gate, cross the road and walk down the street towards the centre of the village. He didn't seem to notice Michael approaching, and he passed by without making eye contact. At least it appeared that somebody was at home, Michael thought as he turned in through the same gateway and made his way across an unkempt garden to the front door.

Frederick Smithieson was an older version of his grandson, Ron Stanton. Despite his great age and dirty clothes, the old man's large frame was still upright and the hand that gripped Michael's was surprisingly strong for someone who must have been in his eighties. He regarded Michael suspiciously with a cold, unfeeling stare, and Michael gained the impression that despite his age Frederick Smithieson was a dangerous man. Michael explained who he was and that he was looking for a lost relative. Smithieson grunted his understanding, and with a brief gesture, he waved Michael into his home. It was disgusting inside, and the cheap air freshener that stood on a windowsill was failing miserably to mask the unpleasant stench of old frying fat and body odour. Dirty plates and old newspapers littered the small lounge, and the cheap settee that was offered to Michael was so stained that he was reluctant to sit on it.

To Michael's relief, Smithieson made no attempt to offer him anything to drink, and instead the old man sat down heavily in a grubby armchair and indicated his readiness to hear what Michael had to say by staring unblinkingly at him. The man's gaze was so disconcerting that Michael fidgeted and felt like a rabbit trapped in headlamps. Quickly, he explained about Flora and his search and that he had been told in the pub that as Fred had worked at Barrington Hall, he might know something of his grandmother. At Michael's mention of Flora, a thin smile cracked Smithieson's inscrutable gaze. The smile became a grin which eventually morphed into an unpleasant hollow laugh.

'Flora? Oh yes, I remember her all right. We all had a piece of that girl at one time or another and it was her that taught me the ways of the world if you know what I mean. She was a right one, a real harlot who was always available for a bit of fun in the stables. I'm surprised that she lasted as long as she did at the Hall, but then again, Sir Roland always had a bit of a soft spot for her. Or perhaps I should say that just like everyone else he particularly liked her soft spots,' he laughed.

'What do you mean?'

'What I mean is that it wasn't only the serving staff that knew Flora well. She was a popular all-rounder you might say.'

'I see. Do you know what her full name was?' Michael asked, failing to reconcile Smithieson's description of Flora with the image of the fresh looking, attractive girl on Marge's photograph. 'I know that after she left Barrington Hall she used the surname Belton, but I need to know her original surname.'

'No, it wasn't Belton. After all, I wouldn't forget Flora's name. How could I? She was my very first,' the old man cackled. 'It was Jamieson, Flora Jamieson.'

Michael didn't know whether to feel jubilant or downhearted. He now knew his grandmother's name, but Smithieson's description of Flora's activities had left him feeling deflated. Fearing further unwelcome revelations he nonetheless pressed on. 'How long did you know her for?'

'Oh, let's see. She must've been up at the Hall for several months. I had a brief thing with her during late nineteen thirty-eight just before she was sacked for bad behaviour. You know, even though she was still seeing me, she was caught with young Will Jones in the potting shed with her skirts up around her neck. Poor lad ran a mile when he heard that Sir Roland had found out. Bill Denton, the butler reported her to the master, and she was sent away the very next day.'

'Did you know she was pregnant when she left?' Michael asked hesitantly, fearing what Smithieson's answer might be.

'Oh yes, the story all came out. But she'd been with so many men in that household that anyone could have been the father. It didn't mean anything to me, and I couldn't have cared less for her or the child.'

Michael's heart sank as his mental picture of Flora received yet another blow. Everything that Smithieson was saying seemed to support what Marge had revealed to Michael about Flora's countless pregnancies and fatherless children, and the sudden reality of her life left him feeling disappointed and a bit angry. It had also occurred to him that the odious man sat opposite could potentially be his natural grandfather, and his stomach churned rebelliously at the idea.

Michael had intended to raise the matter of the stolen papers that Marge had mentioned, but he had heard enough about Flora's activities, and he suddenly felt desperate to leave the squalid house and its obnoxious occupant. He stood up thanking the old man for his time, though he felt little gratitude for what he had learned. Smithieson rose too and followed him to the front door. He looked at Michael darkly.

'Is it the baby's father? Is that what this is all about? If so, I should be very careful if I were you. I couldn't care less for my part, but I can't see the Pendletons being so happy with you dredging up some story about some pregnant whore of a parlour maid. It's all in the past and you'd best leave it there if you ask me.' Michael winced at the man's crude reference to his natural grandmother but nodded.

'I just wanted to discover her surname so that I can find my natural mother,' he said noncommittally. 'You've told me that, so I think my business here in Somerset is finished now.'

The old man nodded and leaned forward threateningly. 'That's very wise, Mr Calvert. Leave the Pendletons well alone if you know what's good for you. Leave Somerset and don't come back. That's my best advice.'

Michael mumbled his thanks and walked away from the front door conscious of Smithieson's eyes boring into the back of his head as he left the front garden. It had been a barely concealed threat of course, and one thing Michael had learned from his time as a reporter was that when people started to issue threats there was always something interesting to be revealed. He might well have learned his grandmother's name, but there was not a chance on earth that he would stop delving now that Smithieson had tried to warn him off.

Chapter 11

Discovery

December 1939

Flora looked down in fear as she watched Frederick Smithieson hammering on the front door of Margaret Belton's house. It was just before Christmas in 1939. She had felt so safe since arriving in London, but it was clear that Sir Roland had found her and that she had lost her sanctuary. There was no time to wonder how she had been traced to the Beltons' house, and so she grabbed a few clothes and rushed out of the back door, past the outside toilet and into the yard at the rear of the building. In more normal times, the poorly lit backstreet was full of grey shadows, but under air raid precautions it was virtually pitch black and she had to move slowly to avoid knocking over the dustbins. However, Flora's eyes gradually adjusted to the darkness and when she peeped round the edge of the gap in the rear wall, she could just make out that the narrow road was clear of people. With a quick glance behind her, Flora left the cover of the dark yard and walked quickly down the cobbles just as confrontational shouts from the front of the building broke the evening silence.

Poor Albert, Flora thought, thinking of his assailant. Despite Smithieson's relative youth, he was a large brute of a man who would use violence without a moment's hesitation if he thought it would achieve what he wanted. Flora had known him for about a year after she had started work at Barrington Hall. He was lewd, and along with the other female members of staff she had tried to avoid him whenever possible. Officially Smithieson worked in the stables, but he was also used casually by Sir Roland to impose discipline on the staff, usually through beatings. She was surprised to see Smithieson now, though, as he had been sent to prison before Flora's escape from Barrington Hall. He must have been released, she thought, and there was little doubt that he was working for Sir Roland again. She thought of Albert, and guilty tears streamed down her face. She knew that he would do anything to protect her, but it was unlikely that he would have the upper hand in any physical confrontation with Smithieson, and she was worried that he might get badly hurt. Over the previous few months, Flora had grown quite attached to Margaret Belton's younger brother. He was more than fifteen years older than Flora and was very proper, but he had a kind heart and what had started as friendship soon developed into something more tangible. More importantly, Albert was not judgemental, and he had avoided asking questions either about Flora's time at Barrington Hall or about her status as an unmarried mother. As she neared the end of the street, Flora checked behind to make sure that she hadn't been followed. All seemed clear and as she emerged from the side street onto the main road the shouting faded away and peace returned to the neighbourhood.

Dodging other pedestrians in the darkened streets, she

headed towards the hospital. Since Jocelyn had been evacuated to Yorkshire, Flora had worked there as a women's volunteer auxiliary nurse. The jobs were menial: mainly cleaning, making beds and emptying bed pans, but the regular nurses liked Flora's sunny personality, and she had soon made several close friends. This was fortunate, because Flora now needed somewhere to stay. The nurses' home was just behind the hospital, and Flora went up to the first floor hoping that her friend, Rose, was off-duty and in her room. She knocked and a small bubbly girl of similar age opened the door. She absorbed Flora's concerned look and stained cheeks, smiled a surprised welcome and without demanding any kind of explanation let her straight in.

It was several days before Flora felt it was safe enough to venture out, and before leaving she wrapped a scarf around her hair to make herself less recognisable. She went out after it got dark, taking a circuitous route to Albert's house which was several streets from Margaret Belton's place. Fortunately, Albert had just finished his shift as a fireman at the local station and he was alone at home. He grinned roguishly at Flora when he opened the door, and the flash of his teeth against his smart uniform made his black eye seem even more incongruous.

'I was beginning to think you might have run away for good, Flora,' he said self-consciously but clearly delighted that his suspicions had been proved wrong. Flora gasped at the dark bruising, and slowly raised a hand to touch the side of his face. She had grown increasingly fond of this gentle giant of a man.

'Oh no, Albert. Are you alright? Did Smithieson do that?'

'Was that his name? To be honest, he was too busy shouting about some papers of yours to tell me who he was!' Albert laughed.

'Oh, I'm so sorry you got hurt. This is all my fault. Look Albert, that man was from the past, from Somerset.

Please don't ask me to explain. I can't tell you what it's all about. It's just too dangerous for me, for you and maybe even for Jocelyn.' She paused as a sudden, more selfish consideration intruded. 'Er, did Smithieson get in? I mean did he get any of my things? Is my journal safe?'

'Oh no, don't worry,' Albert declared proudly. 'I didn't let him across the doorstep, and he went away empty handed. All your stuff's still in your room at Margaret's.' Tears of relief and gratitude started to fall down Flora's cheeks. Albert smiled at her, and gently took her hand. 'Look, girl. I don't know what you've been writing in that book of yours, but if you have secrets from the past then it's no business of mine to go delving into them. You can tell me one day when you're ready. Anyway, the past is the past and it's the future that's more important to me.' Shyly gathering his thoughts, Albert paused for a moment before continuing with a matter that had been preying on his mind for several weeks. 'I wondered if that future might hold something for the two of us…. the two of us together that is?' Flora looked up into Albert's kindly face as tenderness and affection welled up inside. She put her hands on either side of his face and stroked his cheeks before standing on tiptoe to brush her lips tenderly against his.

'You're such a kind man, Albert, but I don't know if I'm good enough for you.'

Fearing imminent disappointment, Albert didn't reply, but he wrapped his arms around her and held her tightly. Flora buried her face in his chest. His uniform was damp from the evening mist and smelled of a curious mix of smoke and camphor. She loved Albert, perhaps not in a heart-thumping, all-consuming sense, but it was love nonetheless and his offer was attractive. She had no doubt that Albert would make a caring husband and father, but Flora's past seemed determined to spoil her future happiness and the last thing she wanted was for Albert to be hurt. Perhaps a compromise was the answer. Something stable but still offering some flexibility should matters take a turn for the worse.

She looked up at his concerned face and took one of his hands. 'I can't marry you at the moment, Albert. Things are just too uncertain: the war, Jocelyn and the past, things like that. But I will live with you as your wife if you would have me, and I'll still come with all the usual promises: in sickness and in health, for richer and for poorer, that kind of thing.'

Albert wasn't shocked, but he looked serious and remained briefly silent while he weighed up her offer. For a horrifying moment Flora thought that he might turn her down, but after a moment's consideration he laughed, raised her face to his and kissed her again.

'Live together in sin? It's not quite what I had in mind, but it's close enough to marriage despite what the neighbours will say.' He hugged her tight and then whispered, 'There is just one thing, though. Does this agreement also mean that you have to honour me in other ways?'

'Oh, I should think so.' Flora laughed, and she pushed him backwards into the house.

Later that same evening, Flora stretched and gazed up at the ceiling of Albert's bedroom with a contented smile on her face. Beside her, Albert slept deeply. A lock of hair had fallen over his black eye, partially concealing it and flattering his face. She looked around the room. It was sparse and clearly owned by a single man, but Flora thought it wouldn't take much to add a woman's touch and make it more homely. A home. She hadn't really had one since Victoria Evans had died and she had moved up to Barrington Hall to work for the Pendletons. The thought of her last employer dampened Flora's spirits slightly. How had Sir Roland found her? Somebody must have let something slip at the hall. She was sure it wouldn't be Cook so she could only imagine it was the butler, Mr Denton. She remembered that the horse and trap they had used to travel to the station had been borrowed from somebody in the village. Had someone else now asked why? Or perhaps the pair had been seen trotting along the road to Taunton and Mr Denton had been challenged by one of the family. Whatever the reason, the appearance of Smithieson at Margaret Belton's house was very concerning, and it was obvious that Sir Roland was not going to let matters rest. She knew Albert would try to protect her, but his house was only a short distance from Margaret's, and she was concerned that it wouldn't be long before she was traced to it. Albert was a strong man and would do his best to protect her, but Smithieson was probably even stronger and had an evil streak to match it. There was no telling what might happen if he caught up with them. Flora simply knew too much, and the papers she had taken from Sir Roland were so damaging to the family that a beating at the hands of Smithieson would be the least of her worries.

She laid back into the pillow. It wasn't just her that was in danger now. As well as Albert, there was Jocelyn to consider too. When the threatened air raids had failed to materialize, Margaret Belton had decided to bring the evacuated Marge back home and she had tried to persuade Flora to do the same with Jocelyn. Flora had been reluctant to do so, partly because she was still worried about the German Luftwaffe, but also because she wanted to be sure that her escape from Barrington Hall had been successful. Now that Smithieson had appeared, there was no way she could bring Jocelyn back to London. The child could be used as a lever and in any case, if Flora was forced to move on again quickly the last thing she would need was a tiny baby clutched to her chest. No, Jocelyn would have to stay where she was. Flora would live with Albert; she would keep her head down and try her best to remain undetected. She looked across at the sleeping form next to her. Poor Albert. Did he know what he had taken on? She stroked his arm, and he stirred sleepily. Leaning across his bare chest, she nibbled his ear and whispered, 'Albert, wake up, I have something very nice for you, and there's a little something I need from you.' Albert stirred, opened one eye and then willingly obliged her.

Chapter 12

An Encounter

Summer 1940

Six months later, the war finally spluttered into life. France had fallen, and the British had carved out a moral victory in the sand at Dunkirk by successfully evacuating over three hundred thousand allied soldiers. The public was jubilant but seemed to have forgotten that most of the Army's equipment had been left behind and that France had capitulated with Britain likely to be the next in line for Hitler's onslaught. For Flora, life at the hospital started to get busier. Many of the wounded came by train from the channel ports to London and other cities, and the hospital wards were soon filled with injured young men. Like the other nurses, Flora was initially horrified to see that many had lost limbs. More troubling, though, were those that were only lightly wounded in a physical sense but irreparably damaged mentally. Every night, the ward would be punctuated with the cries and shouts of those reliving the battle, and Flora spent hours holding the hands of men who would never sleep restfully again.

At the end of June, an exhausted Flora had finished an early evening shift at the hospital and was making her way home to see Albert. It was one of the last occasions that she would make the fifteen-minute journey as Albert's child was growing healthily inside her and she would soon need to stop work. As she walked down the hospital access road, the main gates framed the city to the south. A field of grey barrage balloons rose up on cables from all over the city making the vista seem alien and foreboding. There were few people about and so the familiar well-built figure lurking in a shop doorway opposite the hospital entrance stood out despite the man's efforts to remain concealed in the shadows. Flora saw him as she reached the gates, and she paused just as Smithieson's eyes locked with her own. He was unrushed and looked both ways along the main road to check it was clear before starting to cross over towards her. Flora started to panic. She was in no condition to run away. It was too far back to retrace her steps to the hospital and besides, the access road was shrouded in trees and bushes, and it was much too private. Deciding that forwards was safest, she broke Smithieson's stare pretending not to recognise him and increased her pace. The steps behind matched her stride for stride and her pursuer began to close rapidly. Flora's heart was pounding, and her lungs fought against the space occupied by her baby. She was desperate and was about to run for it when a hand grabbed her arm and pulled her up sharply. There was a prick in the side of her neck as a blade was pressed against her skin.

'Don't even think about screaming, Flora. You won't have time before I cut your voice out.' Smithieson's voice was cold, and he pressed the tip of the knife a little harder into Flora's skin to emphasize his point. 'You've no idea how difficult it's been to find you. Where've you been hiding? 'Ah well, I don't suppose it matters now as we are finally together at last.' He laughed and the hollow sound made Flora's tired legs feel even weaker.

'Leave me alone, Fred. What do you want anyway?' She tried to twist in his grip but was forced to stop as the metal blade at her throat nicked the skin reminding her that her assailant was the one firmly in control. He smiled a humourless grin.

'Hold still or I'll stick you. We can talk about what I want later if you like although I think someone's been there before me,' he leered, nodding towards her swelling midriff. 'But before we get to that, let's talk a bit about what Sir Roland wants first. You took a letter from Barrington Hall that didn't belong to you and the master wants it back. In fact, not only does he want the letter returned, but he also wants his parlour maid back too. Back so that he can keep an eye on her and back so that she can look after him. And you know what I mean about that, don't you, you little harlot?'

Flora remembered the events that had caused her to flee from Barrington Hall and shuddered. 'Please,' she whimpered. 'Don't do this. Please let me go. I'll do whatever you want, Fred, but don't make me go back there. I have a child to look after now and another on the way. I have nothing of the Master's. He's mistaken.'

'No Flora, you're lying. He knows you have it. Is it in that book of yours?' He felt her stiffen, confirming his suspicion. 'Yes, we know all about your diary. It's amazing what friends will reveal with a little persuasion and your roommate at Barrington Hall has told us all about your writing.' He gripped her arm tightly choking off Flora's denials and was about to continue when the sound of voices came floating over the mild evening air. Flora looked behind and saw some nurses coming out of the hospital gates. Her heart leapt at the prospect of rescue. Rose was in the group, and she shouted out a greeting to Flora as they approached. With a look of disappointment, Smithieson quickly transferred the knife from Flora's neck into his coat pocket. He gripped her arm tightly and scowled at her.

'Don't think this is the end of it, Flora. I've found you once and I'll find you again. I know where you work now.' He dropped her arm and without glancing at the approaching group of young women, he turned his face away and walked off briskly in the other direction. Flora almost fell to the pavement as relief replaced fear and the adrenaline rush subsided leaving her weak and exhausted. She staggered slightly just as Rose came up to her.

'Are you alright, Flora? Who was that man? Was he bothering you?' Flora shook her head.

'He was just some drunk, Rose. I don't think he meant any harm, but I'm glad you came along just the same. Will you walk with me for a while until we're sure he's gone?' Rose smiled and detached herself from the rest of the group promising the other nurses that she would meet up with them a little later.

Chapter 13

Blitz

September 1940

It was many months before Flora returned to work at the hospital. The encounter with Smithieson had really shaken her, and for the rest of her confinement she kept a low profile, venturing out rarely and only when it was absolutely necessary. Even Margaret commented that Flora had become a recluse, and she scolded her gently during one of her regular visits to her brother's house.

'You must try to get out and get some fresh air, Flora. You can't stay cooped up in here all the time. It's not good for the baby,' she added, pointing at Flora's unborn child. Flora nodded but she continued to hide anyway as she waited for the baby to arrive.

She didn't have to wait much longer. Flora's son, Andrew, was born in Albert's house at the beginning of September, and he entered the world at the start of a new kind of madness. All that summer, the Royal Air Force had been fighting a largely unseen battle against the Luftwaffe in the skies above southern England. Each night, the news was grim, and the threat of invasion seemed to grow daily such that by the beginning of the month it had become merely a question of timing. Then, Goering changed tactics, and the air raid siren signalled a different form of torture for Londoners. Two days before Andrew was born, a group of German bombers had appeared in the skies over the city and unloaded their bombs. Later that evening, more bombers returned. They were guided by the fires started by the first wave, and they pounded the city until the early hours of the following morning. The noise of the bombardment and the anti-aircraft guns was terrifyingly loud even deep down inside the communal air raid shelter that Flora shared with the rest of her street. Albert was on duty elsewhere in Islington and as she sat shivering with fear Flora had prayed that he would be safe. Little was said during that long first night, and the communal sense of helplessness was only intensified by the occasional cry of a baby further along Flora's row.

Two days later, Flora went into labour. Margaret came to the house to help, and the mewling child was delivered just as the air raid siren signalled another night of torment. It would have been impossible for Flora to make it to the shelter with her new-born child, and so the two women decided to stay inside the house until the all-clear was sounded. With the help of a neighbour, Margaret made up a bed for Flora in the basement of Albert's house. The noise of the bombardment was much louder at street level, and even though most of the bombs seemed to be falling on the docks further to the east, the two women spent a terrifying night holding each other and shielding the baby before the all-clear siren finally signalled that the danger had passed.

That night's bombing set the pattern for the following weeks. Each evening, Flora would make her way round to the street shelter. Albert was working long night shifts on fire picket duties, and so Margaret and Marge would occasionally come to keep her company. She was worried about Albert. The man was exhausted and as the bombing continued night after night, he became withdrawn and worn down by the destruction taking place around him. Albert rarely spoke to Flora about his work and when he did, he tried to spare her by describing it in only the most general terms. One morning there was a particular change though. He had returned home to Flora with bleeding hands and a look of horror that even a thick coating of soot couldn't disguise. Flora saw immediately that it had been a bad shift.

'Oh Albert. What is it? What's happened? Are you hurt?' She hated to see him look so distraught.

Harold inhaled. 'I'm uninjured, Flora, but it has been a terrible night. One that I will never forget.' He then explained that the Islington station had been asked to go further into the city as another borough had received a terrible pounding and the local force were overcome by the number of fires they were trying to extinguish. His team had taken their fire tender and attempted to make it to the agreed rendezvous point but were thwarted by piles of rubble that were strewn across the streets and the fires that were raging through the shops and houses. As the men had attempted to find a way round the mess, they had come across a street shelter that had taken a direct hit. A pale-faced air raid warden desperately flagged them down and the men left their vehicle and tried to search through the rubble for survivors.

'Women and children, Flora,' Albert whispered, glancing at Andrew's sleeping form in the cot beside them. 'It was a terrible thing to see. There must have been thirty or more casualties.' He stopped as tears welled up in his eyes and fell glistening onto his dirty tunic. 'When we got down to them, the chamber was intact but everyone inside was dead. Children too. They were all untouched by the blast but killed by the shockwave. It was like they were sleeping, some in each other's arms. We carried them out and laid them out, one by one, wrapped in blankets.'

Albert's voice finally cracked as the sobs broke through. Flora held him tightly. The damage from the bombing was not only physical but would leave lifelong scars for those that witnessed it at close hand. She knew there was nothing she could say that would ever relieve Albert of the pain of what he had seen, and so Flora clung to him helplessly and willed him to remain strong.

And Albert was strong. Along with many other brave men and women he continued to go out into the besieged city to help. He never complained of exhaustion, and he never again described the horrors of what he found in the blazing streets. Then several weeks later, just after the morning all-clear had sounded, Flora opened the door and was faced by a weeping Margaret. She was with the local air raid warden, and Flora knew from their faces that Albert would not be coming home again. Transfixed by shock, she stood on the doorstep and stared blankly at them unable to allow grief to break through. Margaret took the expressionless woman's hand and gripped it tightly while the warden tried to explain gently what had happened.

'You'll have heard the bombing last night,' he said, his voice shaking with emotion. 'It was louder than usual because they came to Islington for the first time. Packington and Prebend streets copped a packet. Several houses and shops have been destroyed. Albert was with his team trying to fight a fire at the house on the corner where the two roads meet. They were trying to rescue a young girl who was trapped on the top floor. They had entered the property and were making their way up the stairs when the two top floors collapsed. It was very quick and there was nothing that anyone could do. I'm very sorry, Miss.'

Speechless, Flora nodded mechanically as her world fell apart and the wreckage of her life seemed to mingle with the piles of rubble from the destroyed buildings nearby.

From further inside the house, a baby's cry indicated that Andrew had started to shed the tears that seemed so reluctant to fall from his mother. What a world she had brought him into, Flora thought. For several months, Albert had been a mountain of stability, and with the continuing absence of Smithieson, Flora had started to feel more optimistic despite the nightly terror brought by the Germans. Now all that promise was lost, and once again she was left alone with another small child. With a thin smile of thanks to the warden, Flora turned and went silently into the house followed by Margaret. She managed a few steps and had made it to the parlour door when the first tears finally broke through and quickly became a flood of inconsolable grief.

Chapter 14

The Academic

November 2000

Despite Michael's success at discovering his grandmother's surname, he couldn't help feeling a little despondent as he left Smithieson's house and drove up the lane away from Ashill. He was shocked at the old man's description of Flora. At the outset, Michael had been quite prepared to discover some unpalatable truths from the past, and he had been determined to avoid any kind of emotional entanglement. It was meant to be a journalistic endeavour rather than any kind of personal crusade. However, as Michael had gradually uncovered more information about Jocelyn and Flora, the two women had started to assume real personalities with frailties and problems much like Michael's own. He was sure that Marge's description of how Flora had abandoned Jocelyn during the war would make marvellous literary material but his personal connection to those events made them seem particularly vivid. Michael was also finding that it was not enough to uncover the facts, but he needed to understand them too. And that just fed his curiosity.

As he drove back to Taunton, he wondered what happened to Jocelyn after Flora abandoned her in Yorkshire. Had she been brought up by kindly foster parents in the local area or had she been consigned to some soulless orphanage? And how had Jocelyn's childhood experiences affected her later in life? Had they influenced her decision to have Michael adopted or was it a decision made necessary by the social norms of the time? And then there were all these stories about his grandmother, Flora. Marge seemed sure that Flora was running away from something at Barrington Hall. Something that had made the girl fear for her safety. A mistake she had made, perhaps, or something she had seen. If Michael was to believe this, then he could take the view that his grandmother was the victim of the story. But then Michael thought of all the children that Flora had supposedly conceived, delivered and then abandoned. He desperately wanted to believe that Smithieson's coarse description of Flora's life at Barrington Hall was untrue or at least grossly exaggerated. However, the fact that Flora had been sacked for gross misconduct and Marge's description of her as a possible thief with countless babies seemed to lend weight to Smithieson's account. So much time had elapsed since these events that it seemed unlikely that he would ever really get to the truth. But then again, he thought, at least the lack of factual certainty would provide him with the literary freedom to develop Flora's character in any way that he wished once he started writing.

Back in Taunton, Michael left the hire car in the hotel car park for later collection. He intended to return to Leeds that afternoon but before leaving for the station he borrowed the hotel's computer and searched the official index for a record of Flora's birth. He was slightly hampered by the surname Smithieson had provided. Jamieson was a very common name, and his electronic searches revealed pages of likely candidates that all had to be checked carefully. After an hour, however, Michael was certain that there were no birth, marriage or death records for any Flora Jamieson of the right age. Frustrated at his continuing lack of progress and with time to spare until his train departed, Michael abandoned his search and walked dejectedly into Taunton. Passing an attractive medieval church, he made for the main square and stopped to admire the large stone war memorial that stood in the centre. As he did so, he noticed a public information sign directing passers-by to the main library. Michael checked his watch. He still had time to spare, and he wondered idly if the library contained a local history section that might provide some background information.

The library was housed in a modern building next to the tourist office a short distance from the central square. The young librarian smiled at Michael as he entered the building, and she directed him to the local history section at the rear of several large racks of shelving. He stared at the rows of books and magazines as he considered where to start. It was unlikely that there would be any direct references to the serving staff, but everything Michael knew about Flora seemed to bring him back to the Pendleton family. If something untoward had happened to Flora at Barrington Hall, then perhaps there might be a clue contained in the Pendleton's family history. He looked at the books and started to pull them out one by one, but half an hour later he reached the end of the row, and he had found only one brief mention of the Pendletons. It was contained in a book on local architecture which had mentioned the fine Georgian building called Barrington Hall, stating that it had been built by Sir Thomas Pendleton in the early eighteenth century after he had sold the family's successful milling business in the north of England and moved back to his southwestern roots.

Beyond that, there was not the slightest whisper of the family. It was as though they had blended into the Somerset countryside for nearly two hundred years without a mention. Were they unworthy of historical records or just determined to maintain their privacy? Michael wondered. He thought of Emily and Francis Pendleton. Certainly, the current incumbents seemed to be very reclusive.

Michael turned away from the shelving. It seemed that every new approach to his quest was met with a dead end. However, there was one more thing worth trying before he gave up and went home. Michael knew that some libraries held old copies of the local newspaper. If the library had papers that went back to the pre-war years, then it might be worth looking through them. Encouraged by the librarian's friendly demeanour, Michael returned to the main counter to seek her advice. A small queue had formed and after a brief wait, he found himself at the front. Michael explained to the girl that he wanted to do some background research on a local aristocratic family and asked whether the library held any old newspapers that might assist him. The girl could not have been more helpful.

'You're lucky, we were starting to run out of space down in our storeroom and we are about to return our archive of the Somerset Chronicle to the publishers. But for the moment everything's still down there, and if you can give me an idea about the subject matter you are interested in then we could do the research for you. There would be a small charge for the work, but it shouldn't amount to much.'

Michael was impressed with the service and filled out the necessary form using the names Barrington Hall and Pendleton as the main search references and the period between 1935 and 1941 as the main dates. He left his contact number and address and turned to leave. As he did, an attractive woman approached him. She was tall and slim, with dark hair and fine angular features. She was smartly dressed and had a dazzling smile that was instantly engaging.

'Excuse me, my name is Rebecca Holsten. I'm doing a doctorate in History at Bristol University and, without wishing to be presumptuous I couldn't help overhearing your conversation with the librarian. You see, I've been doing some research on the local aristocracy in this area, and I wondered whether we might be able to help each other with our work.' As he sized her up, Michael guessed that the woman's American accent was from the east coast, possibly New York. She looked a little younger than Michael and she had an open demeanour that he found appealing. He smiled to himself. The Americans were always so interested in the British aristocracy, and they were also very forward and uninhibited when talking to strangers. Michael glanced at his watch. He really ought to have been getting back to the hotel to collect his bags and get to the station but there was something he intuitively liked about this good-looking stranger. There was nothing urgent waiting for him at Leeds so it would do no harm to stay an extra night in Taunton. Mentally abandoning any idea of catching the evening train, he smiled back at the woman and shook her hand.

'Hi, my name is Michael Calvert. That's a very kind offer. To be honest with you, I need all the help I can get at the moment so let's talk, but I'm not sure that I have much to offer you in exchange. And so,' he added flirtatiously, 'I shall be equally presumptuous, and ask if you would like to go somewhere for coffee?' Her laugh of acceptance was genuine and infectious, and it lifted Michael's mood.

The librarian directed them to a small café just along the street, and they entered just as the woman behind the counter was starting to think about finishing for the day. She scowled slightly at the late intrusion but scuttled off for coffee and cakes after informing them that there was only thirty minutes until closing time. As they waited, Michael explained how the search for his natural mother had led him first to Marge and then to Somerset.

'All I know is that my grandmother worked at Barrington Hall as a servant just before the war. It's really my mother I want to locate, but I won't be able to find her until I discover more about my grandmother, Flora. Everything I know about Flora seems to centre on the Pendleton family at Barrington Hall. I have visited them, but they have no knowledge of her apart from an old record noting that an unnamed maid was dismissed from the household at around the time that Flora left and went to London. To be honest with you, I don't really know why I'm looking into the Pendleton family; I suppose I was just fishing for something that might be useful, anything really.'

Rebecca Holsten sat patiently listening to Michael's account. 'A personal quest for a lost relative!' she exclaimed when he had finished. 'And I thought you were a fellow academic who might be willing to trade research material. But no matter, I'm studying the local aristocracy and their effect on the regional economy during the nineteenth and twentieth centuries. I've amassed loads of material on notable families in this area, and I'm sure that the Pendleton name sounds somehow familiar. Would you like me to look at what I've got to see if there's anything relevant to your search? It doesn't matter if you have nothing to give in exchange. Your task seems worthwhile, and I don't mind taking a few moments to help you out.'

Michael was grateful. 'Well, if you really don't mind, then of course it would be helpful. I have no other leads now, so this is my only hope really.'

'Rebecca smiled at him. 'That's decided then. Do you live locally? It will probably take me a while to look through my stuff so we could meet tomorrow if I find anything.' Michael explained that he was staying in a local hotel and gave her his card. She slipped it into her bag and stood to leave. She took Michael's hand and looked at him. He was suddenly acutely aware of the touch of her fingers and her brown eyes.

'You know, Michael, our family knows all about lost relatives. My grandmother was a Jewish refugee who escaped to America from Nazi occupied Austria, but much of her family stayed behind and subsequently disappeared. I really hope your search is successful, and if there's anything else I can do to help then I would be only too happy to assist.' Michael nodded his understanding. He instinctively liked Rebecca Holsten, but he found her a little unsettling in a pleasant way that seemed familiar but a little forgotten perhaps. A further encounter with Rebecca was an attractive prospect, and as they parted to go their individual ways, Michael really hoped that she would find enough material in her research to justify a further meeting.

Later that evening, Michael had just about given up on her when she rang. His extra night in Taunton would be worthwhile after all.

'I've found quite a lot about the Pendletons,' she breathed excitedly down the phone. 'There are articles and other references from magazines and newspapers. I'll copy what I have and bring them to you tomorrow if you like.' Michael was pleased on two accounts. He was glad that she had found something that might help his search, but he was also thrilled by the prospect of seeing her again. They arranged to meet at his hotel for a late breakfast and Michael thought it felt like a date rather than an appointment. He hoped she might see it the same way.

*****

The following morning, the stack of papers that Rebecca deposited on one of the hotel's dining tables was impressive, and Michael was surprised that she had managed to assemble such a large volume of material after only one evening's work. She smiled at him. 'What do you think about that then?' she asked proudly.

'I'm genuinely impressed,' he replied. 'You must have a very organized filing system to be able to gather together that lot in such a short time.'

'It's for my doctorate,' she smiled reaching for the breakfast menu. 'You know what a fascination us colonials have for British history. I've got piles of the stuff but at least it's well catalogued for easy access, and as I thought, I had saved references about the Pendleton family.'

At that moment the waitress came to take their order, returning shortly after with a tray laden with traditional fare. As they ate breakfast, Rebecca described some of the information contained in the papers.

'Most of the stuff is about Sir Roland Pendleton and dates to the last century. He was the eldest son of a nineteenth century industrialist called Thomas Pendleton who made his fortune from woollen mills in the north of England. Thomas was originally from the southwest and he eventually sold his business for a huge fortune to move back to the house he had built in Somerset. Unusually, it was called Barrington Hall after his wife's maiden name. He lived a happy retirement on the estate and when he died the family seat was taken over by Thomas' eldest son, Roland. Up until that point, Roland had developed quite a reputation as a playboy in London society, and when he took control of the family fortune, he set up an art dealing and auctioneering business that was also based in London. His younger brother, Maxwell, joined him as a business partner after a short stint in the Army.'

Michael nodded. 'Yes, Pendleton International Art is still going strong today. And you should see the paintings hanging on the wall at Barrington Hall. The place is absolutely stuffed with them.'

'Really?' Rebecca exclaimed with sudden interest. 'I love art. I should very much like to have a poke around their collection.'

'You'll be lucky,' Michael laughed. 'The Pendletons are very private, and when I got caught trying to have a peek in one of the gallery rooms, I thought I was going to be clapped in irons. Retired General Francis Pendleton is very security conscious.'

Rebecca looked at him, a serious expression slowly replacing the laughter in her face. 'Well, if you get the chance to go back, do let me know. I'd love to have a peep.'

Michael would have happily listened to her all day. He smiled at her curiosity and gestured at the pile. 'Is it all about art or is there more?'

'No. there's also quite a bit about Sir Roland's other passion which was horse racing. He used to breed horses and was an enthusiastic sponsor of several races both locally and at more famous courses like Goodwood and Epsom.'

Michael nodded. 'Yes, a man at the village pub told me they had horses at the Hall, but I didn't know the family were into racing.'

'Oh yes, the local papers are full of it. In fact, there was a bit of a scandal in the late thirties. Sir Roland was accused of fixing races by a local bookmaker, but he was eventually cleared of any wrongdoing and successfully sued the man for libel.'

Michael immediately thought of Smithieson. He had been a stable hand at Barrington Hall at the time and would no doubt have been aware of the scandal, not that he would have mentioned it to Michael though. 'Is there anything else?' he asked pointing back at the pile.

'Aside from the racing and art, there are one or two references of a more local nature. Sir Roland wasn't a great philanthropist, but he did occasionally get involved in village affairs. I think he once helped with the cost of repairing the church, and the family used to support things like the village fete. I'm afraid though, Michael, that I didn't see anything that might help you to track down

Flora although I only had time to glance briefly through it.'

Michael shook his head. 'I'm not surprised really, Rebecca. But you've given me a good amount of background information. I'll have a good look through it all on the train home. You never know, there may be something tucked away in an old newspaper article.'

At Michael's mention of returning home, Rebecca's face dropped. 'I saw from your card that you live in the north of England. Do you think you'll be back again soon?' she asked earnestly.

Michael looked down at his plate and used his fork to toy with his food. He knew little about Rebecca, but he was enjoying her company and his imminent departure for Leeds suddenly held little appeal.

'I don't know,' he replied finally. 'Everything I know about Flora seems to lead back here to Somerset but once I finally discover her surname, I can concentrate on her daughter, Jocelyn, my mother, and I don't suppose she would be living locally. In fact, I do have reason to believe that she may be living abroad. My original aim was to find Jocelyn rather than learn anything of Flora, so it may be that I don't need to come back, but, well...' He tailed off, shyness overcoming what he wanted really to say. After a pause, he looked up at her. 'I would certainly like to come back, Rebecca,' he said pointedly.

She smiled at him, and Michael saw that she had received and understood the unspoken message that he had awkwardly tried to transmit. 'Look, 'she said her brown eyes resting reassuringly on Michael's. 'I'm really interested in your story, and I would like to help you. If you do come back, will you contact me? We could meet up, have dinner or something.'

'I would really like that,' Michael replied, relieved that their mutual attraction had been declared and acknowledged successfully. 'I can't thank you enough for putting together this lot,' he waved at the papers. 'I really have to go home today, but I've now got a good reason to come back, haven't I?'

Rebecca blushed as she rose to leave. 'Don't leave it too long, will you. The story of your grandmother could add some real perspective to my work, and I want to hear all about your discoveries.'

Chapter 15

Named

November 2000

Michael spent the journey home looking through Rebecca's papers. They made fascinating reading. Under Sir Roland's leadership, Pendleton International Art had grown into a powerful enterprise as the family exploited social change at the expense of their own class. After World War 1, the British aristocracy had gone into decline as harsh inheritance taxes took their toll. Rich families had been forced to sell off their treasures, and the Pendletons' enterprise had been poised perfectly to send their expensive goods under the hammer. As the company's reputation grew, Sir Roland had come to the attention of the ruling classes, and his knighthood for services to art came at the extraordinary age of forty.

Aside from a booming art business, Sir Roland had also gained quite a reputation as a man of the turf, and the papers were packed with old newspaper cuttings reporting success at the racing track. Rebecca had clumped the racing articles together in one group and as Michael idly flicked through them, he came across a major news report concerning the libel action that Sir Roland had initiated in 1937. A local bookmaker had accused Sir Roland of nobbling his own horses to fix races. The accusation had caused uproar within racing circles and London society, and Sir Roland had resorted to legal action to protect his reputation. The article reported that he had won his case after one of the staff at Barrington Hall admitted to police that he had been solely responsible for tampering with the animals and then betting appropriately. The court exonerated Sir Roland and awarded him substantial damages at the unfortunate bookmaker's expense. As an aside, the article mentioned that the case was particularly poignant for the Pendletons coming only a few weeks after their horse trainer had died in an accident.

Michael sat back and looked out at the passing countryside. Archie, the drunken old man in the village pub had mentioned that he thought Flora's father had died in a riding accident. If that was true, was it possible that her father was the dead man mentioned briefly in the newspaper? From what Michael knew about Flora, the date was about right. He shuffled through the remaining papers to see if there was anything else about it, but he found nothing of note, and it looked like another dead end. He put the papers back into a carrier bag and yawned in disappointment. Was his search really worth the time, effort and expense he was expending? Everything had started so promisingly. His early discovery of Marge with her knowledge of Flora and Jocelyn had boosted his enthusiasm and encouraged him to delve deeper. However, the trip to Somerset had added very little, and his search seemed to have stalled. He had discovered a few scraps about Flora, most of it interesting, some of it conflicting, but none of it had got him any closer to finding his mother. Maybe it was time to accept defeat and write this up as a fictional project. He knew that his adoptive mother had left him some money, but it would be some time before the lawyers sorted out the legal formalities and sent him a cheque. In the meantime, his bank balance was steadily reducing, and it would flash red unless he quickly produced some new work.

As Michael pondered the dire state of his finances, he realized that his expensive trip to Somerset hadn't been entirely fruitless. He had met Rebecca Holsten. The attractive academic had made a real impression, and he knew that if he continued his investigation there was a good chance that he could engineer an excuse to see her again. But much as he liked Rebecca, Michael was wary. It hadn't always been like this he admitted. Since his divorce, he had met the occasional girlfriend, but he had always distanced himself from long-term relationships and he tended to end them quickly whenever he sensed that serious ties were starting to develop. It was a defence mechanism that prevented any possibility of further hurt, but it added to Michael's loneliness, and it left behind a trail of saddened, disappointed and angry women. However, Michael wondered whether it was a little different this time. He had only just met Rebecca, but already he felt at ease in her company. She seemed so trustworthy and self-assured, and there could be no mistaking the mutual attraction. Inside, it felt as though an emotional barrier had started to move, and he knew it was something long overdue.

When Michael left the train at Sheffield to catch an onwards connection to Leeds, he still hadn't decided how to proceed. However, his previous experience had taught him that during any great investigative news story there is often a decisive point when a crucial fact suddenly allows rapid progress. In Michael's case, the obstruction was his grandmother's real surname and the catalyst for its discovery was unexpected. He had just sat down in his next train, when his mobile phone rang. It was Marge and she was triumphant.

'Is that Michael Calvert?' she shouted down the phone. 'It's Marge Belton. How did you get on at Barrington Hall?'

'Hello, Marge,' Michael replied. 'I didn't learn much of use I'm afraid and to be honest with you I didn't much like the Pendletons even though they seemed to be helpful. The only things I learned were that Flora was dismissed from Barrington Hall for gross misconduct and her surname was Jamieson. Aside from that, I met some strange types in the village who knew of her and one pretty much confirmed your assessment of Flora's attitude towards men. A love of life I think you politely called it.'

'Jamieson?' Marge bellowed, ignoring the reference to Flora's love life. 'No, no, that can't be right. Who told you that? Flora's name was Poulter. Flora Harriet Poulter. That's why I'm calling. I was thinking about you the other day and I remembered that there were a couple of ration cards in a box of old things that I kept from the war years. I'm sorry that it's taken a few days to sort it out, but the box was on top of a cupboard, and I needed Mrs Jennison to reach up and get it down for me. Anyway, I was right: the cards were in there. One of them belonged to my mother and the other was Flora's. She left it behind when she finally left us and returned to Somerset. Her name is written on the front. It's definitely Poulter. Once I read the name, I remembered it.'

Michael's previous doubts about the wisdom of continuing his quest melted away and his curiosity flooded back. He was confused. Smithieson had been convinced that Flora was called Jamieson. The man was old and obnoxious, but his memory had been clear, and Michael shuddered as he remembered the reason for the old man's certainty. 'Marge, are you absolutely sure about this?'

'I'm as sure about this as I ever will be. Don't you believe me?' she asked indignantly. 'As we speak, I'm sitting here looking at the card and having a small glass in celebration.' Michael smiled at the phone.

'I can't tell you how helpful this is, Marge. I was a bit stuck and thinking of giving up on Flora to be honest.'

'Give up, Michael? That doesn't sound like the young gentleman that came to see me the other day. Anyway, what will you do next?' Marge demanded.

Michael paused. 'Well, the first thing is to get a copy of Flora's birth certificate. Once I've done that, I shall start to look for other children with the Poulter surname or perhaps a marriage certificate. If I do find records of more children, then there's a chance that they may have got married or had kids of their own. If so, there's every chance of finding a current address which I can use to make contact. Whether any relatives would know anything of Jocelyn is quite another matter, but you never know.'

There was a slight pause on the other end of the line. 'Michael, if you do find Jocelyn would you call me and tell me all about her. You know how responsible I feel for losing her all those years ago. It may be a long time but, it would…. well…. it would make me feel less guilty if I thought Jocelyn's life had been happy and successful.'

Michael reassured the old lady, promising to let her know what he discovered. Marge's memory seemed pretty good, and a ration card seemed incontrovertible so as soon as Michael arrived home, he waded past a pile of unopened mail lying under the front door and switched on the computer to find out what the official records knew of one Flora Poulter. It only took Michael ten minutes to discover the record of her birth. It was registered in Taunton in 1920, and her mother's maiden name had been Halbury. Michael ordered a copy of the birth certificate and then started to look for any marriage records and subsequent children. He was in luck. There were two marriages that looked promising. One was to a man called Harold Wintern in Taunton towards the end of 1945 and the other, in 1955 was to somebody called Thomas Wainwright in Warrington. Michael ordered the certificates, and then started to look in the index for children born under the two new surnames. Again, matters fell quickly into place, and he found a birth for each union. The first child was called Marilyn Wintern registered in Taunton in 1946, and the second was called Carol Wainwright registered in Warrington in Lancashire in 1957.

Michael sat back in the chair to absorb the new information. He would need all the certificates to confirm the details, but it seemed that Flora had married twice and delivered at least six children during her lifetime. Jocelyn had been the first child, followed by Andrew, Agnes and then David. They had all been born in quick succession in London under the surname Belton. To that list he could now add a child from each of her two subsequent marriages. Six children had been born across seventeen years. It was astonishing. He thought about the four children born one after another in wartime London. Marge had told him a little about Jocelyn and he knew that a baby had been born to Albert Belton, but what about the other two? Who were their fathers and what were the circumstances of their entry into the world? Had they been evacuated and then abandoned like Jocelyn, or had they been adopted as Marge suspected?

Michael glanced over to the pile of mail spread out on the floor under the front door. He had rushed past it in his eagerness to get to his computer, but now he remembered that he had already ordered the certificates for the three children born after Jocelyn. He gathered up the scattered envelopes but was disappointed to find only two bearing the central registry office stamp. Wondering what had happened to the third, he laid them on the desk and turned to the details. He squinted at the Registrar's spidery handwriting and saw that they were the birth certificates for Andrew and Agnes Belton. It was David's certificate that was absent. Agnes had been legally adopted and there was no record of her father. Andrew's father was identified as Albert Belton. The child hadn't been adopted but there was no indication of his ultimate fate. Michael paused for a moment. His plan had been to try and track the children through the records to see if he could find a link to a current address of someone who might know where Jocelyn was living. But where should he start? Agnes was now legally anonymous which left only Andrew. An idea came into his head, but it was approaching midnight, and it would have to wait until the following day.

He yawned and switched off the computer before turning reluctantly to the remainder of his unopened mail. He placed the bills into an overflowing pending tray. There was also a letter from his agent asking Michael to let him know when he might expect to receive some more of Michael's work and reminding him in stark terms that it had been several months since his last piece. That one went unceremoniously into the bin. Finally, there was a letter from the Registrar General. Michael had forgotten that he had applied for his adoption records, and he tore open the envelope to read through the details. To his great surprise and relief, the authorities had taken a pragmatic view of his recent application and, noting that Michael already knew his birth name and the name of his mother, they had agreed to release his adoption records without the usual formality of a counselling session. Included in the envelope was a certificate authorising the disclosure of the relevant records and an address for East Yorkshire County Council where his official adoption documents and court papers were stored. Setting aside his fatigue, Michael scribbled a quick note to the council, enclosed the certificate of authorisation and placed the envelope ready for posting on the hall table. With the correspondence complete he crept into bed where exhaustion eventually overcame the facts and possibilities that had suddenly re-energized his project.

Chapter 16

Deceit

November 2000

Michael awoke early the next morning and drank coffee at Lucille's until office hours at 9am. His first call was to the Registrar's Office concerning David Belton's missing birth certificate. The lady who answered was very helpful; she admitted that there had been an oversight and promised to dispatch the missing record straight away.

Michael then turned to the fate of Andrew Belton. Like Jocelyn, Andrew had not been formally adopted, and Michael suspected from his date of his birth that it was possible that he been evacuated and later abandoned by Flora just like his older sister, Jocelyn. In the absence of a formal record of adoption, it was possible that he had been brought up under his own name, either with foster parents or in care. It was another long shot, but Michael was becoming familiar with Flora's methods, and it seemed feasible and worth a try. Michael contacted the main office of the Salvation Army and explained that he was looking for a relative lost during the wartime evacuation. The helpful lady consulted the records, and he was delighted to learn that a child of matching age and names had been raised by foster parents in a small village close to Barnsley. There was no record of an Andrew Belton in the electoral roll for that area, but Michael found an entry in the register recording Andrew's marriage to a woman called Elizabeth Minton who the electoral roll suggested was still living in the village under her maiden name. Was she Andrew's widow or were they divorced? He picked up the phone.

The call that followed was initially easy as Elizabeth Minton was intrigued. She confirmed that the Salvation Army had knocked on their door too, and that Elizabeth knew all about her ex-husband's early life and wartime abandonment. The Salvation Army had put them in touch with Andrew's half-sister, Jocelyn, who had left the country to marry a Swedish chemical academic called Stienerson. It was then that Elizabeth became a little wary as she suddenly remembered the delicacy surrounding adoption contact. She knew Jocelyn quite well, and she challenged Michael to prove his credentials before she would tell him where her friend lived. But by providing Michael with Jocelyn's married surname and her husband's occupation she had already given Michael sufficient detail to track down Jocelyn. Michael thanked Elizabeth anyway, and promised to write to her with his details, but he already knew that he could proceed. Sure enough, after a further two hours work Michael was gazing down at his mother's address and telephone number in Sweden. It was listed under the name Stienerson but with her Christian names as the sole householder. The address was for a small house by the river in a place called Kristianstad. He had found his mother.

Michael was exhilarated, but his self-congratulation gave way to caution when he realized that he hadn't really considered what to do next. It was one thing to identify his mother but quite a different thing to contact her. She certainly wouldn't be expecting him, and she might well take unkindly to Michael bursting unannounced into her life in Sweden. This required some careful thought, he decided, and so whilst he recorded the details of his discovery in his project notebook, he decided that he wouldn't do anything about it until his excitement had died down a little and he was better positioned to exercise some judgment. Besides, his agent's letter had stung his conscience. There was now sufficient material in his notebook to make a start on his article and it was this task that he set about tackling for the remainder of the day.

Had matters ended with Michael's creative work, much of the heartbreak that followed would never have transpired but two mail deliveries over the following days encouraged Michael to embark on a path with disturbing consequences.

The first was a parcel delivery from the library in Taunton containing the results of the librarian's search of the newspaper archive for information on the Pendleton family. Much of it was a duplication of Rebecca's material, but some of the articles were new, and added a more local perspective to what he had already learned. However, now that Michael had unearthed his mother, the Pendletons no longer seemed quite so important, so he only glanced at the papers before filing them with the material provided by Rebecca. They lay there, temporarily forgotten until the postman called again a few days later.

Michael had been typing when the mail flopped onto the mat, and he was pleased to see one of the Registrar's familiar envelopes was in the pile. It was the official record of Flora's birth. As well as confirming the details Michael had garnered from the official index, the certificate recorded the baby girl's father as being Henry Reginald Poulter who lived at an address in Ashill. Most of the information was clear and easy to read, but in one part of the document, the writing had faded with age and had become almost illegible. As a result, Michael almost missed a crucial detail, but when he took it over to the window, he could just make out that Henry Poulter's occupation was a horse trainer. The hand holding the document fell to Michael's side as his astonishment grew. He knew from one of Rebecca's articles that the Pendletons' horse trainer had died in an accident. Separately, the drunken Archie had told him that Flora's father had also died in a riding incident at Barrington Hall. The coincidence was too strong: they had to be one and the same person. Michael turned to the file on the desk and started to root through the piles of paper. Sure enough, the most recent information from the library included a more detailed news article recording the death of the unfortunate man and confirming that his name had been Henry Poulter. The reporter noted that Henry had been found with severe head injuries inside the stable of a mare that was known to be unpredictable. The coroner had agreed with the doctor that Henry Poulter's injuries were consistent with a horse kick and had recorded the cause as death by misadventure. He did however find it surprising that the experienced horse trainer had gone into the horse's stable alone when he knew the animal was difficult to handle and liable to kick out unexpectedly.

Deep in thought, Michael pulled out the article from Rebecca about Sir Roland's libel case and placed it alongside the one from the library on Henry Poulter's death. He studied both items carefully, his mind racing with possibilities. Horses, a death and race fixing allegations. He looked at the first article again. Sir Roland cleared of all involvement, but a member of staff convicted. Who was it? The article didn't say so he rummaged through the pile of papers from the library and found a new item. It was a later report covering the conviction of a member of staff at Barrington Hall for tampering with horses. The name on the paper was familiar and it immediately opened up a barrage of questions. It was Frederick Smithieson.

Michael's head spun. As a stable boy, Smithieson would surely have known that Flora was Henry Poulter's daughter. In which case why had he lied to Michael about her surname? What possible reason could he have for trying to prevent Michael from learning Flora's identity especially after all these years? Was it to do with the parentage of her baby? Perhaps that was why, as Michael was leaving the cottage, Smithieson had tried to warn him off further investigations into the matter. He looked closely at the court report. Smithieson had been sent to prison for two and a half years. That meant that he would have been in prison when Jocelyn was conceived and therefore it was impossible that he was either the girl's father or that he had been involved in an affair with Flora at the time of her dismissal. Michael breathed a sigh of relief as he realized with certainty that despite the old man's lecherous assertions, it was impossible for him to be Michael's grandfather. However, if that part of Smithieson's story was untrue did it also mean that his description of Flora's dealings with other male members of the household was also a lie? In which case, who was Jocelyn's father? Another member of staff or, Michael wondered darkly, Sir Roland perhaps. Maybe that was why she had been forced to flee. There were plenty of questions with no obvious answers and so Michael left the parentage matter untouched and turned to the death of Flora's father. Henry Poulter would have been intimately involved with all aspects of life in the stables and must have known if horses were not running true to form. Did that mean he was involved in the betting scam too? Perhaps the two men had been in it together. Michael paused as a sudden more unsavoury possibility entered his mind. Henry's death had been unusual and unexpected and came about just as the betting scandal was erupting. Perhaps it hadn't been as accidental as it appeared. Maybe Henry had discovered what was going on at the Hall and had been killed to prevent him from revealing the truth. After all, Sir Roland would have had much to lose if his libel action had failed.

Michael sat down. He had set out to find his mother and he had already achieved that so in many respects Flora's story was an unnecessary distraction. However, she was Michael's grandmother, his own flesh and blood, and that made her story even more compelling. One thing was for sure and that was that he had been lied to, certainly, by Smithieson and possibly by the Pendletons. One or all of them had some reason to prevent Michael from making progress and Michael was determined to find out why. He turned from the piles of paper on the desk and picked up the phone. After a few rings, it was answered and when Michael heard Rebecca's voice his reasons for calling became a little diffuse.

'Umm, Hi Rebecca, it's Michael Calvert.'

'Oh, hi Michael. You rang and I'm so pleased. How's the search going? Have you made any progress yet? How was that stuff I gave you?' Michael felt something unfamiliar stir in the pit of his stomach. It was nerves. He wanted the call to go well.

'Well, yes, it was all really useful stuff,' he said unsure of where to begin. 'But I'm pretty sure that somebody is trying to prevent me from discovering any more about Flora. What's more I think it might be related in some way to the betting scandal you mentioned at breakfast the other day.' Encouraged by Rebecca, Michael spent the next five minutes explaining how he had located his mother and describing what he had discovered about Flora and her father. Rebecca listened attentively, occasionally asking questions but always timing her interjections to ensure that Michael didn't lose his train of thought. It was like a trained academic questioning a student on a thesis.

'So, if Smithieson lied about Flora's surname, what was he trying to conceal?' she asked finally. 'Was it something to do with Jocelyn's parentage or something to do with the racing scandal and her father?'

'Well, that's the big question, isn't it?' Michael replied. 'I'm not going to leave it alone though even though it's no longer necessary for my article. I don't like being lied to. It attracts my professional interest. In my experience it means that there's something extremely interesting to learn and I mean to find out what it is.'

Rebecca laughed at Michael's determination. The warmth in her laughter brought the same smile to his face as it had on the first occasion that he had heard it. 'What about these stolen papers that Marge mentioned?' she continued more seriously. 'Do you think they're relevant? What could they have been about? Were they the reason that Flora fled or were they some kind of insurance policy?'

'Well, I'm not at all sure,' Michael replied. 'According to Marge, they were important enough for Sir Roland to dispatch a thug to London to retrieve them. I can only think they concerned one of three things: the parentage of Flora's child, the betting scandal or maybe it was something to do with the family business. Which one, I just don't know. The papers might have been important but I doubt that after all this time they'll still exist so I don't suppose we will ever find out.'

'I wouldn't give up on them that easily,' Rebecca replied encouragingly. 'In my experience, historical papers often contain all sorts of incriminating evidence, and curiously enough, the more damning they are, the less inclined people are to destroy them.'

'Oh, don't you worry about that. I have absolutely no intention of giving up on any aspect of this. I've decided to come back down there and find out,' Michael said firmly.

'Remind me never to place myself on the wrong side of one of your investigations,' she joked. 'You're far too tenacious and I can tell you won't let go. Anyway,' she added more seriously, 'does this mean that I get to have dinner with you? I mean, only if you want to that is.'

Michael loved the hint of uncertainty that had crept into her voice. 'I'd love to meet up with you,' he smiled at the phone. 'I'll come down tomorrow afternoon and we'll have dinner at the Buck Hotel where I stayed before. I'm going to have to decide what to do next, but I expect I'll have to confront Smithieson and the Pendletons to get to the bottom of everything so another visit to Taunton is just what's required. What's more, it seems I now have the benefit of an academic brain behind my efforts!'

Rebecca laughed her agreement and ended the call by arranging to meet Michael at the hotel at eight o clock the following evening. Michael replaced the receiver. His search was becoming more enjoyable by the minute.

Chapter 17

Dinner

November 2000

When Michael made the return train journey to Somerset, he was more preoccupied with his dinner date than the mystery surrounding Flora and the Pendletons. Even though he had only just met Rebecca, he was captivated by her, and the success of the evening had suddenly become quite important. His romantic expectation was an unfamiliar feeling that he hadn't experienced since he had first met Isobel. Michael sighed as the vivid details of his ex-wife's betrayal returned to spoil his mood. He tried to push the memory away, but Isobel's momentary intrusion had done its worst, and when his thoughts returned to Rebecca all he could foresee were obstacles and impediments. He knew that Rebecca liked him but how far did that attraction extend? And how much did he actually know about her? If he was honest, it was very little aside from her academic credentials. And of course, she would only be in the country for as long as it took her to complete her thesis, and then she would return to the US. What would happen then? Would any burgeoning affair just peter out as consequence of all those miles and time zones? There were also more immediate difficulties. Rebecca currently lived near Bristol, several hours away from Michael's flat. Not a great distance compared to the Atlantic but far enough to make any relationship a sporadic and nomadic affair.

It was an impressive list of difficulties but when it comes to practicalities, romance often trumps reason, and Michael's misgivings fell away when he saw Rebecca in the hotel foyer later that evening. She was wearing a dark green dress with black stockings and patent leather high heels that accentuated her tall slim figure. In fact, it was as well that Michael was tall himself otherwise he would have been staring up at her face rather than meeting it on a level. She smiled at him, unable to disguise her pleasure at seeing him again and offered her cheek which Michael's lips brushed with pure excitement and exhilaration. She was wearing the tiniest amount of make-up, and in truth she needed very little as her brown eyes and complexion needed no additional emphasis.

'You look fabulous,' he said feeling a little awkward and unable to conceal his enthusiasm.

'Why, thank you, Sir,' she replied with a curtsy. 'We aim to please.'

'And you most certainly do,' Michael replied with a theatrical bow causing her to blush at the boldness of his praise. He guided her over to the bar, ordered drinks and they sat down to study the menu. Before long, a waitress appeared and took their order before leaving them alone.

Rebecca studied his face. 'Well now, what's the plan? I take it you have a plan. This mystery of yours is far more exciting than any of my historical work and I'm dying to know what it's all about.'

'Well, I've decided to challenge Pendleton first. When I

was there last time, he seemed a little too satisfied at the poor progress I was making and how little I knew. There's something about him. The more I've thought about it, the more I think he knows more than he is telling.' He laughed. 'It's my journalist's nose. It's telling me to pry.'

'Do you think he'll see you again though? He can't have any interest in helping you to investigate an old family betting scandal?'

'Well, actually, I've already arranged it. I called the Pendletons on the train this afternoon and they've agreed to see me tomorrow afternoon. I didn't mention anything about Flora's father, the betting scandal or Smithieson, and I left everything rather vague. I just told them that I had made some further progress in my investigations and wondered if they would see me again.'

'You're going up there tomorrow? Michael, can I ask you a favour? Could I come with you? I'd love to see Barrington Hall, and I could come along as your research assistant.'

Michael smiled. He hadn't relished the idea of going up to Barrington Hall alone. 'Well, if you'd like to come, of course I have no objection, but I should warn you that Francis Pendleton is not a very hospitable host.'

'I'm sure that if he cuts up rough then I can give as good as I can get,' she smiled.

Michael was sure that she was right. There was a strength of character lying behind her warm laughter. 'So, I have a bodyguard now too,' he laughed. 'Anyway, I'd be glad if you'd come along, it means that I get to monopolize more of your time.'

Rebecca smiled but then looked away uncomfortably. For a moment, Michael wondered if his flirtation had slightly overstepped the mark, and there was a short silence which was only rescued when the waitress returned to inform them that their table was ready in the restaurant. Michael mentally kicked himself for his gaucheness, but the moment was soon forgotten as the meal was excellent and the fine bottle of Bordeaux they shared brought a warm glow to their cheeks and loosened their tongues. Rebecca was keen to know about Michael's earlier life and he regaled her with stories from his days on the foreign affairs' desk.

'Why did you give it all up?' she asked finally.

Michael's face dropped. He didn't really want Isobel to intrude on their evening but there was no avoiding it and so he allowed the whole story of the last five years to come out. He had never previously revealed many of the details and there were times when his account became a little disjointed and stuttering as he wrestled with the more painful recollections. However, after several minutes he had set out everything and he sat back feeling strangely purified.

'I've never told anybody much of that. I'm sorry to unload it on you. It's all in the past now and best left there if I'm honest.'

Rebecca leaned across the table and took his hand, as a sad and slightly distracted expression replaced her usual smile. Her skin was cool and smooth, and her finger pads squeezed his palm reassuringly.

'I had no business to pry, Michael, forgive me. I've never been married so I can't lie by telling you that I understand how you feel, but I think I mentioned to you about my family history. My grandparents were Austrian Jews in the Second World War. My grandmother fled to America just before the Anschluss but had to leave all her possessions behind. She also left behind her parents and sister who were all interned and taken to a concentration camp not long after. They were never seen again.'

Michael squeezed her hand back. 'I'm sorry, Rebecca. I know there were thousands of families torn apart on a similar way. It makes my problems and family issues seem a little banal really. What did your grandmother do in America?'

'Well, she settled down, found some work in a gallery

in New York and then married the American owner. They only had one child, who was my mother. Shortly after that, my grandfather joined the Army and was killed on Omaha beach in Normandy in 1944. My grandmother took over the gallery but was never really the same after that telegram was delivered. It was almost as though the wartime loss of her sister and then her husband broke her spirit. She ran the gallery for many years, but her heart was never in it after that, and when she died the business was passed on to my mother who still runs it today.'

As Rebecca spoke, she became animated, her smile faded, and her eyes seemed to burn fiercely. There was real passion behind her story and something else too. It was anger. Not spontaneous red-blooded anger that erupts in the heat of the moment and then quickly subsides, but the kind of long-term anger that sits quietly in the background, always present, but invisible to most and lying unresolved. She concealed it well, Michael thought, and it was only her frown that gave it away. The war had been costly for many families, and the persecution of the European Jews had been a dark chapter in human history. Even so, Michael was surprised that it still generated such strong feelings some two generations later. However, he was conscious that the dinner was in danger of descending into melancholy, and he quickly tried to move onto safer ground.

'And what about you, Rebecca? How did you get into history?'

'There's nothing to tell, really,' she replied as the frown started to fade. 'Like many descendants of Jewish refugees, I was raised in the Fort George area of Manhattan. My father was a lawyer, but he has retired now. I went to a local high school and then studied European History at Columbia University.' She smiled. 'It must be my roots that drew me back to Europe, and after graduating I travelled through Austria and Germany trying to discover what had happened to my old family. It felt like unfinished business or a debt that needed to be repaid to my grandmother and those who were left behind and then lost. I spent months looking through old Nazi records but there was no trace of them, and I eventually had to give up the search. Anyway, during my degree course I became interested in British History and after travelling through mainland Europe I decided to do some postgraduate research at Bristol University studying eighteenth and nineteenth century history, and in particular the role of the British aristocracy on the industrial revolution and Britain's impact on the world. All those lords and barons were the real drivers of your empire, you know. But when their families declined so did the extent of your overseas interests.'

Michael laughed. Her analysis was correct but delivered forthrightly and with a hint of old colonial *schadenfreude*. Typically American, he thought smiling to himself. He was glad, though, that the conversation had moved on to cover the graceful end of the British Empire as the change of subject had allowed family troubles to be set aside and the atmosphere to recover. The waitress appeared to clear their plates and then guided them back to the lounge for coffee and a liqueur. A log fire blazed at one end of the dimly lit room, and they sank into an old leather settee soaking up the warmth as fine quality brandy percolated slowly into their veins. The hotel's other guests had retired early and so they had the place to themselves. Emboldened by their privacy, Rebecca slipped her shoes off and tucked her feet under her legs. As they chatted, they relaxed in each other's company and the intimacy of the moment grew. Gradually, they leaned towards each other, and before long their shoulders were touching, and Michael could feel the warmth of her body flowing into him. It was comforting but her proximity fuelled his desire, and as time passed by, Michael's thoughts turned inevitably towards the end of the evening and other possibilities.

After a couple of hours, Rebecca stretched and put her

feet back into her shoes. 'It's been a lovely evening, Michael, but we really must rest. After all, we've got to confront the mad General tomorrow, and we need to be well prepared.'

Michael took her hand. His heart was beating harder, and he suddenly felt a little tongue-tied. 'Umm. I'm a bit out of practice at this kind of thing,' he said quietly. 'But I really like your company. You could stay if you wanted. Stay here I mean. With me.'

Rebecca turned to face him. Sadness filled her face but there was something else too. Was it pity he wondered as his spirits sank? She squeezed Michael's hand to reassure him and then proceeded anyway with her rejection.

'I really like you too, Michael, and I don't want to hurt you, but this is moving a little fast for me. Would it be okay if we gave it a miss this time? I'm not saying "no, never," just "no, not this time". Would that be alright?'

Michael suddenly felt foolish and embarrassed. He didn't really understand Rebecca's sadness, but he assumed that it was a consequence of his clumsiness and her reluctance to hurt his feelings. He was indeed out of practice, and in his enthusiasm, he had rushed things and now possibly scared her off.

'I'm sorry,' he stumbled. 'That was presumptuous, clumsy, and not at all elegantly put. I hope you don't think any the less of me now.'

She smiled into his face and tried to lighten the moment. 'You're very sweet, Michael. It was beautifully put, and not at all clumsy but as I said, not tonight but maybe another time.' She laughed coquettishly, hugged him closely and then kissed him on the cheek. It wasn't exactly a declaration of future intent but there was sufficient meaning in her intimacy to convey a hint of some future promise or expectation, and it achieved the desired aim of helping to repair Michael's damaged pride.

'I am sorely down hearted and mortally wounded, Madam,' he joked, desperately trying to conceal his disappointment. 'But I should warn you that I am a determined man.' She smiled, getting to her feet and was grateful that Michael had used a little levity to allow a difficult moment to pass.

'What time should we leave for Barrington Hall?' she asked breezily as she collected her coat and bag and moved towards the door.

'Well, the Pendletons are expecting me at 2.30 pm so let's meet here at 2 pm after lunch,' he replied. 'I'm not at all sure what's going to happen when I tell Francis Pendleton what I've discovered about Flora and her father, but it could be quite a quick meeting, and we may find ourselves back outside on the doorstep in pretty short order.'

Rebecca looked seriously at him as they arrived at the lobby. 'I do understand you know,' she breathed almost defiantly. 'It's all about knowing the truth, isn't it, Michael? I can sympathize with that. I spent months trying to discover what had happened to my grandmother's family. But, beyond making available some old records, I found that German officialdom has little interest in helping people like me to rake over the past, and I soon learned to recognize polite disinterest and dishonesty. Don't you worry about Pendleton. I'll know if he starts to lie. He'll be no different to any of the others that I have met like him.'

Michael was taken aback by the determination in Rebecca's final remarks, but he managed to smile a last farewell as she left the warmth of the hotel and disappeared out into the cold autumn night. She was a strong woman he decided as he gazed after her, and their situations were similar in very many respects. But she seemed uncomfortable whenever intimacy loomed, and her look of pity was slightly worrying. Did she also possess some kind of emotional blockage like Michael or was it solely down to his clumsiness and mishandling of the situation? Or perhaps he was missing something about her that was entirely different. No doubt he would find out soon enough.

Chapter 18

Storms

November 2000

When it rains in the southwest of England it can sometimes do so with a persistence that not only leaches the soil but also the morale of all those unfortunates living under the deluge. The day that Michael returned to Barrington Hall was one such day. A late autumnal storm had rolled in from the Atlantic and dumped almost three inches of rain in less than twelve hours. Rivers and streams had broken their banks, roads were impassable in places and old rural properties dripped misery onto their occupants. A fierce wind howled its discontent and whipped around the trees, stripping off the remaining autumnal leaves and testing the resilience of deeply sunk roots. Any that were found wanting were wrenched from the ground and fell like sleeping giants onto sodden turf or grey tarmac. It was as though the very elements were trying to stop Michael and Rebecca as they left the hotel for their appointment at Barrington Hall and almost immediately encountered a fallen tree blocking their way.

Rebecca braked hard to avoid a collision. 'This is fun,' she remarked sarcastically, reaching across Michael to remove an ordnance survey map from an impressive pile inside the glove compartment. 'Can you have a look and see if there's another way while I try to turn round?' Michael looked down at the map surprised that Rebecca owned such an extensive store.

'My research takes me all over the countryside,' she explained as though reading his mind. 'I like to be prepared.' Michael nodded, located an alternative route that took them conveniently through Ashill, and gave her the necessary directions. She was on a mission.

Earlier that day he had risen from a restless night's sleep worried that his morning reunion with Rebecca might be awkward following his failed overtures. However, she had breezed into the hotel lobby as though nothing had gone awry, kissed him on the cheek and firmly took his arm as they walked out to her car.

'I am so looking forward to this,' she had told him whilst leaning up close against him. 'I love old houses. They're so full of history and memories. It makes my work seem somehow real and alive.'

Michael's anxiety had been relieved by her sunny smile, but he didn't share her enthusiasm for another meeting with the Pendletons. He was expecting quite a hostile reception at Barrington Hall, and even before they encountered the fallen tree he was already regretting his decision to return there.

Next to him, Rebecca seemed to be undeterred by either the weather or the unexpected delay and after branching off the planned route, she carefully followed Michael's directions so that they arrived at Ashill barely a few minutes later. Just past the overgrown village sign, Smithieson's house stood unkempt and brooding. When Michael pointed it out to Rebecca she slowed down, and they both looked out half expecting the old man to come out and remonstrate with them. But the house looked unoccupied with the curtains drawn tightly against any outside scrutiny. It was almost as though the owner had gone away on an extended holiday.

'Let's hope he's in when we come back,' Michael said half-heartedly as he remembered the soiled living room and its dirty occupant.

They drove past and approached the green. Just before they arrived, Michael asked her to slow down again as he pressed his face against the glass looking at the house numbers and names.

'There!' He jabbed a finger at the last terraced cottage before the road opened out. 'That is where I believe Flora was born. At any rate that's the address on her birth certificate. It's fascinating, isn't it? She was actually there all those years ago.' Rebecca smiled at his delight, then glanced at her watch and accelerated away conscious that they were going to be late for their appointment.

Ten minutes later, they drove up the drive to Barrington Hall and parked on the gravel. The magnificent Yew trees had withstood the worst of the meteorological onslaught and swayed with a reassuring permanency. Under the leaden sky, the old hall looked much less appealing than before. Everything seemed darker and less welcoming. The window frames still highlighted the graceful lines of the Georgian structure, but nothing was visible through the glass, and they seemed like black featureless eyes, unblinking and forbidding.

'Wow,' Rebecca said gazing up at the lead lined roof and the building's beautifully proportioned features. They surely knew a thing or two about style and architecture in those days, didn't they?' Michael nodded but was unconvinced and led her up the steps to the front door which Mrs Barrow opened before he had a chance to ring the bell.

'Mr Calvert and…?'

'His assistant,' replied Rebecca quickly.

Mrs Barrow made no effort to conceal her disapproval. 'I see. Well, you're expected. Please wait in the hall and I will let Mrs Emily know that you're here.' She closed the heavy door behind them and strode off down the corridor towards the reception room that Michael had visited before. The hall had little in the way of natural light, but the wall lights had been switched on and a row of brass fittings beamed down onto the familiar row of Pendleton grandees. Behind him, Rebecca was making her own investigations.

'Oh look, Michael. Look at this,' Rebecca hissed as soon as Mrs Barrow had disappeared. Michael spun round and saw that she was inspecting the pictures hanging on the wall by the door. She was in front of a small oil painting of a lakeside scene and was excited by the signature. 'This surely can't be real, can it? I think it is you know. It looks familiar and the signature is Turner's. It must be worth a fortune if it's genuine. And here,' she said, moving to its neighbour. 'This is another one. Gee, how many have they got?'

'Rebecca, come away,' Michael whispered hoarsely. 'And for goodness' sake don't touch any of them. The Pendletons are very protective of their collection, and we don't want to upset them before we even get started.' Rebecca moved reluctantly into the middle of the hall but continued to stare at the walls. Was she searching for other grand portraits or just mentally calculating the value of the wall covering?

'There are loads more paintings in there,' Michael said pointing at the closed door that he had peeped through on his earlier visit. 'But they keep that one locked and private.' Rebecca looked over at the door her face filling with interest, and Michael immediately regretted stimulating her curiosity. She quickly glanced down the corridor to check it was clear and then strode purposely over to where Michael had pointed. Before he could object, she grasped the handle, twisted it and gave it a firm tug. But the door remained tightly shut and her face fell. Then she smiled mischievously.

'As you said, entry is forbidden to guests.' Despite his concern at potential discovery, Michael couldn't help but smile at her boldness. She was like a cat burglar, he thought. Stealthy and calculating.

'Come away. Quickly!' he whispered as footsteps approached from the corridor. She smiled, released the handle and arrived at his side just as Francis Pendleton strode purposely up to them.

'Ah Mr Calvert,' he said disarmingly and seemingly oblivious to Rebecca's attempts to breach household security. 'We thought perhaps that you had got lost or had forgotten but in fact you are merely late.'

'Yes, I do apologise. I'm afraid the gale has brought down a tree on the way here and we had to take a diversion. Through Ashill actually,' Michael said pointedly.

'I see,' he said, ignoring Michael's excuse and looking pleasantly at Rebecca. 'And you are?'

'Hello, I'm Michael's assistant, Rebecca. I've been helping him with his research.'

'American too. You have interesting friends, Mr Calvert. Anyway, I'm delighted to meet you, Rebecca. Please both of you come this way.' Seemingly unfazed by the unexpected presence of an additional guest, he led them down the hall to the reception room they had used previously. Michael was unsettled by the man's friendly welcome. The retired general was so full of oozing charm and bonhomie that he seemed to be a completely different person to the one that had first berated Michael for his nosiness and then patronized him during their previous discussion about Flora. The change in the man's demeanour made Michael feel uncomfortable. This was not the real Francis Pendleton. The man was trying too hard to put them at their ease.

They entered the drawing room at the end of the

corridor and Michael introduced Rebecca to Emily who was waiting in her customary seat in the middle of the room.

'Hello, my dear,' she said taking Rebecca's hand. 'When I heard of Mr Calvert admiring our collection, I thought that he must have very good taste, and now I've met you I can see that I was entirely correct.' Rebecca was temporarily speechless and sat down next to the old lady, blushing and self-conscious.

'I saw some wonderful paintings in the hall,' she eventually replied. 'I would love to see the rest of your collection sometime.'

'Well yes, dear, perhaps sometime, 'Emily said vaguely, avoiding any firm commitment. 'But I think we are all here today to listen to Mr Calvert's latest update on his investigations.'

Francis Pendleton walked over to an impressive marble fireplace surrounding a fire and prodded some burning logs with a poker. 'Yes, what can you tell us? We're very intrigued to hear what you've discovered. We know very little about the history of Barrington Hall whilst it was occupied by my great uncle.'

Michael doubted that very much but cleared his throat. Some of what he had to say needed to be broached very carefully if he was to avoid giving offence. He started by reminding the Pendletons how Marge's recollections had led him to Barrington Hall in the first place. They listened patiently and reassured by their polite silence Michael went on to tell them about his visit to Smithieson. He also explained about the death of Flora's father in an accident and how Smithieson had been convicted of nobbling horses during an old betting scandal.

'I don't understand why he told me a pack of lies about her surname. It was almost as though he was trying to put me off the scent, and he even threatened me in a rather obtuse way. Umm, there was something else too, and I don't quite know how to put this without causing any offence, but it seems that Flora was pregnant when she left.' There was a short pause, and Michael was aware that Emily Pendleton was suddenly galvanized. She had stopped staring out of the window and had turned to face her son with a look of undisguised horror as she anticipated what Michael meant to say. Across the room, Francis Pendleton seemed unaware of his mother's discomfort and his face continued to wear a mask of infinite patience.

'Yes, well that would perhaps explain why she was dismissed,' he said reasonably. 'Why should that cause us any offence?'

'Well according to Smithieson, there was some doubt about the identity of the father, and he reckoned it was possible that, er, Sir Roland was involved with the girl.'

'How could Smithieson possibly know that?' Emily Pendleton interjected. 'He was a mere stable hand. What could he know of such matters?'

'Well, I don't know for sure, but according to Smithieson it was common knowledge amongst the staff.'

'Rubbish. The man's a serial liar,' Francis said firmly. He looked unblinkingly at Michael as though challenging him to disagree. His facial expression was controlled and impassive, but Michael sensed that fury boiled just beneath the surface. 'We know about Smithieson. He was a crook and almost ruined my great uncle's reputation with his betting fraud. Do you know, Sir Roland was so soft that he even spoke up for Smithieson at his trial and managed to get the man's sentence reduced slightly? And now look at how he repays the family. He lied to you about the servant girl's surname and he's making unwarranted and false accusations about the parentage of her bastard child. I'm sorry, Mr Calvert, but I think you are a greater fool than you look if you believe any of this nonsense.'

'There's something else too,' Michael continued undeterred. 'Marge seems to think that Flora took some important papers belonging to Sir Roland and that she later had to go on the run when he sent men to retrieve them.'

For an instant, Francis Pendleton almost lost his composure, and a fleeting look of shock passed over his face before the mask fell back into place. It only lasted for a split second, but it was long enough for Michael to notice and wonder if he had struck a nerve. The General eyed him suspiciously. 'Stole papers? What sort of papers?'

'Well, Marge doesn't seem to know. It was something to do with Sir Roland though. We were hoping that you might be able to tell us something about it. Apparently, Flora told Marge that it was a great secret and that nobody should know.'

'And does this Marge know what happened to them? Were they recovered?'

'Apparently not. Flora took all her possessions with her when she returned to Somerset some years later. Nobody knows anything about the papers after that.'

'I see,' Pendleton said with poorly concealed satisfaction. 'And what happened to Flora then?'

Michael paused and he glanced over at Rebecca for moral support. However, she was sat bolt upright staring out of the window, listening intently but remaining determinedly detached. Pendleton was changing the rules of the meeting. Suddenly, he was the one now doing the interrogating and he was giving nothing back in return. Michael's instincts warned him to proceed more cautiously. 'It becomes a bit vague after that,' he said carefully. 'There's a thought that Flora died in an accident not long after, but I have reason to believe she may have survived and perhaps moved away.'

There was a short pause as Francis Pendleton carefully absorbed this latest information. He had noted Michael's caution and realized that his visitor had reached the limits of what he either knew or was prepared to reveal. As a result, General Pendleton finally allowed the superficial veneer of charm to melt away and his expression became cold and threatening. He walked over to Michael and looked down at him trying to intimidate him by his presence.

'Look Calvert,' he spat, 'I think this charade has gone on long enough, don't you? You come barging into our house trying to sully the family name with some fanciful story about stolen papers, threats and the suspect parentage of some child from sixty years ago. But I know what's going on here. You see I've made some enquiries of my own and I've discovered that you're some kind of freelance journalist although as far as I can see you've not published anything noteworthy for many years. Is that what this is about? Are you trying to dredge up some old story just to make a few pathetic pounds? You have no evidence for any of your accusations. They're pure speculation and hearsay. Look. You'd better leave now. You're no longer welcome and if you persist in troubling us then I shall be forced to make a complaint to the police. We have very good relations with the local constabulary, and they are likely to take a very dim view of some washed-up hack harassing one of the county's better-known families.' He paused momentarily before reinforcing the threat. 'We are well-connected, Calvert, and you'd be as well to note it.'

Michael felt invigorated. Despite the highly charged atmosphere, he suddenly felt quite relaxed now that the General had reverted to his true self. The obsequiously charming, retired army officer was an unknown quantity, whereas the school bully full of calculating bluster and threats seemed familiar and somehow easier to deal with.

'I'm sorry that we seem to have wasted your time, Mr Pendleton,' he said knowing that by failing to use Francis Pendleton's military title he would cause the man's blood pressure to rise further. 'As I told you before, the only reason I am here is to research my family tree. There was no professional interest involved. Or should I say there wasn't at the outset,' he added, trumping Pendleton's threat with one of his own.

Michael stood up, meeting the General face to face and recapturing his personal space. He thanked an embarrassed Emily Pendleton for her forbearance and then nodded to Rebecca to indicate that their visit was over. The General had added little that was new. However, his behaviour had been illuminating. He was clearly interested in Flora's story, and he had been unable to conceal his shock at the mention of stolen papers. Michael was now certain that Flora's secret originated in this very building, and it was clear that Pendleton knew far more about the matter than he was letting on. Michael knew he would have to tread carefully, however. By initiating his own enquiries into Michael's background, Francis Pendleton had clearly demonstrated that he regarded Michael as some kind of threat, and Michael was certain that he would make a dangerous enemy. The General was ruthless, cold and very intelligent, and when he spoke there was always a sense that physical violence was not too far away. He would do well to respect that in the future, he thought as Mrs Barrow showed them out of the door onto the windswept steps.

Back in the car, Michael looked at Rebecca who was uncharacteristically quiet and a little preoccupied. 'Well, what did you make of that?' he asked as they drove down the long drive towards the main gates.

'He certainly knows more about this than he's letting on,' Rebecca replied as she leaned forward with a cloth to wipe condensation from the steamed-up windscreen. 'And he seems to be worried about something too. He wouldn't have gone to all that trouble to find out about your background if he wasn't a little concerned about your investigations. The question is, what are they worried about?'

'Hmm, I'm not sure. Emily Pendleton looked alarmed when I suggested that Sir Roland might have fathered Flora's child, but Francis didn't seem too concerned about that, and the only time I noticed a chink in his armour was when we were discussing the stolen papers. What I do know for certain is that I've made enemies of the Pendletons, and we'll get nothing else out of them.'

'Well, there's always Smithieson. We could visit him and challenge his version of events to see if that throws up anything new,' Rebecca suggested as they turned off the lane towards Ashill. Michael agreed. They were nearly at the old man's house, so it made sense. However, when they reached it, Smithieson's house stood dark and as seemingly vacant as it had when they passed it earlier. The curtains were still drawn and there was no reply when Michael hammered on the door.

'I think that's probably as far as we can get today,' Michael said dejectedly as they got back in. 'How about we go back to the hotel and get a drink while we work out our next step?'

Rebecca pulled a wry smile. 'I'm sorry, Michael, but I must get back home and prepare some work for tomorrow. I'm teaching some undergraduates at the University in the morning, and I must make sure that I'm prepared. We could meet up in the afternoon if you want though?'

Michael readily agreed. He was disappointed that she couldn't stay, but remembering his fumbling efforts the previous evening, he decided not to press her. Instead, they fell silent as the car made its way back to Taunton. Michael didn't perceive it as an uncomfortable silence. It was just a moment quietly shared between two friends occupied by their own thoughts.

While Michael and Rebecca continued their ritual dance, General Francis Pendleton seethed. Calvert was making far too much progress, and it was time to intervene as the danger to the family was palpable. His mother was worried about the servant girl's pregnancy, but she was ignorant of a far greater threat than some aristocratic fumble deep in the past. He thought of Calvert. He might

be failing professionally but he was an effective
investigator, and it would be wrong to underestimate him.
Before he died, Sir Roland had disclosed a ruinous family
secret which Francis still hid from his mother. His great
uncle had been certain that it was safely buried, but the
General was no longer so sure. He was worried that
something had been overlooked in the past. A weakness.
Something that might become apparent to Calvert as he
filled in his family tree and combined all the snippets of
information that he gathered along the way. The General
thought that Michael had made a mistake by revealing too
much of what he knew including the names of those who
had helped him. And that had included that damn fool,
Smithieson, he thought angrily. The old man and his
grandson, Ron Stanton, had served the Pendleton family
faithfully for many years, but Smithieson had given away
far more information than he had been instructed to
provide, and he had become a liability. He was just too old,
and it was time he was retired and prevented from telling
any more of his stories.

Making sure his mother was otherwise occupied, he
dialled a number that was clear in his memory but not one
he would ever consign to a contact list.

'Hello. Peter Hargreaves? This is General Francis. I
have a job for you. Smithieson has exceeded his brief and
has become unreliable. I would like you to deal with him,
please, and after that, I need you to go on a collection
mission. There is damaging information out there that
needs retrieving. One way or another. Yes, I will send you
all the details.'

On the other end of the line, the man called Hargreaves
indicated his acceptance of the tasks, and the General rang
off satisfied with the plans he had put in place and pleased
that he was acting in the traditional Pendleton way.
Hargreaves had served in the Army under the General's
command, and he had recently replaced Smithieson and
Ron Stanton as the man to call when unconventional

means were required. He was highly trained and discreet. Sir Roland would have approved, he reflected, gazing up at a gilt-framed portrait of the man that looked down at him from the wall.

Chapter 19

Murder

November 2000

It took less than 24 hours to confirm that General Pendleton was alarmed by Michael's progress. It was late morning at the hotel, and when Michael answered his phone he heard the official voice of the local police.

'Is that Michael Calvert? This is Chief Superintendent Parker from the Somerset Police. I've been asked by the Deputy Chief Constable to call you.' Michael knew what was coming and was impressed. The General was indeed well-connected. After Michael had confirmed his identity, the officer continued.

'Look, Mr Calvert, we've had a complaint from Barrington Hall. Apparently, you've been making a nuisance of yourself with the Pendleton family. I understand that you are some kind of journalist, so you should be well aware of the boundary between fair reporting and harassment. We try to offer the press as much leeway as possible so consider this as a friendly warning. This is a quiet county, and we don't take kindly to our residents being pursued in this way. I should also remind you that harassment is a criminal offence, and if you persist then we will be forced to make this a formal matter. Please leave the Pendletons alone. Is that understood?'

It wasn't a friendly warning at all, but Michael assured the officer that he had completed his investigations, and he promised to stay within the law. Later that afternoon he told Rebecca about it, and she seemed alarmed that the local authorities were taking a sudden interest.

We'd better tread carefully when we go to see Smithieson,' she asserted. 'If he complains too then we could find ourselves arrested. How do you think we should play it?'

Michael was less concerned. From what he had learned about Smithieson, he doubted that the old man would want police involvement. 'Well, I think I will play it straight and just challenge him with what I know. He's lied to me about Flora, and I want to know why. He's a formidable old man but if I confront him with the facts he may fold.'

'Okay, but if he's as old as you say, we'd better be slightly careful. We don't want him to keel over and die of shock or anything like that.'

'Oh, I doubt that very much. He may be old but he's a powerful man who's good for a few more years yet,' Michael laughed not knowing how prophetic their exchange had been.

They left the hotel and followed the usual route to Ashill. The village had always seemed quiet, but it was unusually deserted that afternoon and when they rounded the corner the reason became apparent. A cluster of police cars and an ambulance blocked one side of the road, and Smithieson's house was surrounded by uniformed officers. A police incident sign had been placed to one side, and the front garden and pavement were blocked off by plastic tape. Several policemen were standing around as a stretcher was wheeled out of the house. It was clear that the stretcher was carrying a body, but the occupant's face had been carefully covered. Michael's heart sank. He was sure that Smithieson was the key to unlocking Flora's mystery, but that avenue looked like it had been closed off.

'I hope that's not Smithieson under that sheet. We need to find out. Let's stop and ask a few questions,' Michael said, reaching into his wallet for an old Press Association card.

'Wait, Michael. I really don't think that's a good idea,' Rebecca replied firmly. 'What if there's been some kind of foul play? We don't want to become part of a police enquiry. Think of your phone call this morning. We could end up down at the police station for hours whilst they eliminate us from their investigation.'

'But we don't even know whether that's Smithieson laid on the stretcher never mind whether there's been any foul play,' he protested.

'That may be so, but we're strangers in the village and you've been seen here recently. You even visited the man. It's up to you, but I think we should stay well out of it.'

Michael thought carefully about the phone call. The General had influence at a senior level within the local police, and it would be all too easy to rope Michael into a lengthy enquiry designed to impede his progress. Rebecca was correct, it was better to keep a low profile until they had at least discovered what was going on.

'Okay then, but let's at least go down to the pub. Somebody down there will know what's happened, and I've had a bit of idea. If we can't speak to Smithieson then there's somebody else who might do, but we need his address first.' Rebecca nodded, and they drove slowly past the incident untroubled by the watching police officers standing on the pavement.

Down at the pub, the landlord had called time on the

lunchtime drinkers and the last of the customers were just leaving.

'I'm sorry, we're just closing up,' he said as they came through the door. 'Oh, it's you again,' he added, recognising Michael's tall figure. 'I hope you've not come to cause any more bother. We've had enough of that today in Ashill.'

'Yes, we saw the police cars,' Michael said evenly. 'What's going on?'

'It's old Smithieson,' the landlord said as he wiped a grimy cloth along the bar surface. 'Somebody's done him in. Bashed his head in with a hammer or some such like. Nasty mess too. His neighbour hadn't seen him since yesterday afternoon, and he went round this morning to check that he was well. He found Smithieson lying on the floor in a pool of blood. Stone cold dead he was. Mind you, it's not surprising if you ask me; Fred didn't exactly make friends easily.'

'How do you mean?'

The landlord twirled his sideburns thoughtfully. 'Well apart from being a grumpy old sod, he used to do a lot of dirty work for that lot up at Barrington Hall. It was a family tradition you might say as his son and then grandson did the same kind of work. Keeping the staff in order that kind of thing. If a servant stole something from the family, then they'd let the Smithieson family sort it out rather than call the police. A lot of people from the village worked up there at one time or another and there's quite a few who still have an axe to grind.' He paused momentarily as a suspicion took hold.

'Anyhow, what's any of this to you?'

'Nothing at all really,' Michael replied. 'The real reason I'm here is to try and track down somebody I want to talk to. Do you remember those two men who got involved in that argument the other day. I think one of them was called Arthur Blackford. Do you know where they live?'

'I remember. It was Arthur and his son David. In fact,

it's a bit of a strange coincidence but the three of you were arguing with Smithieson's grandson, Ron Stanton. Anyway, what do you want with the Blackfords?'

'It's to do with my grandmother. You remember. I'm trying to trace my family tree.'

'Hmm, well, it's not a good day for strangers to be poking around. Old Arthur had a quite a quarrel with Smithieson. In fact, if Smithieson's been murdered it wouldn't surprise me if you find the police have already beaten you to Arthur's door.'

'Quarrel? What sort of quarrel?'

'Oh, I don't know, something to do with Arthur's father. It goes back years. Every now and then there's an argument in the pub like the one the other day. I think David even came to blows over it on one occasion. I got fed up with it to be honest and stopped listening to them a long time ago. You'd be best to ask Arthur.' On that note of finality, the landlord reluctantly gave Michael directions to the Blackfords' cottage and turned to collect the used glasses of his lunchtime clients.

The Blackfords' property was just outside the village. It was set back from the road slightly and obscured by a tall privet hedge such that they almost overshot the entrance. Michael knocked on the door and a few seconds later, Arthur appeared on the doorstep. At their previous encounter his face had seemed unusually smooth and youthful, but the face that now peered out was lined with concern.

'Oh, it's you. What do you want? I would have thought that you'd stay well clear of Ashill today with what's gone on down at the other end of the village.'

'Yes, we've heard about Smithieson. Terrible, isn't it?'

'Terrible?' the man echoed. 'That depends on your point of view. I've never condoned violence, but I can't say I'll miss the man. Between the two of them, Smithieson and Sir Roland Pendleton damaged my family terribly over the years, so you'll not find anyone here in mourning.'

Michael weighed up Arthur carefully. Although he was clearly nervous of Michael's visit, he didn't seem overly concerned by Smithieson's demise. On the contrary, there was almost a whiff of satisfaction about him, and what he had just said could easily be construed as a motive for murder. What was the bad blood that had existed between the two men?

'Look, Mr Blackford, I don't want to take up much of your time, but could we have a word with you? It's about Flora, my grandmother, and I suppose, it's about Sir Roland and Smithieson too.'

'I have nothing to say to you. This is not the right time with a man laid out cold on a slab in the morgue. I expect the police will soon be here asking the same questions as you. The village is full of gossipers, and it won't be long before an officer gets to hear about the Blackfords and their feud with the Smithieson family. In fact, it wouldn't surprise me if fingers are already pointing in our direction. We're used to it. After all, they've been doing that for the best part of seventy years.'

Michael's frustration bubbled up. 'Look, Mr Blackford, I think you're my last chance,' he pleaded. 'I've been to see Smithieson as you suggested, and I've also been back to see the Pendletons. Somebody is lying to me about Flora. In fact, I would go as far as saying somebody is trying to prevent me from discovering anything about her. It's all to do with Barrington Hall, but without your help, I'm stuck. All I need is a couple of answers and then I'll leave you alone.'

Arthur looked at Michael curiously. 'They're lying to you, are they?' he asked cautiously. 'I know all about that. They're good at it aren't they?' He paused for a moment, then seemed to reach a decision and stepped back from the door, gesturing for them to follow him inside. 'My son has just popped out to the village shop but shouldn't be long,' he added to warn them that moral support was only just around the corner. They followed him through the front door which opened straight into a living room with a glowing fire. Arthur sat in a wooden rocking chair and waited for them to take up position on a soft settee opposite. He looked at Michael and then asked slyly, 'before I answer any of your questions, perhaps you could start by telling me what you know.'

Michael was a little put out that once again he was the one being asked to do the talking, but he assessed that Arthur would only open up when an element of mutual trust had been established. He therefore recounted everything that he had learned since his visit to Smithieson. As he spoke, Arthur stared into the fire as though Michael was guiding him back through time. He occasionally nodded to indicate that he was listening, but Michael got the impression that he was in some way distracted and that his thoughts were elsewhere.

When Michael had finished, the old man shifted uncomfortably in his seat. A look of turmoil and long-seated anger had gradually fallen across his face. 'My father was a bookmaker,' he said bitterly. 'In fact, he was the bookmaker in your story, the one mentioned in all the old newspapers that you've uncovered. He knew the Pendletons well from their time at the track and he became suspicious when their best horses started to run poorly and against form. On those occasions he noticed that large bets were being made against the Pendletons' mounts. He claimed he had found evidence of horse tampering that went all the way back to Sir Roland and he made a public accusation. It wasn't done out of spite or anything like that but for financial reasons because he'd lost a significant amount of money from the fraud, and he wanted it stopped. He confronted Sir Roland about it at the track one day and in front of several other dignitaries, he accused him of betting fraud. Of course, it was an absolute scandal at the time. It was in all the papers and for a while it even threatened Sir Roland's business activities.'

Michael nodded. 'What happened? How did your father lose the court case?'

'I can't prove any of this, and goodness knows I've tried hard enough over the years, but it seems that Sir Roland got Smithieson to take the rap for him. That was why Sir Roland spoke up for the man at his trial. He owed him a big favour. You see, once Smithieson made his confession as the sole miscreant in the plot then Sir Roland was in the clear. Shortly after that, the slander case went against my father, and he was ordered to pay full costs and extensive damages. He was financially ruined, and his business went bankrupt. It wasn't long after that he took a shotgun from the cupboard just over there and committed suicide.' The old man's eyes glistened with sorrow as he glanced at the locked gun cabinet. 'I've spent years trying to prove my father was right about Sir Roland, and I've repeatedly tried to convince Smithieson to tell the truth. Even my own son, David, had a go. But all we ever got were stonewalling and threats, and we just couldn't prove it. Smithieson's grandson, Ron Stanton, even assaulted David on one occasion and we were eventually forced to let the matter lie.'

'Well, what about Flora's father. Wasn't he the Pendleton's horse trainer?' Michael asked.

'Yes, and this is the worst of it. You see Henry Poulter was also very suspicious. He couldn't understand why the horses performed so well in training and then seemed listless and lacking energy on race days. He started to watch carefully what went on in the stables, and one day just prior to a major race meeting at Ascot, he saw Sir Roland emerging from one of the stables holding a large veterinary syringe. Sir Roland saw him and made up some excuse about finding it on the floor. He even had the temerity to berate Henry as though he was responsible for leaving a dangerous instrument lying about where it could cause some harm.'

'But didn't any of this come out in the court case?'

'Well, that's just it. Henry Poulter told my father that he was willing to give evidence in court about what he had seen. Shortly after, and before any of the stories became public knowledge, Henry was killed, supposedly in an accident at the stables.'

'And that was when Smithieson popped up to take the blame for the horse tampering?'

'Exactly. He must have been well-paid for his trouble as he spent over two years in prison.'

'And what about Flora? Wasn't she working at Barrington Hall by then?' At the mention of Flora, Arthur's expression changed as anger was replaced by something else that Michael couldn't quite place. Was it sorrow or regret? But he couldn't tell, and just as the old man regained his composure and was about to speak, the front door opened and David Blackford staggered into the room, arms full of carrier bags.

'Hello,' he said noting that Michael was back and this time with an attractive assistant. 'I hope you're not bothering my dad about Smithieson again. Not today of all days.'

'It's all right, David,' the old man answered. 'I've told them about the betting fraud and Smithieson. They're not here to harm us as far as I can tell.'

'Well, if you're sure,' the younger man said doubtfully. 'The village is full of police cars, and I expect they'll be along here before too long.'

'You were going to tell us about Flora, Mr Blackford,' Rebecca interjected breaking her silence for the first time. The old man looked carefully from his son back to Rebecca. His son's entrance seemed to have made him more wary and cautious, and for a moment Michael thought he was going to refuse to go on. But the moment seemed to pass, and the old man merely coughed uncomfortably and then continued with his story.

'I can't tell you much, and my memory is fading. But I did know Flora a little. She was a bit older than me.

Friendly though, vivacious and outgoing. She used to work for a lady in the village but went up to the hall after she died. She arrived a few months before the betting scandal and the death of her father.'

'You would have thought her father would have tried to prevent her from joining the household bearing in mind what he suspected was going on at the time,' Michael said.

'Yes, I've often wondered about that. But you know, money and jobs were in short supply in those days. I seem to remember that Flora had lost her cleaning job, and with little employment available elsewhere she probably had no choice. It's also possible that she was unaware that anything was amiss at the hall if her father had kept the matter to himself.'

'Do you know anything about why she left?'

'I don't really, but I remember that it caused quite a stir in the village. Some people said that it was because she was pregnant and there was even a rumour that Sir Roland was the father.' Arthur looked darkly at Michael as he struggled to frame his words. 'I don't know anything about that, and I wouldn't care to speculate,' he said angrily after a short pause. 'For my part, I've often wondered whether Flora had discovered something about her father's death that made her run away. Whatever it was, she left very suddenly and in great secrecy.'

'Did you hear anything about her taking some papers of Sir Roland's?'

'Papers? No,' the old man said casually. 'What sort of thing do you mean?'

'I'm not sure, I do know that Flora went to London and a lady who knew her there told me that Sir Roland sent a man to find Flora. He came to the house demanding to see her and mentioned that Flora had taken some important documents from Sir Roland.'

Arthur looked away as a deep melancholy seemed to weigh heavily on his shoulders. Michael couldn't understand the cause, and for a moment he wondered if

Flora had meant more to Arthur than he had revealed. Perhaps his dejection was merely a consequence of all the old memories and the loss of his father. He debated whether to stop his questioning but decided it was worth one more attempt. 'As well as papers, I've been told about a journal too. Apparently, Flora used to love writing in it and recorded everything that happened to her. I don't suppose you know anything about that do you? If it could be found, it might explain quite a lot.'

The old man didn't look round and seemed lost in his thoughts; there was something else – was it grief? After a moment he shook his head, but it was unclear whether he was denying knowledge of the diary or just indicating that the interview had reached a natural conclusion. David Blackford clearly thought it was the latter and stood to indicate that it was time they left.

'I think my dad has had enough now,' he said pleasantly. 'And it's probably best if you left us now.' Michael agreed, and after thanking the silent Arthur for his help they made their way to the door. As they left, David followed them out. 'You must make allowances for him,' he said apologetically. 'He's lived with this business about his father for so long it's become an obsession. But you obviously made some kind of impression as I've never heard much of that stuff about Barrington Hall and the staff.'

Michael thanked him, but as set off down the path he suddenly stopped and turned back to David. 'Can I ask you something personal,' he asked. 'Your dad never mentioned anything about your mother. What happened to her?'

David smiled sadly. 'I never knew her; she died in the war when I was a baby, and I was brought up by my grandmother.' Michael nodded. He was discovering many similar stories from the war.

Chapter 20

Dancing

January 1941

After Albert Belton died, Flora's life took a turn in a direction that Margaret Belton thought was very much for the worse. The authorities had instructed Albert's landlord to release the property to a homeless family, and Flora was forced to vacate the house and move back in with Margaret and Marge. It wasn't ideal, and she worried continuously about Smithieson. However, there was nowhere else to go, and she had the baby Andrew to consider. It was also handy for the street shelter which was fortunate as the German bombardment was relentless.

Flora hated it. The entrance was surrounded by sandbags, and there were steps that went deep beneath the pavement. There were no home comforts inside, just rows of wooden benches on a concrete floor. It was damp, and the smell of human anxiety mixed unpleasantly with the fumes coming from an earth bucket toilet hidden in the corner behind a blanket. At the start of the Blitz, the occupants were defiant, and the crump of explosions had been accompanied by dark humour and occasional singing. However, the lack of sleep and weeks of bombardment eventually exacted a toll. Spirits remained unbroken but the atmosphere became more sober as the subterranean refugees became worn down by fear and the constant worry of losing their homes. Flora thought the shelter was a dank morgue, and she was worried by the sniffling and coughing of those around her as they spread their germs.

It was a tough time for Londoners for other reasons too. Food was carefully rationed, and there were frequent shortages. It was especially difficult for those with little or no money. On one occasion, Flora found Margaret weeping in absolute despair, and she told Flora between sobs that there was not enough food in the house to feed everyone that evening. Flora hugged her and realized that Margaret had been trying to support all four of them on her part-time cleaner's pay. Margaret's desperation also highlighted that Flora was adding to the household burden without contributing anything. Flora thought about the dank air raid shelter and the lack of food. Was this really the most that Andrew could expect from life? What a terrible prospect. It was the baby boy that was preventing her from returning to work, and she could not bear the idea of being the reason that Margaret and Marge were going unfed. There were many reasons for another child evacuation but none of them made Flora feel any better about her decision to send Andrew north. Opposite Flora, Margaret Belton had no idea that Flora blamed herself for their hunger.

'Are you sure evacuation is what you want for Andrew?' she asked Flora. Marge has returned home and seems to be managing with the bombing alright. Don't you think he would be better off here with us?'

'It's for the best, Margaret. This is no place for a baby. I would never forgive myself if he stayed here and something happened to him,' she replied.

'Well make sure you write the postcard with our address,' Margaret Belton reminded her firmly. 'And don't forget to get the details of whoever carries the child for you. That way we won't lose him.' Margaret hadn't completed her sentence by adding, 'like your daughter, Jocelyn,' but the reproachful expression on her face betrayed her thoughts, and Flora felt a pang of guilt as she was reminded of her baby girl missing somewhere deep in the Yorkshire countryside.

Flora fled from Margaret's disapproval in favour of the dubious sanctuary of the street outside. She spoke to Mr Crofton, the local headmaster, who told her that there were other children fleeing to the countryside who would look after Andrew on the journey. He promised her that they would take good care of the baby boy, and his promise sealed the matter for Flora. As she handed over the baby to a bright-eyed teenage girl at the station, she glanced one more time at the small face staring up at her from inside the blanket. Half of her wanted to hold on to him and to take him back to Margaret and Marge. But other, more pragmatic voices told her that the child would be better served elsewhere. And she was honest enough to know that, even at that tearful moment of departure, it was the last time that she would see Andrew Belton again.

***

After Andrew had gone, Flora contacted her friends at the hospital and managed to regain her old job. She was able to give Margaret a little cash, and whenever possible Flora tried to free up food for Margaret and Marge by either going unfed or by scrounging a meal at the hospital. When she did eat with them, Flora often waited for Margaret to be distracted and then removed food from her own plate and put it onto Marge's, winking and placing a finger on her lips to keep the girl quiet.

Flora's friend, Rose, still lived in her room at the nurses' home, and she was delighted that her friend had returned. She was also a generous girl and was more than happy to make space for Flora who spent many nights curled up asleep on Rose's settee. Rose was vivacious and immediately took charge of Flora's social diary. 'What you need is some fun and laughter,' she remarked one night as they huddled in the air raid shelter in the hospital grounds listening to the distant explosions. 'Let's go dancing one evening. I have lots of friends, men friends, who would love to meet you and show you a good time.' She looked knowingly at Flora. 'Men with money,' she winked.

Flora looked shocked. 'I don't know what sort of girl you think I am,' she remonstrated, 'but if you think I'd…'

'I don't mean that silly. What I mean is that we go out and have a good time at a dance and meet some nice gentlemen who spend their money on us all evening. What happens after that is down to you. It's not a formal financial arrangement or anything like that. It's much more, well, sophisticated. It's about having fun, and goodness knows we need some of that with the war and all this bombing. Besides, you never know when your life might end so you might as well take advantage of it whilst you can.'

Flora wasn't convinced by what was being proposed, but the explosion of a large landmine in the distance seemed to emphasise Rose's point about the fragility of life. Flora also liked dancing, and she had been taught by a real enthusiast. As soon as she had reached the age of sixteen, Victoria Evans had declared that it was time for Flora to prepare for high society. The old lady seemed oblivious to the fact that, in social and practical terms, Flora was as far away from high society as it was possible to be, but she had nonetheless insisted on regular dance lessons. They would move the furniture to one side of the parlour and then spend an afternoon whirling round the room, with Victoria taking the leading man's role and shouting encouragement in time to the music coming from a tired gramophone player. Flora smiled at the memory. Rose was right. It would be exciting to go into town and dance the night away, and it would do her good to make some new friends.

Unfortunately, work intruded for a few days, but later that week, the two women finished a night shift and dashed back to Rose's room to get ready. Flora was astounded by the range of dresses hanging in Rose's wardrobe. Her own clothes had become very worn, and she had repeatedly darned her underwear to keep it going. New items were unaffordable and in most cases unavailable.

'None of these are "make do and mend!"' she exclaimed, looking at Rose's collection. 'How on earth have you managed to afford all of these? How did you get the ration coupons?'

Rose laughed. 'You'll meet Freddy later. He's a real darling of a businessman and can get anything you want: stockings, underwear, clothing coupons, that kind of thing. He even has a Bentley…. with petrol!'

Flora was astonished. 'How does he manage that?'

'I don't know, and you mustn't ask or say anything. He once said he has friends in high places and just winked at me. Anyway, come on, which dress do you want to borrow?'

Flora looked at the array of clothes and felt a wave of gratitude for her friend's generosity. She was ashamed of her plain old blouse and skirt with their obvious repairs, and she was relieved that they could remain concealed in her bag. She found it difficult to choose but eventually Flora spotted a blue silk dress that would flatter her figure and excitedly got changed.

Two hours later, they emerged from the underground station to an Oxford Street that was ringed by piles of rubble and broken glass. The John Lewis and Selfridges department stores had been badly damaged in raids a couple of months earlier, although both shops had Union Jack flags hanging above their entranceways with signs announcing that they were still open for business. They picked their way past the ruined buildings and dodged shoppers and workers who rushed past seemingly oblivious to the destruction around them. It was 4 pm and the light was fading. For some, safety for the next twelve hours would be found on the cramped platform of the underground station. For others, it would be a communal street bunker or Anderson shelter in the back garden. Wherever it was, everyone was aware of the lengthening shadows, and they were rushing for safety.

'Come on, Flora,' Rose said, 'we need to get a move on. The Jerries will be here soon, and we don't want to get caught outside in an air raid.'

They made their way down Regent Street and a few minutes later arrived at the Berkley Hotel on Piccadilly. Flora had never seen such a grand building. It had been built on the site of an old coaching inn and was opened towards the end of the nineteenth century. The entrance was framed by two enormous stone pillars, and it was guarded by two men in top hat and tails who eyed them suspiciously but nonetheless opened the large double doors to let them pass.

'Down here, look,' Rose said, pointing to a carpeted staircase that led to a lower level. 'The beauty of this place is that we don't need to go to an air raid shelter if the siren goes off. They've made a temporary ballroom and bar in the basement so we can stay there and dance our hearts away all night until it's safe to go home.'

They left their coats in the cloakroom and turned towards the ballroom and the sound of band music. Inside, a well-lit dance floor was full of evening revellers dancing an energetic foxtrot to the sound of the Howard Jacobs Orchestra. Civilians and soldiers mixed harmoniously, and there was a hubbub of excited voices, laughter and clapping. Flora had never seen anything like it before and was enchanted.

'Rose, you made it,' a voice shouted from one side of the room. They turned and were faced by a handsome man in his mid-thirties who had left a crowded table and was advancing towards them. He was tall, with dark hair that fell foppishly over his forehead. He had a fashionable moustache and wore a flashy light grey suit that looked as though it had only just come off the tailor's table. He didn't look in any way aristocratic but there was no mistaking the aroma of money that surrounded him.

'Freddy, darling,' Rose cried rushing over and hugging the man tightly. 'I told you we would come. Look at you though. Where did you get hold of that suit? You look like a film star or something.' Freddy laughed and tapped the side of his nose.

'I've told you before, Rose. Friends in high places.' He kissed the giggling Rose and then released her as he noticed Flora for the first time.

'You have a friend,' he said approvingly, and Flora blushed. He oozed confidence, and it was clear that Freddy was a man who knew what he wanted and was accustomed to getting it. Flora suspected that Freddy's women would be treated extremely well but they would be numerous, nonetheless.

'This is my very good friend, Flora,' Rose gushed. 'She's had a difficult time recently and needs some fun and laughter, so I've brought her along to meet some new friends. So, you be nice to her.'

Freddy was shameless. 'Well, that's an easy promise to keep. I'm sure I'll have no trouble being extremely nice to this beautiful young lady. I also have no doubt she'll be very popular, but only if I allow anyone else to monopolize her time,' Freddy replied, making no attempt to disguise his plans for the evening.

Rose punched his shoulder playfully. 'And you keep your hands to yourself Mr Freddy Latimer. Flora is not that kind of girl.'

'A nice girl? Yes, but like you, I'm sure there'll be something to persuade her of my good intentions,' he replied cryptically. 'Anyway, that's for later. Come and sit down next to me at the table and meet the rest of the gang.'

Flora and Rose followed Freddy to a table and sat either side of him much to the disgruntlement of two blond girls who were asked to move and lost their exclusive access. He introduced Flora to the rest of the group and handed her a glass of champagne. He was a charismatic host who commanded the conversation effortlessly, and it wasn't long before Flora was giggling along with everyone else. The other men were deferential, but in many respects, they were like Freddy. They were all in their twenties or thirties, dressed in expensive clothes and they possessed the same self-confidence. Their main topic of conversation centred on the value of certain wartime commodities. Clothing, cigarettes, alcoholic drinks, petrol and even fine foods. They were all seemingly available despite wartime rationing but only if you had the right connections.

Flora was astonished. 'I never knew you could get hold of such things,' she told Freddy during a brief lull in the banter.

He looked at her and smiled. 'I can get you anything you want, Flora. What is it that you would like?'

'Oh, I don't know,' she replied dolefully. 'Even if I had the ration coupons, I don't think I could afford anything. Auxiliary nurses don't get paid a lot I'm afraid.'

'Well forget about the cost,' Freddy laughed. 'If you had the money and the coupons, what is it you would buy?'

'Well, I really would like some new underwear and stockings. And maybe some make up. You just can't get hold of things like that anymore.'

'Leave it to me,' he laughed. 'Before you go home tonight, I'll make sure you have a bag full. And there's no need to worry about money. I'm sure we can think of something else instead. In fact, we could start right now with a dance if you like.'

He led Flora to the dance floor, and for the next three wonderful hours Flora was able to forget about the war waging above her head as they laughed and whirled around the dance floor. Freddy was thoroughly charming, and he made Flora laugh so much that she occasionally had difficulty keeping time with the orchestra. Like food and clothing, laughter had been a rare commodity in the previous two years, and Flora felt a weight lift from her shoulders as she enjoyed the unfamiliar experience. Eventually her feet could take no more.

'Enough,' she cried. 'I've got to sit down before my legs conk out.' They returned to the table where Rose was huddled in intimate conversation with a young man who looked as though he was barely out of school. As Flora approached the couple seemed to arrive at a decision and Rose stood and picked up her bag as though to leave. Flora was disappointed.

'Oh, are we going already Rose?

'Umm, just come over here a moment, Flora,' Rose said self-consciously, and led her friend to a corner where they couldn't be overheard. 'I'm, er, just going out for a moment with that nice young man, Reg. For a few private moments, you know. He's a nice lad and I really like him. He's promised to give me a silk blouse too. You don't mind, do you? You'll be quite safe down here.' She laughed at Flora's shocked expression and gave her a brief hug to offer reassurance and an apology. 'You seem to have made quite a hit with Freddy you lucky devil. He has a permanent room here you know. One of the posh suites, and it's absolutely stuffed with new things that you can't get hold of. He calls it his auxiliary warehouse.' She winked. 'I'm sure you'll be invited up there at some stage this evening.' Flora smiled her acquiescence and decided she wouldn't press her friend to disclose how it was that she was familiar with Freddy's hotel room. Instead, she returned to the table where Freddy seemed energized by Rose's sudden departure and set about charming Flora with more shameless flattery. After another hour, Freddy stopped and looked at his watch.

'Well, the worst of the raids should be nearly over by now. Do you want to come up and we'll see about those things I promised you?'

Flora hesitated for a moment. His offer encompassed more than just a few items of clothing, and by accepting his invitation she was accepting her role in his plan. She had no illusions. Freddy was what Margaret called a spiv. A racketeer. A criminal who profited from national shortages at the expense of the general war effort. But he was also attractive, and he had treated her almost regally for the whole evening. It had been fun, and a welcome distraction from her other difficulties. Perhaps Rose was right, she thought. Things were different in wartime. You had to look after yourself otherwise you'd become another victim. The city was depressing enough with its broken buildings and all that human suffering, and it would be far too easy to succumb to pessimism. She smiled at him and followed him out of the ballroom and up the stairs.

As soon as they entered Freddy's room, he checked the blackout curtains and then switched on the lights to reveal a scene that was so palatial that for a moment Flora thought she must have been transported back to Barrington Hall. The suite was ornately decorated with fine plasterwork and silk wall coverings, and the plush carpets made the accommodation seem warm despite the high ceilings.

'Nice, isn't it?' he grinned.

Flora was astonished. 'Do you live here all the time? It must cost a fortune.'

'It does, but a businessman in my position needs to be able impress his clients, and it only makes a small dent in the profits,' he laughed as he poured her a drink from a silver topped decanter. 'Anyway, let's see what we've got for you.' He walked over to a set of double doors on one side of the room and opened it to reveal a vast wardrobe. The clothes were all new and were suspended from hangers on a long rail. Several suitcases sat on the floor and were bulging with similar promise. Freddy pointed at the clothes.

'Really, these are just my samples. My customers come here to see what's available and then order in bulk. But I'm sure there'll be something that will fit you. Come and choose what you want.'

Flora couldn't believe her eyes. All the clothes were fashionable and high quality; some were made of silk. She rummaged through the row unable to contain her excitement. 'I can't choose,' she cried. 'What can I take? I don't want to be greedy.'

'Take what you want,' he replied grinning at her, 'but leave me a little to sell. Oh, and while you're there have a look in that small blue suitcase, there's some make up inside.'

Flora spent a few minutes sliding clothes hangers along the rail unable to make up her mind. In the end she chose a skirt and blouse, a camisole and some stockings. The little blue suitcase also fulfilled its promise, and a brief rummage yielded some eye liner and a blusher.

'I can't thank you enough, Freddy. You're so kind.'

'Your smile is enough,' he replied gallantly. 'Well nearly enough, perhaps. Anyway, before we go any further there's something else I want to show you.' He walked over to the door and flicked a polished brass switch. The room was plunged into darkness as the light was extinguished, and Flora had difficulty seeing where he had gone. 'Come here and look at this,' he said from the window and raised the curtain slightly to allow a chink of dim light to illuminate her way. 'You won't have seen anything like it I promise you.'

Freddy's room was situated on the top floor of the

hotel and looked out over Green Park towards Buckingham Palace. All the lights in buildings and on streets had been extinguished yet there was enough glow for Flora to make out the eerie silhouette of the city. In the distance, an unbroken row of fires was burning on the south bank of the river, and smoke billowed up into the air, darkening the sky and obscuring the stars. Roaming searchlight beams tried to cut through the impenetrable screen as the operators searched for an unseen foe who had long since returned to the safety of France. The view reminded Flora of a picture illustrating Dante's Inferno that she had once discussed with Victoria Evans. It was certainly a scene from hell.

'Are we safe do you think?' she asked nervously.

'Well, they seem to have gone a little earlier tonight so unless they come back for a second go, we should be safe. Anyway, what's a little danger between friends? It's in keeping with the moment don't you think?' His hand fell onto her bare shoulder, and Flora felt his lips brush the nape of her neck causing the fine hairs that grew there to stiffen and her nipples to harden under the thin silk of her dress. Sensing her response, he turned her to face him, gently lifted her chin and kissed her. Flora gave a small involuntary sigh of anticipation. She had only known the man for a few hours and already she was in his hotel room. But she had come up the stairs knowing what was being silently proposed and there were all those clothes to consider. Yes, it was going to be a commercial transaction of sorts, but it somehow didn't feel that way. Life seemed short. She banished the moral arguments from her mind and wrapped her arms around him, kissing him back hard. She felt his hands reach round and uncouple the clasp at the top of her dress. The zip followed shortly after, and she stepped back to allow the garment to fall silently away onto the floor.

'You really are beautiful,' he said and led her gently from the window to the bedroom.

***

Rose and Flora's visit to the Berkeley Hotel set the pattern for several months and a trip to see Freddy became a weekly event. For Flora, the liaison was not only fun but also a practical arrangement with benefits, and before long she found she had extra money in her purse and a wardrobe to rival her friend's. Clothes weren't the only commodity Freddy had on offer, and on several occasions, Flora was able to repay Margaret Belton's kindness by giving her rationing vouchers. It was obvious that the precious tokens were illicit, but times were really hard and so Margaret gratefully accepted Flora's gifts and merely registered her suspicions with an enquiring eyebrow.

And it was as well that Flora kept in touch with the Beltons for just as the Blitz started to ease in the Spring of 1941, Flora found that she was pregnant again.

The change in Freddy was immediate. 'A baby?' he exclaimed, 'this is no time for having a baby. Look about you, what sort of world is this for a child? Flora, you're a real darling, and we've had a lot of fun in the last few months. I certainly don't want to upset you, but I can't take on the responsibilities of a father. I have my business to take care of. I'm sure it would be better for both of us if you…well if you got rid of it, I suppose.' Flora had been expecting this and waited for him to finish. 'I know of a lady in Soho that can take care of these matters, and I could arrange for her to see you. You wouldn't have to pay anything. What do you think?'

He was so predictable. Flora had no illusions about Freddy. He was selfish and irresponsible, and the moment that she discovered that she was pregnant again, she knew that the affair was over. In fact, she had questioned her own use of the term 'affair' and decided that 'business arrangement' was a more accurate description of the relationship that was undoubtedly now entering its final

185

throes.

'Don't worry about a thing, Freddy Latimer,' she said kissing him on the cheek. 'I don't expect anything from you at all. You've looked after me so well in the last few months. I don't need a woman in Soho to carry out some illegal operation as I have my own way of dealing with these things. Forget about it. Forget about me and the baby. I'm going to disappear for a while to sort things out then one day I'll reappear as though nothing has happened. Perhaps we could even meet up and have a dance, for old time's sake. But I'm not going to impose on you at all.'

Relief filled Freddy's face as he realized that Flora had no intention of holding his feet to the fire. 'Yes, alright, if you're sure. But in the meantime, if you need anything then you just let me know, through Rose perhaps.'

And that was how it ended. Flora never saw Freddy again and a few months later Rose told her that he had been arrested for illegal trading and profiteering and then sent to prison for five years. For Flora, the birth of her third child later that year was a familiar nuisance that required her once more to seek the sanctuary of Margaret Belton.

Flora's surrogate mother was furious. She sat Flora down and gave her an admonishment that was so loud that even the neighbours heard it.

'You have to be more careful,' she shouted at a chastened Flora, ending a long lecture on personal responsibility. Upstairs, Marge heard the diatribe and felt sorry for Flora. She later told her mother that Flora had been sneaking food from her own plate and putting it onto Marge's. Margaret was moved by the revelation and her anger immediately subsided leaving only residual frustration. Sometimes Flora seemed to act so irresponsibly, Margaret reflected, but then she would immediately make up for it with a simple act of selfless kindness.

Flora was relieved to be allowed back into the household, and her confinement and the birth of the child, Agnes, in a local maternity hospital were uneventful. However, the end of the Blitz meant that evacuation as a means of abandonment was no longer an option for dealing with the unwanted child, and so Flora was forced to register Agnes for adoption. It was a common problem, and the authorities were used to dealing with it. The legal formalities were relatively straightforward, and the child was taken from Flora soon after the birth. Flora cried a little at the time, partly for the baby and partly for herself, but she didn't mourn for long, and the matter was soon forgotten especially when the visitor from Somerset arrived.

Chapter 21

Burglary

December 2000

When Michael arrived at his ground floor flat it was obvious that something was wrong. The front door was ajar, and an unfinished cigarette smouldered on the top step. The lights were out inside but Michael could see the flicker of a torch as it swept across his living room. Angry at the intrusion, he crept into the hallway and paused to listen. The entrance to his flat had been forced open too, and he could hear the rustling of paper and the sound of movement within. He thought of General Pendleton, and a drop of sweat ran down his neck as anger was replaced by apprehension. Confrontation or police he wondered, but the matter was soon taken out of his hands and the choice passed quickly from the practical domain to the hypothetical. He had forgotten that one of the floorboards in the hall was slightly loose and it creaked terribly as he crept over it. He froze as the board betrayed his presence and the sound of careful inspection from inside the flat stopped in sympathy.

Events then occurred so quickly that Michael would later have difficulty recounting them to the police constable that attended the scene. Before he had a chance to react, footsteps approached from inside the flat, the door swung open, and a brilliant beam of light blinded him. He had no chance to prepare for the blow that he instinctively knew would follow, and when it came, it was in the form of a violent punch to the side of his face that knocked him to the floor. His head spun and for a moment Michael thought he would lose consciousness. As he fought for sensibility, his assailant followed up with a vicious kick to Michael's side before stepping over him and leaving by the open front door without uttering a word. Stunned, fighting for breath and semi blinded, Michael saw nothing of the man's face, but he sensed that he was muscular and had dispensed his violence in a practiced manner that was carefully metered and deliberate. A professional. A soldier perhaps, he thought remembering the athletic man that he had seen leaving Smithieson's house.

Michael staggered to his feet and locked the front door in case his assailant decided to return. His nose was bleeding, and he groaned as a newly cracked rib protested. Michael grimaced and entered the flat. Just inside, he flicked a switch and light flooded down onto his ransacked apartment. As he surveyed the scattered debris, Michael wondered whether it was just an opportunistic burglary or a something more malign. Drawers lay casually open with their contents dumped on the floor, and his papers were scattered everywhere. The worst mess was around his desk which suggested that it had been the burglar's main interest. Nothing of value was missing. Nothing of material worth anyway. The only things that had been removed were his adoption file and his project notebook. Pendleton, he thought grimly.

Michael reached for the phone to call the police but paused. Should he report the burglary, and what should he tell them about it? He turned the matter over in his mind. This was a worrying escalation. The violent burglary was further evidence of the General's concern, but what was he afraid of, and who else might be affected? Michael's investigation had left a trail, and there was a chance that others around him could be hurt. Like Rebecca he thought, wishing that she had returned with him but glad that she had been spared the violent confrontation. And what about Jocelyn? Pendleton could certainly find her now that he had Michael's notebook. But would he regard her as a threat? Michael knew that if he went to the police and pointed a finger at Pendleton, he would be unable to provide any evidence to support his allegations. He would also have to contend with the General's influence within the police. Michael had experience of the General's access to senior levels of the Somerset constabulary, and it was likely that those links could be brought to bear in West Yorkshire too. It was a tricky decision, but Michael eventually decided to call his local police station and report only that he had disturbed a burglary and had been assaulted by an unknown assailant.

While he waited for them to arrive, Michael returned to the hallway and noticed a pile of unopened mail including two envelopes that were stamped with the mark of the Registrar General. The first one contained the missing birth certificate for David Belton. Michael looked at the details and saw that on this occasion the father was named. He nodded to himself as his earlier suspicions were confirmed. David's father was Arthur Blackford, and his mother was Flora. It was a secret that David's father had kept from his son for an impressively long time, and Michael wondered why. He transferred his attention to the second envelope. This one looked different to those that arrived bearing certificates. Inside there was a covering letter from the Registrar and a second envelope addressed to Robin Belton. Michael's hands shook partly from the delayed shock of his violent altercation but now also in excitement as he realized that Jocelyn had used the Contact Register. It didn't take long for excitement to evolve into disappointment.

Dear Robin

I know you probably won't recognise my use of this name, but it is the one I gave you when you were born. When I gave you up for adoption it was in the sad but necessary expectation that we would never meet again. I was alarmed when the law later changed to allow children to discover and contact their natural parents and to lodge contact details. I know that should you ever read this letter it is because you have embarked on such a search. I therefore know that you will be extremely disappointed to learn that I have no wish for us to make contact or to meet. Whilst this sounds callous, I would like to reassure you that I gave you up for the best of intentions. My life has been full of challenges and a degree of adversity much of it caused by my own mother. As far as I have been able to tell, her influence has extended into many people's lives and usually for the worst. Perhaps I am indeed my mother's daughter, but I was determined that your life would not turn out like mine or hers.

I know that you will feel hurt, but please do not try to contact me. Please just leave me in peace.

I really do hope your life turned out to be happy, fulfilling and productive but I'm sorry that it cannot include me.

Yours truly,

Jocelyn

The hand holding the letter fell to Michael's side in disappointment. This looked like an emphatic end to the story. Jocelyn's letter suggested she had led a rocky life after she was abandoned, and there was real bitterness and anger directed at her own mother. Michael already knew about the retrospective registration of Jocelyn's birth, and he could only guess at Jocelyn's feelings when she had been informed by the Salvation Army that Flora was still alive. She was understandably angry, but why should that antipathy extend to him? He understood that there had been few legal options for unmarried mothers in 1960, and so her decision to have him adopted was understandable. It just seemed a strange reason to deny him contact. And what about the final line of her dismissal? Was his life happy, fulfilling and productive? Certainly, it had been at one time. His adoptive parents had been loving, and his early life had been a good one but only up to the moment of his ex-wife's betrayal. Since then, he knew his star had faded, and he had been bogged down in a personal and professional morass. He sighed, overcome with a sudden melancholy that was only interrupted when the doorbell announced the arrival of the police.

It was a welcome distraction, but only briefly, because there were two police cars which attended Michael's flat that evening. They came separated by half an hour, on different matters, but with a common underlying cause. The first car contained two officers and a photographer who were responding to his report of the burglary. They scribbled notes and took pictures of the mess in the flat. They also recorded the growing bruises on the side of Michael's face and over his ribs. Declining their offer of hospital treatment, Michael stuck to his truncated account of what had transpired, and as they left, he promised to attend the police station to make a statement knowing that the report would quickly go into a box marked 'unsolved.'

The second car to arrive was driven by another detective who was the bearer of terrible news. Marge had also been violently burgled the night before. She had not been badly injured but the scared old lady had been admitted to hospital where the shock eventually resulted in her passing away. The police were treating the matter as murder, and Marge's home help had pointed to Michael as a possible place to start their investigation. Michael explained to them that he was researching his adoption, and that Marge had known his mother. He produced his train ticket and his hotel receipt showing that he was not the assailant, but he did not tell the detectives that his search might be controversial or about Pendletons' likely involvement.

After the detectives departed, guilt weighed heavily on Michael as he realised that he was the one who had told Francis Pendleton about Marge and her recollections of Flora. Michael remained outwardly calm but underneath his anger boiled. Marge. That lovely old lady. How could she possibly have hurt the Pendletons? All she had was a couple of old photographs and some memories that were easily dismissed by her age and the contents of her sherry decanter. There was no need for murder.

As Michael's fury took hold, he was reminded of Arthur Blackford's determination to get justice for his father, and he recognized the similarities with the situation that he now faced. Michael was determined to get justice for Marge, and he had to stop the General from harming anyone else. As his anger gave way to constructive analysis, Michael realized that it was the General's secret that made the man vulnerable. There was no need to respond to violence in kind. All Michael had to do was discover the secret that his adversary was so determined to conceal, and then expose it in the most damaging way possible. He would make sure that the truth really did hurt. He would use it to cut off the General at the knees.

Chapter 22

The Visitor

December 1942

Several months after Agnes was adopted, Flora arrived at Margaret's after a shift at the hospital and was dismayed to learn that there had been a visitor from Somerset. The man had told Margaret that he wanted to speak to Flora and that he was called Arthur Blackford. Flora knew Arthur slightly from her childhood days in Ashill. His parents lived just outside the village and his mother had been a good friend of Victoria Evans. She had never really spoken to him much as he was several years younger than her, and he had always blushed awkwardly whenever she had greeted him. He was certainly not a close acquaintance and that made his arrival in London unexpected and a little worrying.

Flora was angry. 'What does he want and more to the point, who told him I was here?' she demanded of Margaret.

'I think it might have been my sister, Mildred.'

'But she promised to keep it a secret.'

'Yes, I know, but the lad says he wants to talk to you about something important. It's to do with your father. To be honest, Flora, I quite liked him. He's very polite and I really don't think he's here to harm you.'

'My father? Why could he possibly want to talk to me about my father?'

'I don't know. I asked him the same question, but he clammed up and was very secretive.'

Flora sighed. She had heard nothing about Sir Roland, Smithieson or Barrington Hall for over a year and had started to feel safe. However, the unexpected arrival of somebody from the past was unsettling, and it revived all the bad memories of her previous life.

She thought about her father's death and wondered what Arthur knew of it. She had been working at the hall when the fateful day arrived. Mr Denton had found her polishing silver in the dining room and approached her, ashen faced and barely able to speak. He had broken the news gently, and in faltering terms explained about the accident at the stables. Flora had accepted his explanation but a later encounter with Frederick Smithieson had sown the seeds of doubt. It was a few weeks after her father's funeral, and she had been out in the yard hanging out some clothes when the stable hand crept up on her. He had grabbed her around the waist, tried to kiss her and then suggested that they pop into an outbuilding for some fun and games as he put it. Flora protested and Smithieson became angry. He flung her to the floor, turned to stalk off and then stopped and looked back.

'You little bitch,' he had scowled. 'You want to be careful around here. You don't want to have an accident…like your father.' It was a malicious threat, and it made her wonder whether the official account of the accident was true. Her father had been such a careful man who knew horses well and he would never have put himself in harm's way by confronting a dangerous animal. Was it possible that something more sinister had taken place? She was too frightened to press the matter and when she did mention it to one of the other parlour maids, she was advised to stay silent or risk a beating and immediate unemployment.

Flora took the handwritten card from Margaret Belton and studied it. It gave the name and address of a nearby hotel and there was a telephone number which she rang. There was a slight pause whilst the receptionist sent a runner upstairs and then a moment later a polite voice announced the arrival of Arthur Blackford. Flora had a couple of days off, and so she agreed to meet him for afternoon tea the next day. When she entered the hotel dining room twenty-four hours later, she looked around trying to remember what Arthur looked like.

'Flora?' a voice said next to her. She turned and realized that her eyes had passed over Arthur without recognising him. He was no longer the awkward willowy boy that she remembered but a tall handsome young man with blond hair and an engaging smile. She took his hand and allowed him to steer her to a seat at the table.

'You've changed,' she said. 'I'm sorry, but I didn't recognize you straight away.'

'You've changed as well. You're not a girl any longer' he replied, causing Flora to blush and to wonder whether her figure betrayed the extent of her maturity.

'Umm, Mr Blackford…'

'You can call me Arthur, if you want,' he interrupted, shyly.

'Arthur,' she smiled. 'Margaret told me that you wanted to speak to me about my father, and I have to say, I am a little intrigued.'

Arthur smiled back and after pouring them both some tea, he told her all about the betting scandal, the likely murder of Flora's father and his own father's suicide. Flora saw his anger which grew when he told her that his own life had been affected too. After his father died, he had found it increasingly difficult to find work locally, and he suspected that Sir Roland had put the word out that Arthur was not to be employed beyond menial handiwork. He told Flora that he had been tempted to move away but had decided to stay in deliberate defiance of the Pendletons' efforts to discredit him.

'I've spent years trying to learn the truth,' he said bitterly, 'but all I've got for my troubles is a beating from Smithieson and veiled threats from the hall. I have no evidence, and that's why I'm here today. You see, I've heard that you took something from the Pendletons, and I wondered if it had anything to do with the betting scandal, some evidence or something like that. Please tell me you have something to help me, you're my last hope.'

Flora looked at Arthur with mixed emotions. She was furious that somebody had gossiped about her departure from Barrington Hall, but at the same time she felt sorry for the young man sitting opposite. Like Flora, he had lost his father and in distressing circumstances too. Flora had heard household rumours about the betting scandal, and she was aware that Smithieson had eventually been sent away to prison. However, she hadn't known of her father's involvement. The truth of his murder made her reply unintentionally clumsy.

'Arthur, I'm sorry but there's nothing I can tell you about any of this, and I have nothing that can help you with your search.'

'But I know that you have something,' he replied. 'What is it? Is it something that could help me to get that bastard, Pendleton? I just want justice for my father. Call it revenge if you like, but I won't rest until the truth comes out. Surely you want the same thing. What about your own father? If you have something that can incriminate Sir Roland, tell me now and we'll use it to take some action.'

Arthur was clearly determined but Flora wouldn't be swayed. 'Look, Arthur,' she said cautiously. 'What I have or haven't got is no concern of yours. Can't you just accept that I can't help. I promise you that if I had evidence of Sir Roland's involvement in the betting scandal then I would give it to you, but I haven't, and anything else that I have is best left hidden where it is. It's for my own safety.'

Arthur looked deflated. It was dangerous to meddle in the Pendletons' affairs, and he understood Flora's reluctance to get involved. But he had spent fruitless years trying to expose Sir Roland's fraud, and his final hopes of exposing the truth had rested on Flora. He sighed, and Flora immediately regretted the vehemence of her denial as she saw his sweet features darken. There was something about Arthur that was terribly vulnerable. Perhaps it was the grief of losing his father to suicide or the realization that his quest had failed. As Flora studied him, she felt a curious mix of pity and something else. Desire. Arthur was so handsome and yet he was unpretentious and unassuming too. His modesty was entirely different to the attitude of the arrogant men that she had encountered with Rose. He was a genuinely nice young gentleman. She considered her nomadic lifestyle. Perhaps it was time to form a more solid relationship with someone she could trust. Was Arthur capable of providing the life she wanted? Flora thought so, but his search for justice seemed unhealthily intense and that made her worry. Could he be trusted to keep Flora's whereabouts secret, or might he act rashly and leave a trail for Sir Roland to follow?

Another glance cemented her attraction to Arthur and overwhelmed her caution. She took his hand and ignored the sudden look of surprise on his face.

'Look, Arthur, I'm sorry I can't help you, but I'd love to hear more about Ashill and Barrington Hall and whatever's been happening since I left. Perhaps we could have dinner together and you can tell me all about it? That is…if you'd like to.' She took care to look into his eyes.

Arthur squeezed her hand back. He was surprised that she was so forward, but he was flattered by her attention.

Flora had turned into a beautiful woman with an air of cosmopolitan experience that he had never encountered in Somerset even though the local girls competed fiercely for his attentions. He had no idea whether they would ever make a suitable match, but he wanted to find out, and it would give him another opportunity to persuade Flora to show him her journal and any papers. His face brightened, and he beamed his acceptance. He could hardly wait for dinner on the following day.

Arthur wasn't a rich man, but his one-night stay at the hotel became two nights and then two weeks. The first dinner was repeated on the following night by a second, and before long, Flora and Arthur were seeing each other every day. They made an unlikely couple – the younger country boy and the metropolitan beauty – but they loved each other's company, and their differences seemed to fertilize their attraction. Arthur was captivated by Flora's open personality, her self-confidence and her beauty, and he soon forgot about his original purpose. Flora, on the other hand, loved Arthur's innocence and his dry sense of humour. Margaret saw the change in Flora almost straight away and was glad that the burgeoning relationship seemed to be much more stable than Flora's experiences in central London. And at least she wasn't pregnant.

After the fourth dinner, pregnancy became at least a theoretical possibility. Flora had planned a seduction and dressed accordingly. Arthur was too shy to take the lead and eventually Flora had to lean forward and whisper something in his ear. Arthur's eyes widened and she loved his innocence even more.

At Flora's behest, Arthur distracted the inscrutable concierge while Flora crept unobserved up the stairs to meet him on the first floor. His room was plain yet clean, but the surroundings didn't really matter, and Flora made love to Arthur with an energy that surprised her and completely entranced Arthur. He was an inexperienced, yet eager and considerate lover, and as Flora looked down at him at the height of their passion, she marvelled at his youthful willingness to allow her to take the lead during their intimacy. It was satisfying physically and emotionally, and for Flora, it confirmed that what had started as desire had matured into love and a genuine commitment. After a further month they started living together in a rented house not far from Margaret's house, and with nothing to keep him at Ashill, Arthur had found work at a menswear shop. Meanwhile, Flora continued to work at the hospital. They were saving for a better place, and Margaret thought it wouldn't be long before the couple married. Flora was overcome with happiness until one night when she noticed a man following her home.

She had walked out of the hospital gates and noticed him lurking in the same spot that had been used by Smithieson. He was wearing a long coat, and a brimmed hat pulled down over his eyes. He was extremely short and didn't look particularly threatening. More like a watcher than an assailant. She pretended she hadn't noticed him and walked briskly home. The man seemed a bit inept as he followed her, and his efforts to appear innocent were so exaggerated that they were almost comical. But Flora wasn't laughing. She knew that she had been found. This man might not hurt her, but she was sure that another man would be summoned, and he might. As she arrived home, she was relieved to see that Arthur had beaten her to it. He looked confused when Flora came in, switched off the light and peeped through a crack in the curtains.

'I'm being followed by a man, Arthur. He must work for Sir Roland.' Arthur's face darkened with anger.

'Well, we'll see about that,' he said grimly. 'I'm fed up with the Pendleton family. Why can't they leave people alone?' He went to the curtain and looked out. The man was hiding in a doorway across the road. Arthur couldn't see his face, but he could see the man's raincoat protruding from the edge of the brickwork. 'Wait here. I'll sort this out,' he said darkly.

'Be careful, Arthur, he may be small, but he might have a knife of something,' Flora warned. But Arthur's blood was up. He would protect her, and he wanted to prove it.

Flora watched from an upstairs window. Arthur crossed the street and grabbed the man by the lapels and shook him so violently that his hat fell off. Flora couldn't hear what he said, but the man foolishly said something to enrage Arthur who flung him to the ground, picked him up and flung him down again like a rag doll. Flora could almost hear the ribs cracking and hoped Arthur wouldn't overdo it. But he was finished. As Arthur walked away, the man sat up and tried to stand. Arthur turned and the man shrank back in such fear that Flora almost felt sorry for him. Dear Arthur. Not so gentle after all.

Arthur closed the front door behind him. 'Well, he won't be bothering us any time soon,' he laughed.

Flora wasn't so confident. 'What did he say, Arthur?'

'Well, at first he tried to deny that he was following you. Then he confessed, and said he'd been hired by the Pendletons to find you and then follow and report. He tried to threaten us by saying that other men would soon be coming at which point I'd had enough,' Arthur replied. 'He mentioned that diary of yours Flora and some papers. That's what they are after. I wish you'd tell me what's in it,' he added, as the old obsession returned to the front of his mind.

Flora noted his renewed interest in her journal but remained silent about it. 'I think you've made a mistake confronting him like that, Arthur. Sir Roland's men are coming, and now they'll come even quicker. This is exactly what I've been trying to avoid. I think we'd better hide. We can't stay here that's for sure. I'm going to pack some things.'

Arthur's face dropped. 'Let's not be hasty, Flora. I don't see why we should be forced out of our homes by these thugs.'

'Well, I've seen what he's capable of, and I'm going to

Margaret's,' she declared resolutely and climbed the stairs. She went to the bathroom to recover her journal from its hiding place beneath one of the cupboards. As she lifted the leather volume she checked it carefully to see whether anyone had tampered with it since she had last made an entry three days earlier. They had. The tell-tale hair she had left on top of it had disappeared and there were scratch marks around the lock where someone had attempted to pick it. Her heart sank. Behind her, Arthur's face appeared around the door. He looked at Flora and knew that he had been discovered. He didn't wait for her accusation; the look on her face spoke the necessary words.

'I didn't see inside, Flora, I promise.'

A tear fell down her cheek as her heart broke. 'No, but you tried, Arthur. You tried. Don't you see that by trying to snoop you have broken my trust? I promised you there was nothing in this book that you needed to see. Why couldn't you leave it at that?'

He couldn't meet her gaze. 'I'm so sorry, Flora, I just wanted a quick look. For my father. Please forgive me.' But it was too late. Arthur knew that Flora loved him, but mutual trust and security had fled as assuredly as it would for an act of adultery. Even as they spoke he could see that Flora's instinct for calculated self-preservation was already wrapping an impenetrable shell around her broken heart. He sighed. He knew there was no possibility of forgiveness.

Flora blamed herself. What a fool she had been. This moment had been entirely predictable, she reflected, remembering her early doubts. Arthur would always be an unreliable link back to Barrington Hall and one which could be easily exploited by the Pendletons. It hurt to admit it, but this was the end, and with tears tumbling down her face she told him.

'I have spent the last few years running from the Pendletons and now they are coming for me again. I have had knives pressed in my neck, my friends have been assaulted and I have lived in fear for most of the time. You were my chance for a more stable life, Arthur, but it had to be one based on love, respect and trust. You knew this book is my most precious possession and the guarantee of my safety yet still you broke that trust. You may not see it, but it is a betrayal. I cannot live with you, Arthur. It may be an idealistic view of love, but I'd be forever wondering whether I'd play second fiddle to your search. This is over, and I'd like you to leave right now and never return.'

Arguing was pointless, and Arthur's head dropped in anticipation of the years of regret and sadness that lay ahead. He left the following day, and whilst Arthur's mistake did forever weigh heavily on his shoulders, his grief was tempered by an unexpected gift. Several months after he left London, a policeman called at Arthur's home in Ashill. He was accompanied by a social worker and something else: an abandoned baby called David who needed his father. Arthur smiled when he looked at the child. Though he couldn't have Flora, he would nurture their son.

It had been a damaging experience for Flora. She had loved Arthur, and though she was the one that had ended their relationship, it broke her heart to send him away. She hoped that he would see the gift of a son as her way of acknowledging their shared happiness even though it had lasted for only a short time. She had delivered David several months after Arthur left, and on a quiet night in November 1942 she carefully wrapped the sleeping boy in a blanket and left him at the foot of the steps outside the police station with a note identifying Arthur as the father. Margaret was disappointed that Flora had delivered yet another child but at least it was one born in the context of a loving relationship and at least the child would be brought up by one of his parents.

After David left, Flora went very quiet, and for several months Margaret worried that the young woman's experiences might be too much for her. She didn't think

Flora would commit an act of self-harm, but she seemed very depressed, and Margaret kept an extremely close eye on the brooding young woman and tried hard not to leave her alone. It was a dark moment in Flora's life, but it was also the start of a brief period of stability, and she was untroubled by failed affairs or the Pendletons. The house that she had shared with Arthur was compromised so she moved back in with the Beltons and kept looking over her shoulder. There was constant fear, but she was also weary of her transient existence. Like everyone else in wartime Britain she ached for stability and the return of peace. It was time to lead a more settled life, and so although she continued to see her friend, Rose, she avoided the spivs in town and lived quietly with Margaret and Marge waiting for the war to end. One day she hoped she might have a home of her own.

Chapter 23

Sweden

December 2000

The day after the burglary, Michael attended the local police station and provided his statement. He had awoken with a fearsomely dark bruise on the side of his face and nose, and his side ached badly. He regrouped at the café, and stuffed coffee, pastries and painkillers into his mouth while ignoring Lucille's worried and enquiring looks. The main concern, he decided, was that Jocelyn was completely unaware of the developing storm, and she might well be at risk from Pendleton's thugs if the General decided to deploy them. Michael was disappointed that she didn't want contact with him but the sharp pain in his ribs reminded him that her safety should come first and that he should try to warn her. He thought about his dwindling funds but decided their first meeting would be best in person and that he would travel to Sweden.

Michael called Rebecca and related everything that had

happened since they had last met. She was concerned about his injuries and alarmed to learn that the General's threats had escalated to violence. She agreed that a face-to-face meeting with Jocelyn was likely to be more productive than a phone call, and Michael was pleasantly surprised when she asked if she could accompany him to Sweden. He told her he would book two tickets for the flight from Newcastle to Malmo which departed two days later. It would be an early flight, so he offered her the use of his spare room and then managed to conceal his disappointment at her obvious relief at the proposed sleeping arrangements. Rebecca seemed to have raised a perimeter around their relationship. It was a boundary that was close enough to offer hope of future fulfilment, but distant enough for Michael to recognize it as a vague promise that was only implied and without any concrete terms. He had no idea where they were going, and he was worried that he would be let down again. However, when she arrived at the flat, Rebecca seemed to be genuinely worried by the dark bruise on Michael's face, and she hugged him tightly until his wince reminded her of the cracked rib beneath his shirt. He was pleased to see her, and they spent an enjoyable evening together that ended in an empty bottle of wine, a brief cuddle and separate rooms. The next morning, they caught the short flight to Malmo, and after a one-hour drive in a hire car they arrived outside a row of small, neat houses by the river in Kristianstad.

Michael recognized the significance of what was about to occur and was nervous. Long hours of investigation were about to bear fruit, and he was about to meet his birth mother for the first time. Yet he hadn't really considered what to say to her. He was certain that Jocelyn would be angry at his unwanted arrival in defiance of her letter, but he hoped that she might relent once he had told her about the Pendletons. Rebecca sensed his concern and squeezed his arm reassuringly.

'Don't forget what your adoptive mother told you. This is your journey. Just be yourself and everything will work out. Remember you're also here to protect her. And don't forget Marge either.' Michael was bolstered by her encouragement and opened the car door.

It took only a short conversation with Jocelyn's neighbour for Michael's moment of self-discovery to be put on hold. There was no reply from Jocelyn's house, but their knocking had encouraged a cautious man to emerge from the house next door. Rebecca's smile encouraged the man to set aside the doubts raised by Michael's bruised face and he told them that two men had arrived the day before and left Jocelyn hospitalized. Michael's chin dropped. Once again, Pendleton had been one step ahead of him. He must have tremendous resources or influence to be able to act so swiftly. Or maybe he had help? An unwelcome and distressing idea started to form in his mind, and he glanced at Rebecca, as suspicion and doubt bubbled up. She smiled back so disarmingly that Michael instantly dismissed the nascent idea that had started to form, and he silently berated himself for doubting her.

Reassured by Rebecca's smile, Michael was nonetheless worried about the way his search was unfolding, especially at the indiscriminate use of violence which seemed to mark every step he took. He already felt guilty that his indiscretion had resulted indirectly in Marge's death, and now he had brought danger to Jocelyn's door too. Should he continue? Whatever the Pendletons were trying to conceal it must pose a huge threat to the family who seemed willing to deploy any means necessary to prevent the truth emerging. The truth pitched against violence. It seemed asymmetric but, remembering his pledge to avenge Marge, he decided that he was now too far along his chosen path to give up. He thanked the neighbour who asked Michael to deliver a get-well card.

'She is on Corridor 4 at the hospital', he said in faltering English. 'Her daughter is there with her.'

A daughter? Michael had been so wrapped up in the mechanics of his search that he hadn't considered the possibility of half siblings. Had Jocelyn told her new family about the small accident she had in England before she started a new life in Sweden? He thought it improbable given the contents of her letter to him. It was more likely that she had kept Michael's birth a secret. A clean break with the past. Renewal. If so, he knew he would have to proceed carefully. He had no wish to blunder in and clumsily blow apart Jocelyn's new life, and he knew that unless he acted considerately she would never accept his intrusion.

It took only a few minutes to get to the hospital but there was enough time to formulate a quick plan. They would identify Jocelyn's side ward and wait for her daughter to leave the room before they entered. Rebecca agreed but told Michael that she thought his first meeting with his mother should be a private moment. She would therefore stand guard outside and only come into the room when invited. Michael nodded, and they made their way up to Ward 4 blending in with the other visitors. Clutching the neighbour's card, Michael sat next to Rebecca in the busy corridor, and they waited within sight of a door with a card pinned to it bearing the name, J Stienerson. A few minutes later, an attractive woman left the room calling back to the occupant in accented English that she would return later. Michael's heart suddenly raced. His half-sister. That was Michael's cue, and he rose, knocked on the door and looked in at the angry woman lying in the hospital bed with her arm in a sling. She looked at him with cold recognition.

'Hello, Michael. I've been wondering when you'd arrive. You can't take no for an answer, can you?' Michael blinked. This was going to be difficult.

Chapter 24

The Explosion

1942-1946

Flora would have to wait more than two years for the war to end, but during that time she stuck to her self-made promises. There was no nightlife, unsuitable men or babies, just a simple life spent quietly at the Belton's. Mercifully, there was no sign of a renewed threat from Somerset either, and though Flora stayed vigilant, she started to relax. The war passed slowly, and for a while supplies became ever more difficult to find as the U-Boats took their toll. However, the arrival of American soldiers and the successful allied invasion of Normandy gradually lifted the national mood, and victory in 1945 eventually restored peace to the tired and shattered country.

As the national celebrations gradually subsided, Margaret told Flora that her sister, Mildred, was coming to visit London. She had recently retired from Barrington Hall, and she wanted to see Margaret and Marge now that the war had ended, and it was safe to make the journey. Margaret was looking forward to seeing her sister, but she knew visitors from Somerset caused Flora great consternation and so she warned her of Mildred's impending arrival and gave Flora the opportunity of temporarily staying elsewhere.

'I think it will be alright, though, Flora,' she said reassuringly. 'Mildred has left Barrington Hall, and now that her husband has died, she has moved away from Ashill across to Taunton. She didn't like some of the goings-on at the Hall, and she understands that your safety depends on her discretion.'

Flora wasn't entirely convinced, but it had been a long time since she had been threatened by the Pendletons, and she owed a great deal to Mildred and wanted to thank her personally. Not only had Mildred organized Flora's escape from the Hall but she had also pointed Flora towards the warmth and simple kindness of Margaret and Marge who Flora loved as though they were her own family. So, after carefully weighing the risks, Flora eventually decided to stay for Mildred's visit, with no inkling that her decision would result in an unexpected marriage.

When Mildred eventually arrived, she came with a man who she introduced as her cousin, Harold Wintern. Harold was fifteen years older than Flora, with a kind face and an air of total reliability and honesty. He had served in the Army and had been demobbed after he was wounded in the leg by an artillery shell fired as the Germans retreated from Normandy. Despite his recent wartime experiences, Harold had a ferocious sense of humour, and he soon had Flora in fits of giggling as they flirted outrageously. Mildred glanced knowingly at Margaret who discreetly winked back. And so it was that only a few short months later, Flora married for the first time. Margaret had never seen her looking so happy, and even when Flora discovered that Harold wanted them to live near his Mildred in Taunton in Somerset, her excitement and optimism remained undimmed. Mildred reassured her that she would be far enough away from Ashill to be safe from the Pendletons, and so Flora joined Harold to live on the edge of an attractive village called Nailsbourne a few miles outside Taunton. Their semi-detached cottage was comfortable and well-appointed, which was just as well as the couple had recently become a family with the arrival of their daughter, Marilyn. Flora loved her new life in the countryside, and she took regular evening walks to settle the baby and to breathe in the fresh Somerset air. She became a creature of habit, wallowing in domestic contentment.

***

It was on a fine evening at the end of August 1946 that Flora left the house for one of those regular walks. The late summer air caressed her skin, and it smelled earthy and fertile. Harold was at home setting the table, or probably napping she smiled to herself. She looked down at the sleeping form in the pram. Marilyn was fast asleep and similarly content as mother and daughter slowly made their way down the lane. In the distance, Flora could hear an approaching tractor. The noise grew louder, and eventually Norman Brompton waved and came to a standstill alongside her. He stopped the engine.

'Now then, Missy,' he smiled toothlessly. 'Me and Mrs Brompton are still waiting for you and Harold to come up to Grange Farm for tea,' he grinned, feigning offence. 'And not forgetting the beautiful, Marilyn, of course,' he added gesturing to the sleeping child with a smokeless pipe that usually dangled from the side of his mouth. 'Mind you,' he added, I expect you won't have time today, what with your visitor an' all.'

'Visitor?' Flora asked anxiously. 'We're not expecting anyone today, what makes you say that, Norman?' The old man noted Flora's concern, and to buy time for his thoughts, he carefully restored the pipe to its usual spot.

'Well, I know your next-door neighbours, the Rostrons, are away on holiday so I assumed that chap with the motorcycle was just parking up to visit you. He was in that little glade across the road from your front gate. Funny though, now I think of it, he was behaving a little oddly. Maybe he had a puncture. I have been cutting the blackthorn hedges up there recently, and there are a lot of thorns lying around.' Flora's mouth turned dry, and she thought of Harold. From his seat on the tractor, Norman noted her concern. 'Are you alright, Missy? Is there a problem? Should I come back with you?'

Flora considered his offer carefully. A few weeks earlier she had been chatting with Rose on the phone, and Rose had mentioned that she'd bumped into an old friend of Flora's from Somerset. She told Flora that the man had been charming and that she had given him Flora's contact details thinking it would be nice for her to meet up with him. At the time, Flora had immediately thought of Sir Roland and his men, but as several weeks had passed without incident she had gradually convinced herself it had been a harmless enquiry.

She looked at Norman. The Bromptons were a really nice couple, and the Winterns were regular visitors to Grange Farm. It had been a long time since she had last crossed swords with the Pendletons, and she didn't want to alarm the neighbours unnecessarily. Perhaps it was just a breakdown she told herself optimistically, and so she told Norman that everything was in order and that his help was unnecessary. However, it was a bit unsettling, and Flora decided to exercise a little caution by returning home using the path at the rear of the cottage. She wanted to have a good look at this man to ensure that her optimism was justified.

Reassured that all was well, Norman gave a last wave of his pipe and departed in a cloud of diesel fumes. Flora felt suddenly alone as she pushed the pram and its sleeping occupant along the path that led home. At the field, she walked quietly past the ruminating sheep, then through the woods and past the byre.

When she arrived at the last tree, she stopped and peered around it. The rear of the cottage was silent, and all she could hear was the cawing of restless rooks. She pushed the pram forward and looked in through the kitchen window fearful of what she might see. The afternoon had grown old, and the evening shadows would soon pass away into the night. She could hear the faint sound of the radio, but she was surprised that Harold had not yet switched on any lights. Leaving the pram by the back door, she crept down the side of the house and peered cautiously across the road. It all seemed quiet and then a small movement betrayed a man hiding in the shadows amongst the trees. He was looking at his watch and then leaned forward to look down the road. He was waiting expectantly, she thought; unquestionably waiting for her.

She retreated to the back door and gently opened it. The smell of gas and petrol was overpowering in the kitchen and her heart sank as she recognized what it meant for her husband. Taking care not to cause a spark or alert the man by switching on a light, she tip-toed into the parlour and there was her poor Harold slumped forward, unseeing and immobile in a sea of red cushions. She almost wept aloud as grief and shock framed the dreadful scene, but self-preservation and maternal instinct ran deeply too. There would eventually be time to mourn Harold, but she had to get away first and her first priority was Marilyn.

Flora returned outside and paused as a scheme began to develop. It was a crafty one. Sir Roland clearly wanted to kill her, but what if he succeeded? Once he believed that she was dead he would call off the dogs and stop searching for her. The house was a bomb. If she could trigger it without getting hurt then she could run away leaving everyone else to suppose that she had died. It would have to be a clean break though. She would have to deceive her friends and surrogate family by leaving them in ignorance. They would grieve her loss, and a tear fell down Flora's cheek as she considered the hurt she would cause.

She sniffed away the guilt and forced herself to consider the practicalities. She looked at the bag hanging on the handle of the pram. It contained a few items for the baby and her purse. It wasn't much to make a fresh start, but she would have to manage as there wasn't time to get anything else from the house. Then she thought about how to trigger the explosion without hurting herself. She needed some kind of fuse. She returned to the kitchen and took a box of matches from the windowsill. There was a tea towel hanging on a nearby hook and she dabbed it in a pool of petrol before returning outside and laying the items on the ground by the back door. Flora removed the bag from the pram and hid it amongst the trees before returning to collect Marilyn. She ensured that the baby was securely wrapped in the blanket and then carried her back to the coppice where she laid the child on the ground next to the bag. Flora had just set off back to the house to complete the final stage of her plan when Marilyn stirred and let out a brief cry of protest. Flora looked back, momentarily uncertain, but decided to press on. She had to act quickly. The child's cry had pierced the evening's peaceful decline, even outcompeting the chattering rooks, and Flora was sure it would have been heard by the man at the front. She pushed open the back door, shoved the pram inside and quickly picked up the damp cloth and the matches. The first two matches failed but the third spluttered and took hold, and when she held it to the towel there was a whoosh, and the flames leaped up so high that her hand and wrist were scorched. Ignoring the pain, she tossed the burning cloth into the kitchen and closed the door.

The explosion was gigantic, and Flora was knocked off

her feet and halfway down the garden. The back door came with her. It had been blown off its hinges, but it shielded Flora from a deadly shower of broken glass and rubble that flew out from the destroyed house. Flora fought against unconsciousness. Her ears were ringing, blood dripped down a gash on her forehead and she could smell the fire that was already leaping up from the petrol-soaked timbers. As adrenaline overcame dizziness, she pushed away the protective back door lying on top of her and staggered to the tree where Marilyn had suddenly fallen silent. She looked down to check her daughter, terrified of what she might find. The baby gazed up at her and gave a reassuring smile. She was fine.

Flora glanced at the house and saw that it was completely destroyed. A pair of pram wheels poked out from the rubble, and a fire fuelled by petrol-soaked timbers was consuming the grim contents of what had lain in the parlour. She needed to get away quickly. Whispering a silent farewell to the man she had loved so much, Flora scooped up the meagre remnants of her life and made her way back to the woods. She paused at the byre and thought about the future. There was time for one more task if she was very quick.

Chapter 25

Motherly Love

December 2000

Jocelyn glared at Michael from her hospital bed. There was no denying his bloodline.

'You look just like my mother, Flora, but I sincerely hope that is the extent of any similarities,' she said, without making any effort to hide her feelings on the matter. Michael was about to reply when she changed tack. 'What is it that you've done, Michael? What is it you want? Elizabeth warned me that you were searching for me, and I expect you have read my letter asking you to leave me alone. You knew I didn't want contact yet here you are. And you seem to have brought trouble with you too,' she added, waving her arm and grimacing at the sudden pain.

Michael fidgeted and looked at the floor. There

was no denying the truth of her accusations, and he wished he had been better prepared to explain his unwelcome arrival. He braced himself and looked up to confront her anger. Jocelyn was a slight woman with remarkably similar features to those he had observed in Marge's photograph of Flora. She was now in her early sixties, but the years couldn't obscure her good looks even though they were currently shrouded with suspicion and anger.

'I'm really sorry, Jocelyn,' he said, hoping that the use of her first name would reassure her that he was not looking for a new mother. 'My curiosity was encouraged by my adoptive mother who recently passed away. It started off innocently enough, but my search seems to have disturbed some dark secrets from the past which are now out of hand and are threatening to harm those around me. Please can I reassure you that I have no intention of disrupting your life here, or your Swedish family', he added, thinking of the half-sister who had been present in the room a few minutes earlier. 'Yes, it's true that I initially set out to find you, but once I read your letter, I respected your sentiments, and I am only here now because I became concerned for your safety.'

Jocelyn's anger subsided a little. Michael seemed to be genuinely concerned for her welfare, and he had clearly weighed up the implications of visiting her unannounced. He was polite and thoughtful which was a good start. Jocelyn also wanted to know why she had ended up in a hospital bed. Her instincts shouted that Michael was trustworthy, but they also pointed to a sadness about him. Perhaps it was her rejection or maybe the recent loss of his mother. Either way, she felt an inexplicable urge to comfort this stranger son that she had created and then given up many years earlier. Was it maternal instinct? No, Jocelyn thought, that was going too far, and she pushed the notion firmly aside.

'Well, you're here now and it seems we have a lot to discuss,' she said quickly to introduce a practical aspect to the emotionally charged atmosphere. 'On the whole, I think that I had better go first. Draw up that chair', she instructed.

Over the next half hour, Michael sat and listened to Jocelyn's account as she filled in some of the gaps of what he knew. She confirmed her wartime evacuation, and Michael noted her bitterness as she described how she was abandoned by her mother and brought up by kindly foster parents who had later died, leaving her in local authority care. She explained that the children's home had been secure, but it was cold, functional and unloving. It had left her feeling cheated out of parental love and a normal childhood, and she had left it at the earliest opportunity. She had attended teacher training college, but her education was interrupted by pregnancy following an affair with a young estate agent from Scarborough. She glossed over the details of Michael's adoption, and he understood that it was too early to discuss such an intensely personal matter, so the matter passed by unexamined. It was at that stage of Jocelyn's story that her regret began to give way to visible anger as she confirmed Marge's account of the Salvation Army investigation and their shocking discovery that Flora was still alive and living in Lancashire. Jocelyn had been especially outraged to discover that she was not the only child that Flora had abandoned in such a callous way. The Salvation Army had also found her half-brother, Andrew, who had experienced a similarly difficult upbringing caused by Flora's neglect.

'The problem was that Flora never registered my birth and I needed a passport to come to Sweden with my husband,' she explained. 'When Flora was eventually located, she was persuaded to provide an affidavit to allow my birth to be registered retrospectively. I will never forget that odious woman when we met briefly at the solicitors' office in Warrington. She was rambling about why she had abandoned me and Andrew, and she talked about other children who she had delivered and then lost or given up. If you ask me, she was an irresponsible, selfish and heartless bitch with no sense of right or wrong, and I'm glad I never saw her again.'

Michael was taken aback by the depth of Jocelyn's anger. Her early years had clearly been difficult, and it must have been a great shock to discover that her mother had been alive throughout Jocelyn's childhood. But he wondered if the strength of her feelings was entirely justified. He paused as the rage drained from her face. Anxious not to cause her further offence he constructed his next remarks with great care before delivering them.

'You know, Jocelyn, I have been following Flora's path quite carefully, and I think there may be more to the events that you have described than perhaps either of us realise. I too was shocked at Flora's wartime behaviour, but I have found evidence of a secret that Flora had uncovered which might place her actions in a different light. It is the same secret that is endangering us today,' he added gesturing at Jocelyn's arm and his bruised face. 'I'm sure that if we could solve her mystery then we would be able to explain and understand her actions.'

Jocelyn looked at him in disbelief, and Michael realized she would take some convincing.

'I've heard this before. She mentioned it to me in Warrington and it sounded most unlikely but then again,' she admitted, 'I wasn't exactly listening.' Michael's heart raced when he heard that Flora had mentioned a secret too. He was closing in on it.

Chapter 26

Affidavit

1946 to 1999

From the byre, Flora watched the assassin appear from the side of the blazing house. He spent a moment surveying the ruins, but he soon left, and Flora heard his motorbike roar into life and then fade away into the distance. As the noise subsided so did the adrenaline, and it made way for grief and wet cheeks. She suddenly felt very alone as she realized that if she followed her plan for a new life then she would never see Margaret and Marge again. It made her terribly sad, but her old life had been blighted, and it was always her loved ones, like Harold, who were the worst affected. She thought of the children too. Yes, at times it had seemed expedient to lose them, but Flora had also feared that they would be endangered or used to get at her, and they were poorly served by her itinerant lifestyle. And when she had left them, it was always in the hope that they would find a better life than one provided by a mother who was always on the run. Well, this would be the last occasion she swore to herself. She had to break any personal connections that could be used to find her. She would leave her friends and surrogate family to grieve her memory, and she would go far from the Pendletons' reach. It would be a second life. Sir Roland had stolen the first, but anonymity would cloak the second. It would be lonely at first, but she would find new friends, and this time she would take a companion. Flora glanced down at her sleeping daughter. This one wouldn't be left behind.

And that second life started the moment Flora fled across the fields. She wanted anonymity but it would have to be achieved in stages. All she had was Marilyn, a small bag and an important letter that she had rescued from its hiding place in the byre. It wasn't enough to make it alone and she would need a little help to get started. There was only one couple she could trust, and when she arrived breathless, bruised and crying at Grange Farm, Norman Brompton looked at her bleeding and fearful face and understood that the young woman was in danger and that there was a need for secrecy. He was relieved that mother and baby had survived the explosion, but he was worried by the idea that it had been caused deliberately, and his pipe wobbled anxiously in the side of his mouth as he absorbed the implications.

The Bromptons were a kindly couple, and they took in Flora and Marilyn, bought them both some new clothes and let them stay concealed at the farm until Flora's face and hand had healed. They were discreet and kept her presence a secret despite the furore that erupted locally after the explosion. Flora never explained the danger that she faced, and the Bromptons didn't press her on the matter. After two weeks they gave her a few pounds and arranged for her to stay at a cousin's house in Warrington. Flora was relieved and grateful, and when she finally took the train north it was with a new sense of optimism that for once proved to be well-founded.

After staying with the Bromptons' relations for a short time, Flora left suddenly and lived under an assumed name. She found work and eventually managed to forge a happy life with her daughter, Marilyn. Before long, the peace she enjoyed evolved into domestic stability when she met and married a gentle widower called Thomas Wainwright who gave her a sixth and final child who they named Carol. Flora was untroubled by the Pendletons who assumed that she had died in the assassin's explosion, and the past made only one final assault on her life, and that was in 1968. It was only a brief intrusion, and it was a bit unpleasant. However, no danger resulted, at least not for Flora and not until after her life had ended.

***

Two Salvation Army officers had knocked on the door. Thomas was out with the girls and Flora thought the visit had a charitable purpose. She went to the door preparing to open her purse but was shocked when they asked her if she knew Flora Belton, or maybe Wintern. Alarmed, she had initially prevaricated but admitted her role once they told her that it was about the retrospective birth registration of two children called Jocelyn and Andrew Belton.

The Salvation Army were not judgemental, and Flora was relieved that she wasn't asked to explain why she had abandoned the children. She agreed to provide an affidavit and a few weeks later she attended the offices of Brown, Putnam and Willow a partnership of well-known local solicitors who she had used previously to lodge some letters and her will.

She took the oath inside an oak-panelled room and provided the affidavits as requested. She was about to leave when she noticed a woman at the back of the room who had been observing her with utter fury. The similarity with the girl's father was astonishing, and Flora knew without introduction that the woman was her first child, Jocelyn. She guessed that an unpleasant confrontation loomed, and she attempted to leave down an alternative aisle. But the waiting woman blocked her way intent on confrontation.

"Hello, Mummy,' Jocelyn greeted her sarcastically. It's been a long time, hasn't it? What happened? Did you forget to collect me? No, I don't think so,' she said, answering her own question. 'You abandoned me because I was terribly inconvenient. Was I spoiling your social life?' she demanded with a bitterness that lashed Flora's conscience and left Jocelyn feeling elated.

Flora looked at her estranged daughter with deep regret as she recalled the wartime evacuation and everything that had followed. Would the past ever leave her alone? she wondered. She understood the hurt and rejection boiling up inside the angry woman who was blocking her exit, and a tear fell. There had been so many tears during Flora's life, but this single drop felt like a deluge as she looked at the angry face of accusation confronting her. She had tried to act correctly to protect herself and the child, but she could tell from her daughter's expression that she wouldn't be granted the opportunity to explain. But what about the danger? Did it still exist? It seemed unlikely, but Flora decided that she could make one final act of contrition by leaving something that might protect her daughter if it became necessary.

'Umm, it's Jocelyn, isn't it? Look I understand why you are angry, but please listen to me. I did what I did for good reasons. We were both in danger, and I wanted to protect you. It was the same for the other children too.' Her voice tailed off and the single teardrop fell to the floor as Jocelyn snorted at the improbability of her mother's explanation.

'It's true,' Flora insisted weakly. And then sorrow, guilt and regret overwhelmed the clear explanation that she had intended to provide. Structured reasoning was replaced by rambling, and her voice tailed off. 'It's all to do with the lady playing the harp,' she mumbled without clarification as one disconnected thought managed to dominate all the others that were competing to join her explanation. She looked at the door hoping that her solicitor would return to rescue her and recovered slightly when she heard approaching footsteps advancing purposely along the corridor. Their meeting was nearly at end, and she turned to Jocelyn for one last try.

'Look, there's not enough time to explain everything but if you ever feel in danger of something, something from the past - my past - then I have stored a letter here that might help you. It can only be released after my death, and I urge you not to read it unless you absolutely must.'

Jocelyn heard her words, but she wasn't really thinking about their meaning. Years of bitterness had just been released. She had confronted her estranged mother, and she felt triumphant now that Flora had seemed to wilt before her. Her mother was a rambling and shameless wastrel, just as Jocelyn had always imagined, and her feeble words of explanation were incomprehensible and unworthy of even passing consideration. Yet the sudden release of pent-up emotions left Jocelyn feeling a little empty, and suddenly she just wanted to get away. Away from the memory of her troubled childhood, and away from the worn-out woman stood before her who had caused it. Neither woman spoke, and Jocelyn turned from Flora, pushed past a startled solicitor who had just arrived at the doorway and set off on her journey to Sweden and the new life that awaited.

The confrontation had not gone quite as expected but Jocelyn felt satisfied that she had finally made Flora a feature of her past rather than the present, and she never gave it a second thought. At least not until thirty years later when Michael's unexpected arrival at the hospital reminded her of human frailties and her own mistakes.

Chapter 27

Acceptance

December 2000

Jocelyn finished detailing the events of her only meeting with Flora and became quietly reflective, her anger spent. She had spent much of her life blaming her mother without a nod to her own mistakes. But Michael's arrival had suddenly shone a light on them, and she recognized there had been an element of hypocrisy in her behaviour. She felt a little regretful, and the moment became more poignant when Michael gently told her that Flora had died the year before in 1999.

Michael had listened fascinated as Jocelyn filled in the gaps in his understanding. His quest to discover his genetic inheritance seemed to be nearing completion. He had found his natural mother and grandmother, and he had discovered much of interest about their lives. But there was one remaining fact to tease out. What was the secret that Flora took to her grave? What was in those papers held at the solicitors' offices in Warrington? Were they the source of the danger that had grown increasingly serious as his investigations took shape? He owed it to Marge to find out.

He considered the lady with the harp and wondered if she lay at the heart of the mystery and what it could mean. Perhaps she was someone Flora had met at Barrington Hall or maybe it was about something that had occurred during Flora's time in wartime London. If only Flora's journal could be found. It might explain the mystery and it would provide an intimate record of Flora's thoughts and the reasons for her actions. But overhanging everything, there was the question of Flora's reliability. Certainly, she was flighty, possibly fanciful, but he had also remembered a detail from her death certificate. She had died with dementia, and Michael wondered if her rambling conversation with Jocelyn had been an early indication that all was not well. If so, her recollection of events might well have been wrong or confused. He kept those thoughts to himself. Only the letter could provide an explanation, and only Jocelyn could access it.

However, before exploring her appetite for a visit to the UK, Michael first had to explain to Jocelyn how it was that a man called General Francis Pendleton had sent men all the way to her door in Sweden and put her in hospital. It took some time to bring her up to date, but when he had finished, Jocelyn was impressed by the determination and attention to detail that Michael had demonstrated during his investigation.

'My, my,' she said. 'You really have been busy. I had no idea that it was possible to link so many strands together to find someone.' She laughed. 'And there was me thinking I was safely hidden away from my past too!'

'Yes, but the question is: are we still in danger? Did you tell the men about Flora's letter at the solicitors' office?'

'I'm afraid I did, Michael, but only in the most general terms,' she replied. They were twisting my arm and going on about Flora and some stolen papers. I remembered Flora had said something about a letter and that it might be useful if I ran into trouble, so to make the men stop hurting me, I just told them that all the papers were safely locked up and would be released if they didn't go away. It seemed to do the trick, and they stopped the beating and disappeared. I didn't tell them that everything is stored in Warrington.'

Michael considered the risk. Jocelyn hadn't disclosed enough for the General to find them if they went to Warrington to get the letter although they would need to ensure they weren't followed from the airport. It looked to be a reasonably safe venture, and he was about to propose it when he remembered Rebecca was waiting outside.

'I'm not alone, Jocelyn, I have a friend with me. Would you like to meet her?' Jocelyn nodded and Michael went to the door and beckoned a fidgeting Rebecca. She was itching to hear how the meeting had gone.

When Rebecca entered the room the two women smiled at each other and exchanged greetings. Jocelyn looked at her carefully. She certainly made a beautiful companion, but Jocelyn had noted that Michael referred to Rebecca as a 'friend' but not a 'girlfriend' and she wondered if that was significant. He certainly hadn't mentioned a wife or family. Perhaps that would follow.

Michael quickly brought Rebecca up to date by summarising Jocelyn's meeting with Flora thirty years earlier. Rebecca listened carefully and was full of the same questions as Michael. She seemed galvanized by Jocelyn's story and was particularly intrigued by the lady with the harp. Michael saw that she was about to leap in and try to persuade Jocelyn to release the papers, but he thought that any persuasion might be more successful if it was delivered by him, so he flashed a warning look at his impatient assistant and turned to Jocelyn.

'I know you are still angry with Flora, but don't you want to find out about the mystery? If Flora was telling the truth, then the answers are in the solicitors' vault at Warrington. We could leave them there to gather dust, but we might continue to be in danger from those who for some reason still feel threatened. Alternatively, we could go and have a look. We have one slight advantage,' Michael added, 'The General has no idea where the secure storage is located so we should be able to go there safely.'

Jocelyn stared through him deep in thought. She sighed, 'I don't know, Michael, two days ago I was living in peaceful ignorance of any of this. Now the past has come knocking on my door, opening old wounds and creating new ones,' she added, looking down at her arm. As those men left, they threatened to harm my family here if I told the police. Flora said it was about the past and maybe we should leave it there.'

Michael's disappointment rose but he understood Jocelyn's reluctance. He had burst into her life and brought violence with him. She was clearly angry with Flora's wartime antics, although Michael thought this anger was a little unjustified. He thought about his adoptive mother who had wanted him to learn the truth of his adoption as a vehicle for personal renewal. Jocelyn didn't seem like someone who needed to follow a similar path but perhaps the truth would at least allow her to resolve a difficult period in her life. In that sense, natural mother and son were similar. Michael needed to persuade Jocelyn to join his quest but to illustrate his point he would have to admit to some home truths about himself and reveal matters that were intensely painful and private. Michael didn't know it, but this would mark the moment of acceptance that his adoptive mother had sought when she had placed her letter to him in her biscuit tin of memories.

He looked at Jocelyn and began. 'I went through a particularly difficult divorce. To be honest, I was as much to blame as my ex-wife. Afterwards, my adoptive mother watched silently as I allowed my private and professional life to fall apart. To my great regret, we never talked about any of this before she died, and all I have left on the matter is a final letter encouraging me to find you. She understood that I might end up frustrated and dismayed by what I uncovered, but she knew it was the journey of self-discovery that mattered rather than the outcome. It was about the truths I learned, and the people I met along the way,' he said meaningfully as he glanced across at Rebecca who carefully avoided eye contact.

'And I now wonder if that applies to you too, Jocelyn. Is your journey complete or do you want to understand what really happened in wartime Britain all that time ago? It's your heritage if you want to reclaim it. We have only just met, but I think you would want to know the whole truth especially now that some of it has been partially revealed. If I'm wrong, and that's not what you want then we will go away and leave you in peace. If you agree, then we should go to Warrington, and quickly before anyone else gets hurt.'

Michael finished his pitch and felt cleansed by the experience. Both women looked at him in awe but for different reasons. Jocelyn smiled at the bravery of his honest self-examination. Her natural son was a complex man, but his insight was uncannily correct. Yes, her fury with Flora was close by, but it had already become nuanced by the partial explanation she had heard from Michael, and she did indeed want to know the full story. Yes, she could follow her instinct to ignore Flora and remain comfortably in Sweden but that was intellectually and emotionally lazy. She too wanted the truth, and so long as Michael agreed to keep her Swedish family in ignorance then she would go with him and face her past.

'Very well,' she said after careful consideration. 'I may come to regret this but let's go to Warrington and find out what's hidden there.'

Across the room, Rebecca was also moved by Michael's speech but for different reasons. She knew about his failed marriage but his willingness to expose his own weaknesses was impressively honest and his bravery was entirely at odds with her own duplicity. She had tried to remain aloof, but she thought that she was falling in love with Michael and there lay the problem. She had a task to perform first. An unpleasant task with an uncertain outcome; one that would test Michael's obvious feelings for her to the limit. It might well result in the catastrophic failure of their relationship. She hoped it wouldn't, but the truth of her own heritage had to come first. Afterwards, she would turn to Michael to see what could be salvaged from the wreckage.

Chapter 28

Duplicity

December 2000

As soon as Jocelyn was discharged from hospital and had made creative excuses to her family, the trio caught a morning flight to Manchester Airport. There, Rebecca left them explaining that she had to make a short visit to Bristol as there was an urgent university matter that needed her attention. She promised to return to Warrington, and she asked them to book her a hotel room in case she managed to come back early. It seemed a hasty decision.

Michael and Jocelyn hired a car. As Michael drove down the ramp from the carpark he noticed an Audi with dark windows pull out from a bay at the end of the row. The car followed the same route, and Michael realized they were being followed. He couldn't outpace a car like that he thought but how do you slip a tail? Jocelyn spotted that something was wrong.

'What's wrong? Are we being followed?' she asked.

'I'm not sure,' he lied.

She laughed. 'Good try, Michael, but you can't fool me. Why else would you be glued to the mirror?' He was about to respond when the matter was taken out of his hands. They had just entered a roundabout which was large enough to require occasional traffic lights. Michael had tried to judge their progress around the junction such that one of the lights would turn red forcing the car behind them to stop while they sped off. Unfortunately, he misjudged his second effort, and he was forced to brake quite sharply. Behind them, the Audi braked sharply too but a large 4 x 4 vehicle behind the Audi was unable to stop in time, and there was crash as it rammed into the back of the Audi. The lights then turned green and as Michael drove away he saw both cars stationary, doors opening and angry gestures. Michael laughed and described what had happened.

'It couldn't have been better if I'd planned it myself,' he told her. Beside him, Jocelyn was more sceptical.

'It seems like quite some coincidence to me,' she said. 'But if it was deliberate, who could have helped us out?' she asked.

'It would have been quite a feat of planning to orchestrate an accident like that, but I suppose it is theoretically possible,' Michael replied, doubtfully. 'But whoever it was, we are no longer being followed and this is our hotel.'

They checked in, and Jocelyn called Brown, Putnam and Willow who confirmed that they still retained Flora's letters. They agreed to release them as they already had a copy of the affidavit proving Jocelyn's relationship to Flora and they gave her an appointment for the following afternoon.

That evening, Michael sat with Jocelyn at the dinner table, and they exchanged memories and all the details necessary to paint a broader picture of their respective lives. They chatted easily, and any difficulties caused by the manner of their first encounter soon melted away and they quickly became comfortable in each other's company. It wasn't like mother and son; it was more like two old friends who had lost touch and were renewing their acquaintance by catching up on their news.

As the evening drew towards an end, Jocelyn gently asked Michael about Rebecca. He described how he had met the academic and how her knowledge of the Pendletons had helped him to reveal much of Flora's story. For a moment, Michael inadvertently let down his customary guard, and he admitted to Jocelyn that he liked Rebecca but that something seemed to be holding her back and he was confused by her on-off behaviour.

'It's really not my place to interfere, Michael,' she said, breaking a thoughtful silence. 'But are you absolutely sure about Rebecca? Was it a chance meeting in the library? I don't want to say this, but delightful as she is, I'm a bit concerned about her. When we were at Malmo Airport waiting for our flight, I saw her in deep conversation with a foreign looking man. They seemed quite animated, maybe arguing, but they clearly knew each other. Perhaps it's the recent burglary that's made me overly cautious, but I wouldn't want to see you get hurt again. And what could be so important that she has to rush off to Bristol only to return 24 hours later?'

Michael's feelings fought against his logic for control of his judgement. He was certain that Jocelyn's description of what she had witnessed at the airport was accurate, but he refused to speculate on the implications until he had the opportunity to ask Rebecca about it. However, Jocelyn's remarks were unsettling and reminded him that he had briefly questioned Rebecca's loyalty too. However, Michael didn't want to succumb to unhealthy suspicion, and he pushed aside the darker side of his imagination.

'No, Jocelyn, I agree that it's strange behaviour but I'm sure there'll be an innocent explanation. I'll ask her about it tomorrow.'

Jocelyn observed Michael's conflict, and she didn't want the evening to end on a sour note, so she hid her disagreement and told him that he was probably correct and that she was just being paranoid. This lifted the mood, and they bid each other goodnight on a high note before retiring to their rooms.

In the morning at breakfast, the question of Rebecca's reliability was entirely forgotten as they speculated excitedly and ever more wildly on what they would uncover at the solicitors' office. Michael thought it was a family matter, and in a moment of misjudged familiarity, he revealed that he suspected the identity of Jocelyn's father was some kind of monstrous scandal that the family were trying to conceal. It might even concern a will he added, hoping that humour would reassure Jocelyn who looked alarmed that her uncertain parentage might be clarified unpalatably by the secrets hiding in the vault.

As breakfast ended, Michael's phone rang. It was Rebecca who sounded flustered. She had missed her flight but was going to catch the next one which would make her late. The meeting at the solicitor's was scheduled for three o clock, and she would have to meet them there.

'Damn academics,' she breathed self-deprecatingly down the phone. 'We are so disorganised, it's a wonder we ever complete our work.'

Michael laughed, 'I doubt that very much,' he replied thinking of how quickly Rebecca had raided her research material for information on the Pendletons. She blew a kiss down the phone which Michael caught and returned. With mutual attraction reaffirmed, the call ended.

The rest of the morning passed so slowly, and Michael and Jocelyn were beside themselves with impatience by the time they needed to depart for the solicitors' office. It was a fifteen-minute walk, but they set off in plenty of time. Jocelyn's injuries had included a twisted knee and since leaving hospital she had been walking with the help of a stick. Michael was careful not to rush her, and fifteen minutes became twenty.

The solicitors' office was imposing. They passed by an impressive brass plate grandly listing the partners, and they found Rebecca waiting for them in the entrance hall. She hugged him and kissed him on the mouth with unexpected feeling that both Michael and Jocelyn noted with pleasant surprise. A receptionist pointed the way, and a few minutes later, they sat in the same oak panelled room where Jocelyn had confronted Flora some thirty years before. A clerk disappeared off into the bowels of the building to fetch the document and as they waited, Michael noticed that Jocelyn had fallen silent. He understood that the opening of the document was an important moment for her. Home truths were about to be revealed, and he wondered if the scene of her confrontation with Flora made a suitable place to learn the truth. It was a private matter, he decided.

'Shall we do this back at the hotel, in private?' he asked her gently, suddenly aware of Rebecca nodding vigorously beside him.

Jocelyn looked at him and smiled at his perception and consideration. 'How do you know me so well and so soon' she laughed. 'Are you reading my mind?'

Michael looked at Rebecca who ignored his glance, sitting impassively waiting for the clerk to return. He remembered he needed to ask her about the man at Malmo Airport, but before he could mention it, he heard footsteps coming along the corridor. The sound was soon followed by a slim man who was breathing heavily from climbing the stairs up from the vault.

'Here you are madam, I think this is what you have come for,' and he offered Jocelyn a small envelope bearing some marks from the aging process and some writing in a hand that Michael and Jocelyn immediately recognized from Flora's affidavit. There was no message on the outside of the envelope. Flora had simply entitled it 'The

Haberstock Letter'.

'Does that mean anything to you?' Jocelyn asked turning the envelope over in the hope that there might be more. Michael shook his head and looked at Rebecca who turned pink at his scrutiny and joined in with his silent denial.

'Well, I am certainly looking forward to opening it,' Jocelyn said firmly. 'But I think it is best done at the hotel.' She placed the envelope in her bag, thanked the clerk for their services to her mother over the years, and they set off back to the hotel.

As they marched along, Michael noticed that Jocelyn had upped the pace. She was clearly excited, he thought, and they continued to make good progress until her phone rang. It was the solicitors again. They were terribly sorry to inconvenience her, but they had found more papers and asked Jocelyn to return for them. Her sore leg was protesting, and she looked at Michael for help. He nodded his assistance, and so she asked the caller if they would release the papers to Michael as her proxy ....and son, she added, mischievously. The firm confirmed that this was acceptable especially as the remaining papers were mainly administrative. Michael was happy to do the legwork, but he was worried about Jocelyn's safety while he was away.

'Are you sure you'll be alright, Jocelyn? I shouldn't be long.'

'I can look after her,' Rebecca interjected, turning to Jocelyn. 'We could get afternoon tea while we wait for Michael to return. How does that sound, Jocelyn?'

'That's an excellent idea, my dear,' the older woman replied before turning to Michael, laughing. 'I have an American bodyguard, Michael, I'm sure I'll be fine.' He laughed too and relaxed a little. It might be a good thing if the two women spent some time alone together, he thought. It might allay some of Jocelyn's concerns. As he turned to walk away, Jocelyn promised to wait for him before opening the letter and she laughed when he shouted back as he walked away.

'It's probably their bill they want to give you. Flora's left you the bill to pay!'

Thirty minutes later he was back at the hotel to find Jocelyn ashen faced at the reception desk. She mouthed something at Michael which looked like the words, 'She's taken it.' However, before he could ask, the manager was continuing the conversation that had been in progress when Michael had arrived.

'I'm sorry, the manager was saying, 'I saw your friend leaving on the back of a motorbike about ten minutes ago. I'm sure she'll be back, though. After all, Miss Travers has not checked out yet.'

Jocelyn was incredulous. 'Miss Travers? Who's she and how can our friend have checked out as she hasn't checked in yet? Her flight was delayed, and she has only just arrived.'

The manager was confused. 'No, I'm sorry madam, but she arrived late last night and stayed in the third room that you booked under your name. She registered as Jane Travers.'

Realization dawned, and they thanked the manager and walked up the stairs to Jocelyn's room. Rebecca had deceived them, and Michael heart sank as the cold slap of betrayal started to play its tune again. Jocelyn had seen it in her, but he had been too dazzled to make the same assessment. It seemed moot, but for completeness, Michael asked Jocelyn to relate what had happened.

'Well, while you were back at the solicitors, Rebecca – if that's her real name – and I returned to the hotel. I put the letter in my bag which I left in my room. We were going to have afternoon tea, but Rebecca told me she would meet me in the dining room because she wanted to check in first. After twenty minutes there was no sign of her, so I returned to my room to find it open with my bag discarded and the letter taken.'

Michael looked at the lock and decided it could be

easily picked. He used the phone and asked for the manager. Michael reassured him that there would be no adverse publicity but only if the manager let him into Rebecca's room. Otherwise, Michael declared solemnly, it would have to become a police matter. The worried manager scuttled off to find a master key, and five minutes later they were inside while the manager lurked furtively in the corridor. It was clear the room had been used for a night stop as the bed was unmade, and a half-eaten meal was ready for collection. In her rush to get away, Rebecca had abandoned a small rucksack containing some overnight necessities, and Michael searched it carefully hoping for clues. The main chamber contained nothing that could help to identify their thief, but Michael thought that a couple of pages of notes he found in a side pocket might be useful and he shoved them into his own rucksack for later inspection.

He thanked the manager for his assistance and suggested to Jocelyn that they take stock over tea.

'I expect that Rebecca was working for the General, so it looks as though he has won,' Michael told her at the tea table. 'He has secured whatever was in that letter, and by doing so he has removed the only lever that we had to secure our safety. Flora took it as an insurance policy, and we could have used it for the same purpose. The question is: will he be satisfied to leave it at that or are we still in danger?' He paused, reflecting on the end of their failed search and was struck by the irony of the situation. He looked at Jocelyn and recognized shared disappointment. 'It's funny, isn't it? Safety seems to have played a major role in Flora's actions, and yet we have been prepared to forgo safety to search for the truth of our heritage. But it has all gone,' he added sadly. 'It looks like Pendleton's agent, Rebecca, has robbed us of it.'

He went quiet at his own mention of Rebecca. She had betrayed him by cynically exploiting his feelings for her, and Michael felt his heart harden another notch as the old ways reasserted their dominance. Opposite him, Jocelyn observed his bitterness and tried to add a more positive atmosphere by steering the conversation away from Rebecca.

'You know, Michael, I'm glad we have met. We may not have found definitive proof of Flora's intentions during the war but since we met, I have been able to at least consider that I might have misjudged her. That is positive so I am going to take this new positivity home to Sweden where, unless you object, I intend to tell my family that I have met my lost son who has forgiven me. If it goes well, I hope you will meet them one day, but that must be their decision not mine. In the meantime, I know I will never be your mother, but I hope I can be your friend.'

Michael smiled at her honesty and her poorly disguised attempt to cheer him up. 'There was never anything to forgive,' he replied truthfully, 'and yes, you will always be my friend.'

Chapter 29

Sophie's Discovery

December 2000

Michael was miserable on the journey back to Leeds. Christmas lights shone around him, but the festive spirit sought easier prey than the man staring glumly into the distance. His mission was a failure, ending in duplicity and another failed relationship. He had returned the hire car and said goodbye to Jocelyn at the station. She had decided to return to Sweden, but first wanted to visit Elizabeth at her home near Barnsley. Michael and Jocelyn had shared a great deal in recent days, and they had developed an easy friendship from a mixture of shared bloodline, adversity and disappointment. Michael was certain that Flora's trail had gone cold, but he promised Jocelyn that he would stay in touch. Suddenly reluctant to part, they had hugged and then caught separate trains.

As he made his way home, `Michael considered the article he had started. There was still enough material to create an interesting story based on his experiences of the past few weeks, and he felt that the inconclusive end of his search had released him from an obligation to write factually. Missing facts could be replaced with fiction, he decided as he considered how to complete the story and the papers that he would need.

Back in Leeds, he stopped at the café and bought a takeaway coffee. Lucille noted the absence of banter and the fading bruises on Michael's face and wondered what new catastrophe had befallen him since his previous visit. She saw the fresh lines of cynicism and renewed disappointment in his eyes, and as she prepared his drink his sadness seemed to weigh on her too. She shrugged it off. No wonder he doesn't have a regular girlfriend, she thought bitterly.

As Michael entered his apartment, he was pleased to see that the locksmith had repaired his damaged door, and after reading the short note pinned to the door, he collected the new key from his upstairs' neighbour.

Inside, he went straight to his desk and started to arrange his papers which were still scattered from the burglary. Once order was restored, he remembered the notes that he had found in Rebecca's hotel room. Emptying his rucksack, he also came across the additional legal papers that he had collected for Jocelyn. He cursed. In all the drama at the hotel, he had forgotten to give them to her. He set them aside, intending to mail them to Sweden, and then scrabbled around in a side pocket where he discovered a folded piece of paper bearing Rebecca's handwriting. This was what he wanted. The paper bore the kind of notes you would scribble whilst discussing a matter with someone on the telephone. Short phrases or single words seemingly unconnected to the uninformed observer but making complete sense to the writer. There wasn't much. But at the top was Pendleton International Art. Underneath, there were some names, some of which he recognized. Sir Roland, General Francis, Emily and finally his own, Michael Calvert. An arrow then led across the page to Barrington Hall and under that were more names: Flora Poulter, Haberstock and Hofer and then a date, 1938. Finally, and with the emphasis of a double underscore, Rebecca had written the words, Musik II.

He sat back wondering what it could all mean. Over the last few weeks, he had discovered that General Pendleton wanted to secure some kind of letter or papers that had been taken by Flora, and by using Rebecca as his agent he had succeeded. Michael had no idea what the letter contained or what threat it posed to the Pendletons, but he thought it was either to do with a personal scandal, possibly involving Sir Roland, or it concerned the family's business affairs. He looked again at the name of the business. Was all this about art, he wondered, remembering the side room at Barrington Hall and the gallery he had glimpsed before the General slammed the door shut. But then who were Haberstock and Hofer? And why did this date back to events that took place more than sixty years ago? Although he couldn't yet answer his own questions, Rebecca's notes had provided a fresh avenue of investigation, and he carefully filed them before leaning back in the chair to consider his dwindling bank balance and the article that he urgently needed to complete.

As his thoughts roamed, the winking answering machine finally managed to attract his attention, and he was pleased to hear his daughter, Sophie. He had been expecting a hostile response to his note, but she sounded pleased with his overtures and asked if she could visit him in Leeds on her way south from Scotland to spend Christmas at home. He picked up the phone and called his daughter. Sophie seemed pleased to hear from him.

'Oh, Hi, Dad. I had almost given up on you.' He smiled at the phone. It was good to hear her voice after such a long time. He knew that the acrimonious divorce had hurt Sophie badly. She had been spared the grim details marking the precise moment that her parents' marriage finally collapsed, but she had decided in a fit of adolescent certainty that her father was to blame anyway. Michael had made matters worse by gradually drifting away so he was relieved that her pleasant salutation seemed to be without fresh recrimination. She was growing up rapidly and was already into her second year at university. He regretted missing so much of her childhood, and he hoped that her proposed visit to Leeds might provide a good opportunity for a proper reconciliation.

'I'm sorry, Sophie, I've been away for a week or so.'

'Oh, anywhere nice?' she asked, and without doubting his excuse.

'Well, it wasn't a holiday; I've been on a kind of a mission researching my next article. It has become really quite interesting, actually.'

'Ooh! A mission. That sounds very exciting,' she replied as her curiosity grew. 'Go on. Spill the beans!'

'Well, it's rather complicated, but you know how I was adopted at birth. Well, before your grandmother died, she encouraged me to seek out my natural parents so that is what I have done. The problem is that I have also disturbed an old mystery which I've been trying to solve.'

A brief silence indicated Sophie's sorrow at her grandmother's recent passing, but her excitement prevailed. 'Mystery, what mystery?' she demanded.

Michael grew cautious. 'Well, I'm not sure you should get involved as it has involved a lot of danger, and there are those that seem intent on preventing me from uncovering the secret. It's very complicated and I'll tell you everything when you visit.' But then an idea formed in his mind. 'Actually, Sophie, if you promise not to interfere you might be able to help me with one aspect of the work.'

The mention of danger merely aroused Sophie's interest further. She was delighted to be brought into her father's secret even if she had to remain on the periphery of his search. Full of indestructible youth, she doubted that the danger would ever extend to her, and she swore that she wouldn't interfere. 'I promise, Dad. Now come on, what is it?'

Michael looked at Rebecca's notes. 'I think it might involve art. Do the names, Haberstock or Hofer mean anything to you?' Her excitement grew even more. The History of Art was her subject at university. The line was silent as she searched her memory.

'I'm sorry, Dad. Those names do seem slightly familiar, but I can't quite place them. I'll have to think about it. That's not much to go on, though. Is there anything else?'

There was. 'Well, the word "Music" might come into it, too. I have seen it written down and it was spelt in a funny way with a k at the end and followed by the number Eleven or it might even be Roman numerals for the number Two as they look similar.' Then, remembering Jocelyn's account of her encounter with Flora at Warrington, he continued: 'Someone else has also indicated that it might have something to do with a lady and a harp, but I can't be certain of that as it was raised during a bit of a rambling diatribe, and it might be from someone unreliable, with memory problems.'

Sophie was determined to help. While her father had been speaking, an idea had started to form, but she needed to consult a particular reference book at the university library to see whether it had merit. She told him that she would come to Leeds three days later and she promised to tell him if she managed to unearth anything in the meantime.

The call lifted Michael's spirits, and he sat back and enjoyed the prospect of a friendly visit by his daughter. At least something in his life was going in the right direction. He returned to the desk and was about to start writing when he noticed the papers that he needed to return to Jocelyn. He idly shuffled them noting that his prediction of an unpaid lawyer's bill had been correct. There was also an itemised list of items deposited by Flora including a record of a will which someone had marked as being actioned the year before. It was all routine stuff he thought until a small envelope that had been sandwiched between two larger ones dropped onto the floor. When he rescued it, he was surprised to see it was addressed to Jocelyn in Flora's hand with the date 1968 written on it.

Michael paused. He didn't know much about Flora's final years in Warrington. This letter might fill in the gaps in his understanding of his family roots and provide good material for his article. And what about the Haberstock letter that Rebecca had stolen? Did this second envelope contain clues about that? The temptation to open it almost got the better of Michael's judgement, but it was not his name on it, and it was not his to open. He thought of Jocelyn and her poisoned image of Flora. Michael's account of Flora's wartime life, drawn largely from Marge, had partially persuaded Jocelyn that Flora's motives might be more complex than she had first assumed, though Michael knew that she still wasn't wholly convinced. It was possible, perhaps even likely, that this new envelope might provide definitive and highly personal evidence that would prove the matter for her either way.

He picked up the phone and tried to call Jocelyn to ask permission to open the letter, but there was no reply from her phone or from Elizabeth's landline. Having spent most of the day travelling and considering how to complete his article, he decided to leave her a message and try again the next day.

***

The following day was certainly eventful. It started well enough with coffee under the watchful gaze of Lucille but when Michael returned to his flat, he discovered he had missed calls from Sophie and then Jocelyn.

He pressed 'Play' and heard his daughter who was bursting with excitement. She had all the answers.

'Dad, I think I know what this is all about. It's not a harp it's a lyre, and it features in a painting by Gustav Klimt called Die Musik. But there were two versions of it. Musik I is hanging in a museum, but Musik II was destroyed, along with many other important paintings, in a fire in 1945 when the SS destroyed a castle in the face of the advancing Russian Army. Karl Haberstock was Hitler's art dealer and Walter Hofer was Goering's. Klimt paintings are highly collectable and many of his works started life on the walls of a small number of Jewish families living in Austria. The Nazis often referred to Klimt's work as degenerate art but agents like Haberstock nonetheless looted his works on behalf of senior officials who placed them into their private collections. If you think you've found one it would be world news, but I think it's more likely to be a copy of some kind. Please let me know what you're up to, it's absolutely fascinating.'

So, it was about art after all. He thought of the painting he had seen hanging in the General's gallery and the effort the man had expended to impede Michael's investigation. That painting wasn't a copy, he concluded. It was the real thing. No wonder the General was trying to hide it. It would ruin the family if it became known that they had been trading in looted Nazi art. He thought of Marge. Yes, this was precisely the kind of information he needed to get justice for her, but he would need to consider what was the most damaging way to make the secret public. He picked up the phone to speak to Jocelyn and was astonished to discover that she already knew all about it.

Chapter 30

Confession

December 2000

Jocelyn was stewing with anger as she made her way from Warrington to Elizabeth Minton's house near Barnsley. Rebecca, if that was her name, had not only stolen her property, but she had also denied Jocelyn the opportunity to learn more about her past. She was also upset because Rebecca had abused Michael's trust and piled more hurt on a man who she knew was already haunted by a previous betrayal. It took a special kind of cynicism to act so callously, she thought, and Michael was well rid of her.

By the time she arrived at Elizabeth's her anger had reduced to a simmer, but it started to boil up again when a day later she had received an unexpected call.

'Hello? Jocelyn?'

There was only one American voice that would be calling Jocelyn. 'What do you want, Rebecca?' she replied icily. 'If that's your real name. Haven't you caused enough damage already?'

'No please, listen. My name really is Rebecca Holsten, and I want to explain, but I'd like to come and see you as its complicated.'

Jocelyn remembered the beating she had received. 'What? You want to know where I am so Pendleton can send his thugs around to beat me up again?' There was a pause on the other end of the line and an intake of breath. It sounded like sudden realization and the shocked denial that followed was adamant.

'No, no, please Jocelyn. Is that what you think? But it's not like that at all. What gave you that idea? I don't work for Pendleton. No, never. I work for my mother. And I'm ringing because Michael is in danger.'

Jocelyn noted Rebecca's intake of breath and the rushed explanation and decided that it sounded like the truth. She would proceed cautiously though. 'Very well, Rebecca, I'll meet you, but it must be somewhere public. When do you want to come? I'm staying with a friend near Barnsley.'

Rebecca paused for a moment while she consulted a map. 'I can be there in two hours, but we must hurry.' She sounded genuinely worried, so Jocelyn agreed to meet her at a café that she remembered from a previous visit.

Across the room, Elizabeth looked at Jocelyn enquiringly, but Jocelyn just shook her head. There was no need to bring someone else into it, 'I'm very sorry, Elizabeth, I know I've only just arrived, but I need to go out. It sounds rather urgent.'

Jocelyn took a taxi, and Rebecca was already waiting for her when she walked into the cafe. She looked anxious and beautiful. No wonder Michael liked her, Joycelyn observed silently. But was she reliable?

It didn't take long to find out. Jocelyn took a seat opposite Rebecca, ordered a coffee and then listened in awe to Rebecca's explanation. The reasons for urgency soon became apparent.

Rebecca took a deep breath. 'I come from a Jewish family that used to live in Austria at the turn of the last century. My great grandparents loved art and built up a valuable collection. In 1938, the Nazis confiscated it all. My grandmother managed to escape to America, but the rest of my relatives were interned and died in the camps. At the end of the war, there was an allied investigation into stolen art that suggested that my family's collection was destroyed by the SS as the Russian Army advanced on them and defeat became inevitable. However, my family have heard persistent rumours over the years to suggest that one of the paintings survived and was hidden in a private collection owned by the Pendletons. We hired a law firm in Tel Aviv to investigate, and after two years of research they are getting close to a result and have even deployed some men who are preparing to force entry and secure the painting.'

Rebecca paused to drink coffee and to think as she approached the difficult part of her account. 'Unfortunately, and quite by chance, Michael's research into his family history has intervened. We had to confirm that he wasn't working for the Pendletons, so I piggybacked onto his search. However, as his ancestor, Flora, has guided him closer to the truth, we have become worried he might act clumsily and ruin our operation. We have been watching the Pendletons and their men closely for nearly a year. The reason I disappeared yesterday was to get an update from our operations team. It is as well that I did because you were followed from the airport, and we had to intervene to ensure that you were unmolested. The key to our operation is the Haberstock letter. It is a vital document for a number of reasons. It proves that the painting was stolen from my family, and it is the only evidence that the version in Barrington Hall is the original painting and not the fake destroyed by the SS. It also shows that it was purchased by the Pendletons from the Nazis. If that fact became known it would ruin the reputation of the Pendletons and their business, which is why the General has been acting so aggressively to prevent Michael from making progress.'

'But why take it from us?' Jocelyn asked. 'You could have just explained.'

Rebecca fought back tears. 'It was a bad mistake which is why I'm here now. You see I've been fighting divided loyalties. We decided that the letter was so important that we should facilitate your trip to retrieve it, and then take it for safekeeping.' She wiped her eyes. 'The thing is I really regret that decision. The whole business has become increasingly difficult because I really like Michael, and I think I may even be falling in love with him. I know he is confused and hurt by my hot and cold behaviour, but I've been like that because I was torn between my family and my feelings for him. But I can't bear the deception any longer which is why I have come to you today. I know you are worried about me, so I have brought you something to convince you that I am telling the truth.' She reached into her bag and withdrew an old envelope and laid it on the table. It was the Haberstock letter. 'Without this document, that painting is worthless,' she said. 'Please look after it.'

Jocelyn picked up the letter and thought about its importance not only to this woman's family but to the entire art world. The provenance of a hugely important work of art rested on it remaining safe. Jocelyn knew Rebecca was aware of this and the fact that she was willing to put it into Jocelyn's hands was proof enough of her good intentions.

'That's unnecessary,' she said quietly, and slid the envelope back to Rebecca. 'That is an important document for anybody who appreciates art and wants justice for the victims of genocide. In my opinion, it belongs to you, and in any case, you can look after it far better than me. `But, Rebecca, what is it you want me to do?'

Rebecca dried her eyes relieved that she'd managed to

convince Jocelyn that she was telling the truth. 'Well, we need to stop Michael. I think he may attempt to confront the General to get justice for the old lady, Marge. But if he attempts to do it alone he may well get hurt. We have watched the General for a long time. He is ruthless and has armed men with military experience. This is not something that Michael should be taking on. We're also worried that the General might destroy the painting if he thinks that the story is about to come into the open. We need to tell Michael what's going on, and then ask him to allow us to finish our operation. He won't listen to me any longer, but he might listen to you, Jocelyn.'

Jocelyn had first-hand experience of the General's men. She certainly knew that bit of Rebecca's account was correct. And then she thought of Michael confronting General Pendleton and his men despite being alone. Foolish? Undoubtedly. Brave? Immensely. But it was also unnecessary. It would be far better to leave this to the experts, and it would still result in justice for Marge.

She smiled to reassure Rebecca. 'I'll see what I can do but you'd better keep quiet. He's very upset with you.' She picked up her phone and remembered that Michael had left a message the day before which she had forgotten to return. It was something about the extra papers the solicitor had found. There was a lot to discuss. However, her first call went unanswered and as they waited for him to return her call they chatted easily, and Jocelyn began to appreciate why Michael liked the American woman so much. She was charming.

Chapter 31

Ransom

December 2000

When Michael and Jocelyn finally managed to speak, Michael was relieved to learn that Rebecca was not the General's agent after all. It was fascinating how quickly the different strands were coming together. Sophie had told him about the identity of the painting and now Rebecca had admitted her role in its planned recovery. He was still angry with her deceit though.

'Is Rebecca still there?' he asked Jocelyn, suspiciously.

'No,' Jocelyn lied. 'But don't judge her too harshly, Michael, she seemed to be genuinely regretful, and I think she has strong feelings for you. It might even be love.' Opposite her, Rebecca's eyes turned glassy as she wondered if the damage was irreparable.

'Well, we'll have to see about that later,' Michael replied, 'but if I understand correctly, I'm being asked to step back and let Rebecca's team deal with the General.'

'That's right, Michael, and I agree with Rebecca. The General is dangerous. He has armed men, and I really think you should leave it to the experts.' Michael paused. It made sense. Why risk further danger?

'OK, I will step back but on one condition. I would like exclusive rights to break this story. I want revenge for Marge and…well… to be honest, I desperately need the cash,' he added. Rebecca smiled and nodded at Jocelyn.

'I'm sure Rebecca will agree to that, Michael,' Jocelyn reassured him. 'I think she understands how much effort you've put into this so far.'

As the call ended, Michael looked at his computer. He had better get writing. This story was huge, and it would be syndicated globally. There would be justice for Marge and instant relief for his wilting bank balance. He started his article and was making good progress when he received an alarming call that completely changed the situation. It was from his daughter, and she was with the General's men.

'Dad is that you?,' she sobbed. 'These men have taken me. Please do what they say or they're going to hurt me, and Dad…' The phone was snatched away.

'Listen carefully to your daughter, Calvert,' an anonymous voice threatened. 'If you want to see your her again you must do exactly as you are told. If you deviate or involve the police that will be the end of her. Bring the papers to Somerset and wait for our call. Remember, your daughter's life depends on it.'

The line went dead, and Michael's head reeled. This was becoming very serious but what should he do? He could try to persuade Rebecca to release the Haberstock letter but that would remove all evidence of the painting's provenance and even if she would agree to do it there was no guarantee that the General would allow matters to end there. Alternatively, he could try the police but that would endanger his daughter, and the General had proved his influence extended deep into officialdom. That was too risky. Finally, he could leave it to Rebecca's men to mount a rescue. He picked up the phone and called her.

'Michael, I'm so sorry,' she began but Michael cut her off.

'We do need to talk, Rebecca, but it will have to wait until later. There's something I need to tell you.' He went on to explain about Sophie and asked her whether her men were capable of mounting a rescue. She was shocked.

'How long have we got? she asked.

'About 48 hours I think; they haven't told me yet.'

'Forty-eight hours!' she exclaimed. 'Is that all we have? The law firm's operatives are all ex special forces and I'm sure they are capable of mounting a rescue mission. But I don't know if they can be ready in time. I will have to check and call you back. But in the meantime, Michael, don't do anything rash.' He noted her concern but ended the call before her feelings could be explored. There would be time for that later.

It was then that Michael glanced down and saw Flora's letter to Jocelyn. In all the drama, he had forgotten to ask Jocelyn if he could open it. If it supported the Haberstock letter it might help to secure Sophie. He knew he should ask permission, but the situation had changed, and he opened it anyway. It turned out that Flora wanted to provide her daughter with the explanation that she had failed to deliver at the solicitors' during their difficult encounter. It seemed she could offer proof of her intentions too.

Dear Jocelyn

I wasn't surprised at your anger today and when I look back at some of the decisions that I made as a young woman I feel deeply ashamed. I know there is little I can do to persuade you that there were some very good reasons for what I did, but I want you to know that for the last thirty years I have been on the run from a family called Pendleton. I used to work for them as a parlour maid, but I was exploited and abused by the Master, Sir Roland who, I'm ashamed to say, is your father. It was a terrifying time, and after he made me pregnant, I had to run away to London. But I did something very stupid before I left. I took some papers as a sort of insurance policy. They would have ruined the family's reputation and their business if they had become public. I thought that it would make them leave me alone, but I was terribly mistaken, and for years they tried to track me down or use my children as a lever. You will have seen The Haberstock letter by now, so I don't need to explain the threat it poses to the Pendletons. I have instructed the solicitors to release it to you should you ever feel threatened but be wary of wielding it.

However, that letter is not the reason that I am writing to you. It was dreadful to see you so upset today, and I didn't explain myself at all well mainly because I didn't want you to be exposed to any danger. I am sure that after your anger subsides a little you will one day want to learn the truth of what I did in my life, not just the facts, but my reasons. When you do, I hope you will come to think of me as a different person than the one you seemed to imagine today.

There is no time to tell you everything here, but I want to share a secret with you that may help. For a great many years, I kept a journal. It details my innermost thoughts and the actions I took. There was a serious attempt on my life in 1946 when a man hired by the Pendletons tried to blow me up in a booby-trapped house in a place called Nailsbourne near Taunton. My first husband was killed, and the house destroyed, but I managed to escape with my daughter to hide quietly in Lancashire. As I ran away, I left my journal hidden in the roof of an outbuilding at the back of the house near the trees, and as far as I know it is still there today.

Our lives are too short to waste time looking back at events that we can't control, but I understand that human curiosity drives us to learn about our roots and heritage. The important thing is our forebears should not just be judged solely by their actions but by their motivations too. I hope that I have already said enough to convince you of my good intentions but if not, the journal exposes my every thought, and I ask you to judge me on that record.

I really hope that you achieve inner peace and that I have not totally poisoned your life.

Your mother, Flora

Michael set down the letter and considered the latest twist on his family tree. It had suddenly become quite nauseating. Her letter indicated that Sir Roland was Michael's grandfather and Francis Pendleton was his second cousin. One of the men seemed to have sexually exploited Michael's grandmother and the other was threatening to kill his daughter. Two men. Both relatives. Theoretically bound to him by blood, but it was blood that had been imposed on an unwilling servant girl.

He thought of Flora, and her past actions started to make sense. No wonder she had fled from Barrington Hall and tried to hide in London. He was impressed with Flora's perceptive and remarkably philosophical remarks about family and history. And the note was so well written too. How had a servant girl managed to be so well educated? But there were more pressing matters to address, and Michael's thoughts returned to the gist of Flora's remarks. He was disappointed that she had presupposed the reader's understanding of the Haberstock Letter. But it was the journal that interested him. Pendleton knew that Flora had kept a diary because Michael had mentioned it to him at the Manor, but the General thought it had been lost in the explosion at Flora's home. This could be useful. Michael was worried about leaving his daughter's life in the hands of Rebecca's team. What if they botched a rescue or they were unable to get there in time? There were too many uncertainties, and he needed a back-up plan. The diary might be the answer. If Flora had written a record of the events that so threatened

265

the Pendletons then he might be able to use her journal to arrange a deal on his terms: The journal in exchange for Sophie. It was only a backup plan, but he had to go to Somerset anyway, and there would be time to retrieve it but only if it was still in her hiding place.

He looked at his watch, grabbed a rucksack and rushed to the station to catch the next train to Taunton. As he walked down the street he became aware of a man following him. At first he wasn't sure, but he became certain when the man followed him around a circuitous test route. Whose man was it? Rebecca's or the General's. He couldn't be certain, but he had to lose him. As Michael went around a corner he dodged into a narrow pedestrian access and hid in a doorway. As he peeped around the edge, Michael saw the man rush past searching the crowds ahead. Eventually, the man realized that Michael had given him the slip. He reached into his pocket for his phone and reported that the target was mobile and no longer under surveillance.

Chapter 32

Old Records

December 2000

During the journey back to Somerset, Michael's phone rang. It was his ex-wife who had stopped calling him years ago. It was so unusual that he took the call. She was crying.

'Michael, what is going on? Sophie's not answering her phone, and then a man telephoned. He was going on about a missing letter and threatened to harm Sophie if it wasn't returned. We were warned not to contact the police. What have you done?' she asked, ending on an accusatory note which Michael ignored.

'Hello, Isobel. I don't have much time to explain, but I want to reassure you that I have this in hand. I've been researching my ancestry, and I seem to have disturbed a secret that threatens the people that have taken Sophie. They will return her unharmed if I give them some papers that I have uncovered. I am on my way to them now, but in the meantime, you must remain patient, and we must

267

comply with their instructions.'

'Why should I trust you to sort this out? You'll just make matters worse.'

Michael understood her scepticism, but he needed to prevent police involvement. There was little in his recent life to reassure his ex-wife of his competence to rescue their daughter, and so he decided that fear was the only way of ensuring her silence.

'Actually, Isobel, you have no choice. You need to understand that these are people are utterly ruthless. If we are discovered going to the police, then it is highly likely that we won't see our daughter again. You must give me the space to fix this. Sophie's life depends on it.'

The gravity of the situation hit home, and Isobel started sobbing. Michael softened his tone and told a white lie. 'Look, Isobel, I have what they want. I haven't received my instructions yet, but this shouldn't take more than a day or two. In the meantime, try to be brave, and I promise to keep you updated as matters progress.'

Isobel's tears stopped. She hadn't heard Michael speak with such gentle reason for a very long time. She sniffed. 'Very well, Michael, please bring her home, and I'll wait for your call. And Michael…you stay safe too.'

The conversation ended on an unusually accommodative note. She had awoken his usual bad memories, but the bitterness had been absent, and it had been replaced by their shared concern for Sophie. This was new, Michael reflected, as he returned to the task in hand.

***

The afternoon was drawing to a close when he arrived in Taunton, and Michael needed to move quickly. He knew that it was risky to pin his hopes on the journal. There was no guarantee that it was still in its hiding place after all the years since Flora's escape, and what condition was it in? A damp outbuilding was a poor place to store a book, and the diary might have disintegrated or become illegible. It was also possible that the old building had been demolished and the site cleared for redevelopment as the village expanded. And there was one final, more immediate difficulty. Flora's letter had identified the name of the village but not where Flora's house had once stood. He had a plan for that, but he needed to buy some items first because his search would have to take place that evening in the dark. He found a hardware shop and used a tired credit card to buy some stout boots, a few basic tools, a jemmy and a powerful torch. Stuffing them into his rucksack, Michael rushed to the hire car office anxious to get there before it closed. His funds were low and so he had to settle for a small Fiat. It was hardly the stuff of spy movies, he reflected wistfully as the car struggled up a hill, but at least he was mobile.

Michael took care to ensure he wasn't followed and checked into a different hotel. He had just used his room key when General Pendleton called.

'Calvert?' he barked. 'Where are you? I hope you've got what I want. Your pathetic family has caused enough damage over the years and it's time to draw a line under it. I don't know what that meddling servant girl thought she was doing stealing that letter, but my great uncle's business affairs were nothing to do with her in 1938, and they're nothing to do with you now. I want it back. And don't think you can write about it afterwards. I have the resources to reach deep into your family if you are ever tempted to break silence. Know this too: I have your daughter, and her safety depends on you following my instructions to the letter. If you blink, deviate or call the police she will disappear. Permanently.'

Michael thought of the man leaving Smithieson's house, and he was certain the General meant what he said.

'Look, Pendleton, I'm not interested in your family's ancient history,' he lied, 'I just want my daughter back. I'll give you what I've got but you need to tell me about the arrangements for the exchange.'

Satisfied that his threats had secured Michael's compliance, the General set about detailing his orders which were straightforward and direct. Michael was to go to Barrington Hall at 3pm on the following afternoon. He should bring the Haberstock Letter with him which the General would examine before Sophie was handed over. He warned Michael that the house would be guarded, and that if he didn't comply with the instructions then neither father nor daughter would leave the house alive. The General dismissed Michael by warning him not to be late and rang off.

Michael thought about Sophie. He didn't have the Haberstock letter, and he was relying on Rebecca's men arriving on time. What if they didn't? He hadn't heard from Rebecca, and he had no idea whether her men were even planning to mount an operation never mind when. He rang her to find out and she was shocked by the 3pm deadline.

'So soon,' she exclaimed. I'm so sorry I haven't called, Michael, I've been waiting to hear if the arrangements for a rescue operation could be put in place. I know Sophie's life depends on this, so I'll ask again. I'll do my best, Michael, and I promise to call you when I know. Are you at home?'

Michael told her he was back in Somerset and the line fell silent as she absorbed the implications. 'What are you doing, Michael?' she asked nervously. 'Please don't put yourself in danger. I don't want you to get hurt.'

'Well since we spoke, I have discovered the location of Flora's diary and I'm going to get it later tonight. I know I told you that I'd stay away from Barrington Hall, but Sophie's life is at stake. If your men haven't made it by the deadline I'm going to try and trade the diary for Sophie's life. I can't stand by and do nothing.'

'But the General and his men will be armed,' she pointed out.

'I know, you don't need to remind me, but I will be

armed too, even if it's only with a book,' he laughed. 'But listen, I have to go and find it now. I'll call you for a final update at 2pm tomorrow before I get into position. We'll speak then.' With that the call ended.

He picked up his rucksack which clanked as the tools inside competed to see which one could make the most noise. He stuffed a coat in the bag to muffle the sound and set off to Nailsbourne. After fifteen minutes, he entered the village and was worried by the extent of the new housing around the periphery of the original hamlet. Did those houses now cover the site of Flora's old house? The pub stood in the middle, and it was very different to the one he had visited in Ashill. The new houses at Nailsbourne had transformed the village from a close-knit community to a less personable commuter town, and this was reflected in the pub's clientele.

Nobody noticed Michael as he approached the bar, and the conversation continued at the same volume as those around failed to notice the stranger amidst them. Michael looked around in disappointment. He had hoped for an Archie, a village sage who knew everything and everyone. Someone who would remember the explosion and delight in telling Michael and the rest of the pub all about it. His spirits sagged. Any sages had fled a long time ago, but Michael went to the bar anyway and asked to speak to the landlord. A busy man in his fifties approached from a rear office. He feigned patience as he listened to Michael's enquiry about the old gas explosion, then shrugged and started to turn away.

'I'm very sorry but I have no idea about what you're talking about. Look, it's very busy…' he added, retreating. Then his manners got the better of him and he turned. 'But there is an old chap who used to come in here. I think he was a policeman, and he might remember. But I haven't seen him for a while and I'm not sure if he's still alive.' The landlord gave Michael quick directions to the man's home and retreated into the back office.

A short drive brought Michael to a small corner-terrace cottage that was the final old building on an expanding High Steet. He knocked on the door, and after the rattling of chains and locks, it was opened by an old man whose professional suspicion immediately identified him as a former policeman. Michael introduced himself and explained that he was researching his grandmother whose life had ended in a tragic gas explosion in Nailsbourne just after the war. He told the retired policeman that the landlord had suggested that he drop by to see whether he could remember anything about it.

The man nodded, clearly familiar with the details. He asked for identification and satisfied with Michael's credentials, he introduced himself as Peter Wilkinson and invited Michael in. Twenty minutes later, Michael was on his way. Sergeant Wilkinson had a good memory. He had confirmed Michael's knowledge of the explosion, but he had added an interesting fact. There were some in the police station who thought the explosion had been suspicious. There were whispers in the village too, and the finger had been pointed at someone from a place called Ashill. The retired policemen thought the implicated man had been called Blackstone or perhaps Blackwood, but he confirmed that there was no evidence whatsoever to implicate him and the coroner had recorded the three deaths as accidental. He finished by telling Michael that he had wondered if someone with a grudge had been trying to frame the unfortunate suspect but as a young and inexperienced constable, he had kept silent, and the case was closed. Michael immediately thought of Sir Roland and his vendetta against the Blackfords, and he silently congratulated the retired policeman on his early professional perception. Then, very casually Michael asked where the house had been, explaining that in the morning he might pay his respects to his late grandmother if the site still existed. 'Oh, I think so' the man replied, and Sergeant Wilkinson gave Michael the directions he needed. Michael thanked him, and when he drove away he had no idea that Sergeant Wilkinson had picked up the phone and was dialling an old friend.

Chapter 33

The Byre

December 2000

Michael had no intention of waiting until the following morning before searching for the journal. He was impatient to see whether it was still in its hiding place and to read its secrets. But there were practical considerations too. His search had to be at night to avoid unwanted scrutiny, and he would need time to study the journal to confirm that it posed a sufficient threat to General Pendleton to guarantee Sophie's safety. The retired policeman's directions were precise, and Michael was relieved that they took him beyond the built-up area to unlit fields and quiet seclusion. Eventually, he arrived at the gap in the hedge that he was seeking. He glanced across the road at a clump of trees that were bisected by a narrow farm track and thought it would make an excellent place to park. The natural cover concealed the small car nicely, and Michael would have found it ironic had he known that sixty years earlier the assassin had chosen the same discreet spot to conceal his motorcycle.

Michael rescued his rucksack from the rear seat and exchanged his shoes for the new boots. He took out the flashlight, checked it was working and slung the bag with the remaining tools over his shoulder. As he crossed the empty road, the moon emerged from behind a solitary cloud and lit his way. He glanced up at the clearing sky and was strangely encouraged by the sight of Orion seemingly standing winter guard over him. The moon made the torch redundant, and the natural light was strong enough to reveal the remains of the house that had once stood beyond the gap in the hedge. Mounds of rubble had become overrun by a carpet of small shrubs, weeds and ivy which snaked across the uneven ground threatening to trip the unwary. The jungle of brick and vegetation was passable, but only just. He dodged an unruly Buddleia that had taken root in the remains of the front wall and picked his way down the side of the ruins. At the rear, he stood close to where Flora had crawled bleeding from underneath the protective back door. He ignored the ruins around him, and looked beyond the end of the back garden where he could just make out a group of trees. He was close now, and the realisation made him inexplicably cautious even though it was highly unlikely that anyone could see him going about his task. Slowly, and as quietly as he could manage, he made his way towards the coppice. The last thing he needed was to turn an ankle or stand on a concealed nail. The sheep in the nearby field stood up and eyed him considering noisy flight. But Michael moved with such care that they elected to remain immobile with their reflective cats-eyes fixed eerily on the visitor. He reached the trees and peered through the shadows. And there it was.

The disused byre had been partially consumed by 60 years of undergrowth, and for a moment Michael thought the shadowy form was just part of the hedge line. It was only small, and one end of the roof had collapsed under the weight of the vegetation. Orange tiles that were tinged with the green patina of age and damp had fallen onto the floor, and Michael hoped that Flora's diary wasn't underneath. If sturdy roof timbers couldn't survive the cold and damp, then what chance was there for the diary? Michael took out his torch and the impatient beam of light eventually showed him the best way in. At one end of the building where the roof was still standing, he saw a split stable door. The top half had fallen off its hinges and lay casually on the ground like an unwelcome doormat. The lower half was more secure, but Michael still had to spend several minutes hacking at the Ivy with a knife before he could free the door sufficiently to squeeze past.

The scent of damp and decay permeated the building. He looked up at the roof and wondered about the condition of the remaining roof timbers. Those clay roof tiles are heavy he thought looking at the scattered pile on the floor at the other end of the barn, and he would need to be careful to avoid a further collapse. He slowly ran the beam of the torch along the roof starting at the damaged end. It was covered with a waterproof roof felt that was fastened to the underside of the timbers with rusty tacks. The felt was faded but looked undisturbed. Frustrated, he was about to transfer his attention to the fallen tiles when he noticed that at the very end of the wall, in the corner where it met the roof slope, the felt sagged slightly and was no longer properly attached. Michael dodged round a pile of rotting feed sacks and stood on tip toe as he stretched up and reached inside the void. His hand fumbled around, urgent fingers searching for contact, and when they eventually touched the parcel it was heavy, and he struggled to lift it with one hand. He carefully brought it down, lowered his heels back to the ground and shone the light on his discovery. It was larger than he had expected, and it had been wrapped in an oil cloth secured by string that was tied in a bow. The parcel had been wrapped with great care, and it reminded him that Christmas was only two weeks away. It was Flora's gift from the past and Michael was jubilant at his discovery.

He reached inside a pocket for a penknife but found it was unnecessary as the rotting string broke easily, and the oil cloth fell away. Flora's diary was bound in leather which had turned dark brown in protest at the harsh conditions and the oil that had preserved it. The lock looked a little corroded, but it was intact, and Michael was pleased to see that the catch was still closed. It looked undisturbed and just waiting for Flora's key. Michael instinctively wanted to force it open and start reading straight away, but if he lingered too long someone might notice the car and discover his trespass. He imposed reluctant reasoning onto his impatience and stowed the precious book in his rucksack before turning around to find the twin barrels of Arthur Blackford's shotgun hovering menacingly just in front of his nose.

Michael stepped back in alarm, but the barrels followed him. What was Blackford doing here? The man holding the gun answered Michael's silent question.

'So, you've found it,' the old man said softly. 'I have wanted this book for so long that I'd forgotten what it looked like. I always assumed it was destroyed in the fire when I discovered that she had died here in a gas explosion.' He gestured at the rucksack. 'That book will prove my father's innocence.' Arthur's eyes glowered at the thought of his father and of those that had anonymously tried to finger Arthur for the gas explosion. 'Hand it over. Now.'

'Arthur, please,' Michael said gently as he started to worry about the state of the old man's mental faculties and his judgment. 'There's no need for this. At least make sure the safety catch is switched on,' he added, trying hard to conceal his fear. But Michael's attempt at reason was interpreted as defiance and his words inflamed Arthur. The old man snorted, and the barrels wobbled even more erratically as his hands started to shake.

'I'm afraid you're going to have to hand over that diary right now, and without any argument,' he threatened, voice rising. 'Don't think I won't do it. My father WILL get justice!' he shouted.

It was then that a movement in the darkness behind the doorway caught Michael's eye and he could have kissed the ground in thanks when David Blackford calmly stepped forward.

'Please put it down, Dad. This is not what we agreed when Sergeant Wilkinson called about Michael's visit. The gun was only meant to be for our protection.' He glanced at Michael. 'I have no idea what you're both talking about, but I don't think Mr Calvert intends to hurt us.' However, Arthur's judgment had been undermined by age, ill health and years of brooding determination. He wasn't listening to his son, and he looked at David blankly while emphasising his resolve by tightening his grip on the gun and waving it around Michael's face.

Michael realized that Arthur had become dangerously unbalanced, and there was a grave risk that events could run away with unpredictable consequences. He needed to distract him, and Michael chose the biggest weapon he could think of to do it.

'Have you told him yet, Arthur?' he asked the old man, casually.

Despite the sudden change in tack, Arthur blinked his immediate understanding of what Michael intended to reveal. 'Don't,' he said, half pleading and half threatening, and he raised his weapon even closer to Michael's face. Michael pretended to ignore the old man, and he turned to David who was standing behind Arthur looking on with alarm and confused disbelief. It was not really the best moment to break this kind of news, but it was unavoidable.

'I think it's time you knew, David. You see, you're correct. I would never hurt either of you. I couldn't.'

Michael said evenly. 'We are tied by Flora's blood. She was my grandmother, and I have to tell you that she was your mother, which makes you my uncle.' The weapon dropped to Arthur's side. Unknown to Michael and David, his threats had been as empty as the cartridge chambers of the unloaded gun that he had waved in Michael's face.

The old man's face sagged in resignation, and he sighed as painful memories of Flora and their separation flooded back. It was a secret that he had kept from his son for sixty years.

'It's true, David. He's telling the truth. Flora Poulter was your mother. During the war I had an affair with her. We were living together but then I foolishly tried to read that journal, and she caught me and threw me out. Sometime later she disappeared after delivering you. You were brought to me by the police, and I made up a cover story that your mother had died in the war. I had to protect you because Flora was being pursued by the Pendletons for something that she had taken from them. I was worried that if they discovered that you were her child then they would use you to get at her. It's complicated but I'm certain everything is explained in that book,' he said, pointing at Michael's rucksack.

At the mention of the Pendletons, Michael thought of Sophie. Everyone wanted Flora's diary. Arthur wanted it for justice and revenge, Flora's wartime children wanted it to understand their mother's behaviour and Michael needed it to buy his daughter's safety. He looked at Arthur and was relieved that for the moment the gun was still at his side and pointing at the floor.

'I understand you want Flora's journal to prove your father's innocence, Arthur, but Pendleton has kidnapped my daughter, and I need to trade the book to get her released. If I don't give it to him then he has made it clear that she will be killed. Your father has passed away now but my daughter's life has only just begun. You must let me give it up."

David had been listening intently and he stepped forward and put a comforting hand on Arthur's arm. 'I agree with him, Dad. We must let Michael take it. A young girl's life now depends on it just as Flora's life once depended on it too.' He turned to Michael. 'I have just one request though. Before the journal passes into the General's hands would you read it and take some notes. I would very much like to understand what Flora was thinking when she left me with my father.'

Michael understood. There were several of Flora's children who wanted explanations too. He would have time to make a transcript if he started tonight, and it was a small price to pay for Sophie's release.

However, standing beside Michael, Arthur Blackford didn't think it was a reasonable accommodation at all. His last opportunity to avenge his father was about to disappear into Barrington Hall, and he looked meaningfully at the two other men as the wild look started to return.

'I'm outvoted,' he said angrily, 'but if I can't have the book, then I'll have to find another way,' and without explanation he pushed past his son, gun in hand, and stomped out into the night. Michael and David chatted for a while and then returned to the spot where the Blackfords had parked their car only to find that Arthur had driven off. David Blackford looked embarrassed.

'I'm sorry about all that, Michael. I suspect that my father is starting to lose his mental faculties. I'm worried about the guns though, and I think they'll have to go. We can't have behaviour like that. Would you mind giving me a lift?'

Michael agreed, and he was relieved that there was no sign of Arthur when he let David out of the car at the Blackford's home in Ashill. Michael promised to get in touch with him once he had finished reading the journal and had traded it successfully. He left David searching for his father and drove the short distance to his hotel. There, he called his ex-wife to reassure her that he still had matters in hand and that he expected to secure Sophie's release the following day. Isobel was still anxious, but she was satisfied that Michael seemed to be making progress and promised him that she would keep the matter private.

Michael rang off. Despite the late hour and his growing fatigue, he knew that he had to read the diary straight away. He rescued a penknife from his rucksack and turned to the old book laid on the desk. This was quite a moment, he thought as he started to work on the lock. It didn't take long, and the catch soon sprung open as the mechanism submitted to his efforts.

Michael opened the leather cover and on the inside leaf he saw Victoria Evans' theatrical message to Flora explaining her gift of the leather-bound journal. Michael breathed a silent thanks to Flora's mentor and skipped past it until he was faced with Flora's handwriting which to his relief was unaffected by sixty years of enforced captivity in a damp dungeon. Michael picked up his notebook and went in search of what he needed to outwit the General. It was contained in two long diary entries towards the end of Flora's written account. They described Flora's secret and once he had read them Michael knew for certain that the diary was a powerful weapon.

Chapter 34

The House Party

December 1938

The domestic staff at Barrington Hall were exhausted by the preparations for the Pendleton's annual Christmas party, but the work was complete, and the Mistress finally seemed to be content. The house was full of seasonal trappings, and Lady Pendleton hoped their guests would bathe in such festive spirit that they would feel it was oozing from the very fabric of the building. First impressions count, she thought, looking at the giant tree standing in the hallway as a welcoming and highly decorated sentry. Elsewhere, each room had been garnished with holly and fir which were crowned with tinsel and edible treats. In the corner of the ballroom, the instruments of a small but highly regarded dance band stood ready to perform. Connecting doors had been opened to allow guests to flit between the dancefloor and a neighbouring dining room that would soon be loaded with the best seasonal fare that she could source. Even the staircase and bedrooms had been finished with subtle decorations all to emphasise the hosts' hospitality and the Pendletons' total commitment to their guests' enjoyment. The only room that was closed and locked was just off the hallway. It was closed to guests because it contained Sir Roland's art collection which was just too valuable for general viewing.

Such was the importance of the event that Lady Pendleton had taken personal control of the preparations. Everything had to be perfect. The guestlist included local gentry whose influence Sir Roland cultivated for a rainy day. Others on the list were important and influential society figures, who the Pendletons wanted to nurture as potential business clients. But above all, it was important to build the family's reputation, so it was crucial that nothing was overlooked. Her personal involvement had made the work of the staff impossible at times as she hounded them by first directing their efforts in one way before changing her mind and redirecting them in another. But, yes, she was now satisfied, and she even directed Mr Denton, the butler, to reward the staff with a small glass of seasonal sherry.

While Lady Pendleton surveyed the decorations, Flora was in Sir Roland's office watching him button up his trousers while she used her handkerchief to rid herself of the evidence of their recent activity. As usual, her visit to his office had started with the pretence that her attendance was voluntary, and as usual the man had initially been full of warm familiarity and witty seduction. However, now that his physical exertions were complete, he had again become distant. She knew he was about to dismiss her with the certain authority of his class, and she fully understood the nature of the gradient that lay between the aristocratic master and his servant. She sighed at the hopelessness of her situation and remembered how her initial excitement at Sir Roland's attentions had quickly been replaced by fear and loathing.

Flora had worked happily at the hall for nearly a year but following the consecutive deaths of her village mentor, Victoria Evans, and then her father, Flora had suddenly found herself without any relatives or close friends. She was lonely, and when the Master eventually noticed her, she was flattered that he seemed to understand her predicament and that he showed a keen interest in her welfare. Soon enough, those brief enquiries of concern became more familiar especially when he learned of her interest in art. While the Mistress had been out for the day, he had summoned Flora and petted her ego with a tour of the various portraits that hung in the reception rooms. Cook had warned her that Sir Roland's attentions were not right, but when he had invited Flora into his office, she had accepted with all the foolishness and adolescent innocence of her age.

In the office, he had told Flora how much he had become attracted to her and how much he enjoyed talking to her about art. It was barrage of false flattery and exploitation which the lonely Flora lapped up gratefully. He made her feel important, and even when he made a clumsy attempt at physical intimacy, she had not resisted him, naively assuming that the loss of her virginity to her master was just a natural extension of her lowly position and a part of growing up. But since that first occasion, Sir Roland had become more demanding and presumptuous, and he had stopped even a pretence that Flora was anything other than his disposable plaything.

But Flora had then taken a decision that would resonate for many years. In the absence of a confidant, she decided to record the affair in her journal. Night after night in her shared room at the top of the house she carefully deployed ink to describe her encounters with Sir Roland. She brushed over the most explicit details of his ruthless disregard for her, but his cruelty was clear to the reader. And she was an especially diligent scribe when it came to recording other conversations that she overheard.

One of these took place a few days before the Christmas house party. She had been cleaning in the corridor near the entrance to Sir Roland's office when she heard voices approaching. One was Sir Roland, and the other was a man she knew from previous visits. He was from the German Embassy, and his name was Karl Haberstock. Flora had recently started to hide from Sir Roland's attentions, and she decided that this was one such moment for discretion.

There was a small broom cupboard in the corridor that was adjacent to Sir Roland's office. It was a bit close, risky even, and she would have to remain completely silent to avoid discovery, but the voices were getting louder and she'd run out of time to make other arrangements. Darting in, she closed the door just in time and noticed a small hole in the wall that had been caused by a picture hook inside Sir Roland's office. The picture and hook had been made redundant at some point, but the hole remained, and she glimpsed the two men as they entered the office and passed beyond her narrow field of view. She couldn't see them, but their conversation couldn't be missed.

Sir Roland knew his visitor well. Haberstock was Adolf Hitler's art dealer, and the man was an excellent source of paintings at good prices. Under Sir Roland's joint stewardship with his brother Maxwell, Pendleton International Art had prospered, but the two brothers hadn't been selective when it came to the provenance of the art they traded. Within some very private and discreet circles, their company had developed a reputation as the vendor of extremely rare and unusual paintings. These paintings often had a shady past but were on sale for private collections that would never be viewed publicly. It was a highly lucrative business, and Sir Roland regarded Haberstock as one of the Company's best suppliers and therefore worth cultivating. As the two men exchanged pleasantries and chatted about the excellent market conditions, it became apparent that Haberstock was abusing his position to skim off some of the profits from Hitler's growing collection. It was a dangerous game to play.

'I just don't understand your liking for this Jewish art, Sir Roland,' Haberstock told his host. 'It's degenerate.'

Sir Roland disagreed. 'Well, we think that one day it may become quite valuable, and this one is for my own private collection.'

'Well. It has certainly taken a lot of effort to get it to you,' Haberstock replied. 'And much risk too which I'm afraid is rather expensive,' he added, getting swiftly to the point. 'This painting was kindly donated to the Austrian state by its Jewish owners who wanted the state to preserve it. I can provide you with a signed document which records their gracious generosity. The Fuhrer was concerned for its safety, and I was instructed to bring it into his private collection where it could be kept safe. Now, I have a friend called Walter Hofer and I paid him to arrange for a copy of the painting to be made. The forgery has gone into the Fuhrer's collection and the original will come to you if we can agree the price.'

Sir Roland blinked. He knew enough about the Nazi Party to know that Haberstock was taking a great risk.' Karl,' he replied anxiously, 'you must be careful. Think of the consequences if you are discovered.'

The German laughed at his concern, and he was pleased that he had probably increased the final agreed price by another ten percent. 'Don't worry, Sir Roland, I have taken steps to ensure that I will never be discovered. Hofer and the forger have since received visitors who have ensured their silence, and the bill of sale I shall provide will show the painting was sold by Hofer's Gallery at 68, Augsburgerstrasse in Berlin. It cannot be traced to me.'

Sir Roland looked at Haberstock and admired the cunning that had been sewn into the deception. It was ingenious.

'And what about price, Karl? Remember I am a regular customer.'

'Well, these arrangements are expensive I'm afraid, Sir Roland, and because war looks likely, I would need paying in gold bullion…'

Flora heard the two men argue for a few minutes, and then agree the quantity of gold that Pendleton would supply. Haberstock promised he would deliver the painting along with the bill of sale when he attended the Pendleton's house party. He ended by reminding Sir Roland that the receipt should be kept safe, and that it would be wise to keep the painting hidden until its provenance had faded into history. Sir Roland promised to comply, and they discussed delivery arrangements until Haberstock's driver arrived to take him back to the German Embassy.

Once the men had left the office, Flora crept out of the broom cupboard and conjured up an excuse for her lengthy absence to a doubtful housekeeper. That evening, she wrote a detailed record of what she had heard. She didn't understand it fully and she knew nothing of the terrible events that were taking place in Europe, but she knew the painting had probably been stolen and she ended her diary entry with a single understated comment: 'This is very wrong!'

Sixty years later, Michael silently agreed and turned the page. He saw that Flora's next entry was about the events of the house party, but that she had written it three days afterwards. When he had finished her grim account, he understood the reason for the delay.

Flora's duty at the Christmas Party was to walk around the house with a tray of champagne. Mr Denton had issued her instructions. She was told to wear a clean uniform and a new white pinafore. She was to be polite; she wasn't to talk to the guests unless addressed and under no circumstances was she to eavesdrop. She was to fade into the background, yet always be available to lubricate the guest's enjoyment with her tray of brimming glasses.

Flora's record of the party skipped over the details of the revelry, and she left it to future readers to imagine ball dresses, the crowded rooms, and all the self-indulgence of the high society event of the year. She merely noted that her instructions from Mr Denton had been clear, and that she had done her best to adhere to them until she was spotted by Karl Haberstock.

He approached her, immaculately dressed in a pristine dinner jacket with a starched shirt sporting a winged collar. As he took a glass from Flora's tray, she noticed that his cufflinks were in the form of discreet swastikas which were the only visible sign of his political leanings. Haberstock knew that British society opinion was divided over the rise of Hitler and his intentions, so he had dressed conservatively for the occasion to avoid giving offence to any of Sir Roland's guests.

His eyes rested approvingly on Flora, and such was his arrogance and presumption that he didn't even try to conceal that he was studying the outline of her body beneath her maid's uniform. His inspection was deliberately long, and she shuddered when he licked his lips as though savouring her flavour. He continued to study her in minute detail, and then finally he looked up into her face and said just one word: 'Nice.'

A familiar voice from the side increased her alarm. It was Sir Roland.

'Nice? Yes indeed, Karl, I see you have found, Flora.' He lowered his voice. 'She is very *nice* to me regularly,' he bragged, as though Flora wasn't there and allowing his emphasis of the word, 'nice' to ensure his meaning was unmistakeable. The recollection of his recent physical activities with Flora stirred Sir Roland's imagination and he smiled as a new and daring idea coalesced. He thought Haberstock was just the kind of man who would like his proposal.

'Karl, we have just concluded an excellent deal this

evening and we need to celebrate. Perhaps Flora can help us to celebrate too. That is: all three of us together,' he added to remove any doubt about what he was proposing. 'She performs well in her service, and you wouldn't mind, Flora, would you?' he added threateningly whilst enjoying the deliberate ambiguity of his words. She gulped in fear, almost dropping the tray and desperately looked around for help. But there was nobody in that house who would intervene on her behalf. Who would believe her? Sir Roland read her mind. 'Don't be foolish. There's nobody coming, Flora.' he said replacing feigned civility with scorn and menace. 'Do exactly what you are told.'

He turned pleasantly to Haberstock. 'What do you say, Karl? The German looked at Flora's outline again as though he was weighing up the value of what lay beneath her uniform. Neither man was homosexual, so the proposed activity would be a shared experience where individual satisfaction would be achieved by the simultaneous exercise of power at the servant girl's expense. Haberstock was immediately aroused by the idea of such unbridled domination, and he smiled pleasantly.

'Do you know, Sir Roland, that kind of celebration sounds like an excellent idea.'

Sir Roland had read his man well. He glanced around furtively and turned to Flora before lowering his voice again.

'Go immediately to my office and wait there for us,' he growled. 'Don't talk to anyone or try to run away. If you do, I will arrange for you to be fed to the pigs. Remember Mary. Do you understand, girl?'

Flora understood only too well. But the thought of what lay ahead filled her with dread. She understood Sir Roland's predilections and she could imagine the sexual acts that the two men were slavishly anticipating. But it was the implied use of violence that really frightened her. Would they beat her too and what would happen to her afterwards? She remembered Mary, the maid who had preceded her, and knew that like Mary she too was just an expendable commodity.

Flora saw the excitement and anticipation in their faces grow when she nodded in capitulation. She walked slowly away with the tray with the feeling that she was now under sentence. Her progress was slow as she wanted to avoid drawing anyone's attention to her journey beyond the margins of the party. The Mistress who was always on the lookout for skiving staff was nearby, but she was engaged in small talk with the Lord Lieutenant, and she didn't notice Flora as she left the hallway or when she stopped to place the tray on a stone ledge just behind the staircase.

Beyond the staircase lay the corridor leading to the Master's office and a library that was closed for redecoration. Right at the end, there was an auxiliary staircase behind a concealed door that led up to the servant's quarters and to the side of that there was the entrance to a large orangery. When she arrived at the office door, the terror at what was about to unfold behind it made her knees weak and tears started to fall. But as she despaired, a distant memory inexplicably rose up and marked the moment that Flora's adolescence gave way to womanhood. It came from an unlikely source, but it was one that she had often seen. It was the opening line of Victoria Evans' words in the front of the diary:

For your lifetime of trials and tribulations that you must face bravely if you are to triumph…

Victoria's preface was part of a longer theatrical exhortation to encourage Flora to record her life in the journal, but the old Lady's opening words now seemed like distant encouragement to face adversity whatever it might be. Was she being brave? No, she decided. It wasn't brave to accept the cruelty that the two men were about to inflict on her, and it wouldn't guarantee her survival anyway. She might only be a servant girl, that was true, but Victoria had believed in her ability to triumph. But only if she was brave. Her resolve started to return, but hearing male voices coming along the corridor she hastily took refuge in the broom cupboard.

Flora sensed that the two men had been discussing the physical practicalities of what they had planned for her, and she was relieved that this part of their conversation had ended by the time they came within earshot. Instead, she heard Haberstock tell Sir Roland how much he was looking forward to this new experience and how grateful he was that his host was facilitating it. She could sense their greedy anticipation. Flora held her breath as the office door opened just beyond her hiding place. The two men entered, and she heard an angry exclamation at her defiance.

'That damn girl. Where the hell has she gone?' Sir Roland shouted as Haberstock stayed silent and looked wistfully around the room. He saw the furniture in a new light as he imagined what might have taken place in the office.

'Right, that's it,' Sir Roland decided. Then he remembered his guest. 'I'm terribly sorry, Karl. Please don't worry. We'll find her and bring her back. She can't have gone far. And when we do…' He left the sentence unfinished hoping that the inferred promise of a future threesome would soften Haberstock's obvious disappointment.

The German looked at Sir Roland. By discussing their shared physical requirements of Flora, the two men had crossed a line of familiarity, and they now shared a secret which he was confident they would try to share again. The legal risk was entirely Sir Roland's as Haberstock had diplomatic protection. So, he shrugged off his physical disappointment and reassured Sir Roland that he would welcome another visit when it was a suitable time.

'Don't worry, Sir Roland. We can certainly try again,' he said optimistically to his relieved host, and then returned to another pressing matter. 'By the way, I have bought you the bill of sale for the painting as we discussed. I came to the party early to escort the painting and personally ensure that it was safely delivered. You will find it crated and stored in the library next door. In the meantime, there is the small matter of payment.'

Sir Roland noted that the business relationship seemed to have survived the disobedience of the servant girl. 'Thank you for your understanding, Karl. I will let you know when she is back….and available. Now about that gold. I have it here for you, ready in a briefcase.'

Flora heard the safe opening, followed by the sound of the catches on the case snapping open as Haberstock looked inside. He didn't need to count the bars as he knew it would be the correct amount, and the latches quickly snapped shut. It was then that Flora heard a new voice advancing down the corridor. It was Lady Pendleton.

'Roland, are you in there? Please don't tell me you're working tonight.' The safe quickly slammed shut. There was the sound of rustling paper being drawn from a pocket. '

What about this?' the German whispered.

'Don't worry,' Sir Roland replied taking the bill of sale, 'I will lock it away later.'

Moments later here was a knock and Lady Pendleton waited. Not even Sir Roland's wife was allowed inside his private office unless invited. He went to the door and opened it.

'Oh, I'm sorry for interrupting,' she said seeing Haberstock beyond her husband and noting the heavy briefcase at the man's side. 'It's just that some of our guests are looking for you, Roland.'

'That's alright, Lady Pendleton,' Haberstock interjected. 'We were just finishing, but I'm afraid I must leave. There is an urgent matter to attend to at the Embassy, and they have asked me to return.'

'Oh, that's a terrible shame, Mr Haberstock,' she

replied, unaware that the two men had originally gathered in the office for a different purpose. However, she was concerned that if a small number of guests started to leave it might provoke a general exodus. Deciding that Sir Roland's presence was crucial for shoring up the party, she ordered him to join her. Their voices soon faded along the corridor.

Inside the broom cupboard, Flora knew she had to leave quickly as it wouldn't be long before a search was raised to find her. Satisfied that nobody was around, she emerged from her sanctuary and started to move to the hidden servant's staircase. She stopped and looked at the office door. She tried the handle and looked in. Everything was as she remembered, but then she noticed the envelope on the desk. It was the receipt for the painting which Sir Roland had been unable to lock in the safe following Lady Pendleton's unexpected arrival. She picked up the envelope and put it inside her pinny. It was only later that she would discover that the receipt was accompanied by an incriminating letter that was intended to be a thankyou note that would be destroyed once read. She picked it up and set in train a series of events that spanned decades.

Chapter 35

Revelations

December 2000

Michael almost wept as he read Flora's account of the party. That poor girl, he thought, and the sheer evil of those two men. How could anyone treat another human being with such casual disregard and depravity? Especially one so young and vulnerable. In Flora's letter to Jocelyn, she had identified Sir Roland as Jocelyn's father, but she had skipped past the terrible circumstances of the conception. These were now clear from her diary.

It made him think of Sophie. She was now a similar age to her great grandmother who had once served drinks at the Pendletons' party. Like Flora, Sophie had effectively been fatherless too, he observed guiltily. And now she was in similar danger from the same family. His family.

As Michael compared the two girls he thought about Flora and how wrong his initial judgements had been. Her actions, especially regarding the children, had at first sight seemed irresponsible and cruel, but in the light of what he'd just read they were quite clearly motivated by maternal instinct and terror. Yes, she had acted irresponsibly at times, but he was certain that the unread parts of the diary would reveal that her behaviour was a consequence of her age, fear and the relentless wartime conditions. More philosophically, Michael recognized that his ancestry search had uncovered the facts of Flora's life but not their context which had only been revealed when he had found the book before him. It was almost as though Flora was next to him, grateful for the opportunity finally to explain.

He thought about Sophie's fate. He still hadn't heard from Rebecca whether her team could mount a rescue operation before the General's deadline expired. Her continuing silence was disturbing. He didn't want to act single-handedly though he would if necessary. He couldn't abandon his daughter, but would the diary be enough to secure her release if he was forced to act alone?

He considered the General and what he wanted. The reputation of Pendleton International Art would be ruined if it became known that the family owned a valuable painting stolen from its Jewish owners and sold to them by Hitler's curator of art. The man's priority would be to save the family and the business. He would want to hang onto the painting but not at any cost. If forced, Michael thought the General would try to get rid of the work by hiding or destroying it. Without a painting, it would be straightforward for the General to refute a servant girl's diary from sixty years ago as the sole evidence of the family's misconduct, especially as the painting was officially deemed to have been destroyed in a fire. He might be able to refute the Haberstock letter too although the General couldn't be sure of that without reading it.

Michael sighed. The Haberstock Letter and Flora's diary together might have been enough to exchange for Sophie but when Flora took the decision to hide the two sources separately, she had made it difficult for her grandson. As matters stood, the only weapon Michael could wield was a servant's account of what had taken place. It was ironic that Sir Roland had been able to abuse Flora because he knew nobody would believe her, and now General Pendleton was likely to rely on precisely the same doubts to avoid justice and preserve his family's dubious reputation.

Michael was especially concerned about what the General might do when Michael told him that he didn't have the Haberstock Letter. He thought the man's first reaction was likely to be disbelief. But what would he do to extract the truth? Michael didn't want to contemplate the answer to that. He knew enough about the General's willingness to reach for the stick, and he had men to help him. But the violence had only ever involved two foot-soldiers. Was that the most he could expect to encounter? Plus the General of course. Michael had no training whatsoever for a physical confrontation that was likely to include the use of weapons, but he needed to know what he was up against. He had to be at Barrington Hall at 3pm but he could go slightly early and scout the area. Hopefully, he would watch Rebecca's men make their assault but if not he would go to the Hall and try to use guile and the diary. It was all he had.

As he considered his preparations, Michael remembered he had promised David Blackford that he would take notes on the contents of Flora's journal before he gave it up to Pendleton. It was a sincere promise made to a man who had just discovered his true parentage but wanted to understand it. Michael understood that wish intimately and so he would keep to his word. It was the early hours of the morning, and he was desperately in need of sleep, but he picked up his notebook and returned to Flora's diary.

Chapter 36

Inferno

December 2000

When Michael finally finished reading Flora's journal, he stowed his pen and tore the used pages from his notebook. He stuffed the notes inside a hotel envelope, addressed it to David Blackford and locked it in the room safe. Michael hoped that one day David would get the chance to read the actual diary for himself, but if it was lost later that day then Michael's notes would hopefully provide a satisfactory record.

Michael had learned a great deal more about his grandmother and her life, but he knew Flora's story was now complete, and he should concentrate on rescuing his daughter. It was early morning, and he wanted to get to Barrington Hall at least two hours before the 3pm deadline. On the way, he would need to stop and buy some more items, but there was still time for a quick nap. He put the 'Do Not Disturb' sign on the door and picked up his phone to set an alarm call. It had been on silent mode since his visit to the byre but there were no missed calls. He lay down hoping that sleep would come soon. It did eventually, but it wasn't restful, and his dreams reflected the dread of what might await him later that day.

***

Three hours after the alarm went off, Michael found a sheltered spot to hide his car about a mile from the entrance to Barrington Hall. He had awoken feeling fatigued, dressed in dark clothes and eaten a plain hotel biscuit he discovered in the room. He was unshaven and might have appeared a bit disreputable to anyone ignorant of his mission. On his way to the Hall, he went to a country outlet where he bought a pair of binoculars and a scarf that could double as a balaclava. He wasn't trained in covert surveillance, but he knew that his white face would stand out against the countryside's muted colours unless he disrupted his outline. It would also protect him from the approaching December frost that was heralded by a sky that was cold and windless.

Michael decided it was too risky to take the journal with him, and so he reluctantly locked it in the boot. If he did need to trade it, the book could be handed over once Sophie had been released and he could be certain that an exchange would be honoured. He had decided to retain the tools he had purchased for his search of the old byre, and he removed the new binoculars from their box and added them to the rucksack. He turned to the map. He had chosen an observation point surrounded by trees on high ground to the west of the hall. He hoped the setting winter sun would blind anyone looking up at his position and that the light would be favourable for him to watch the house and anyone guarding it.

He glanced at his watch nervously. He was approaching the point of no return, and he still hadn't heard from

Rebecca. He decided to call her. At least he could tell her what he was planning to do. He dialled the number. She answered immediately, but the mobile phone coverage was terrible, and though he could recognise her urgent tone, he couldn't make out what she was saying. All he got were a few broken snippets that added nothing to his understanding.

'I can't hear you,' he told her. 'Listen, I'm at Barrington Hall. I don't know if your men are coming, but if nothing happens by 3pm, I'm going in. And, Rebecca, if things work out badly then I'm sorry. I'm sorry that we never really talked about how we feel about each other.' There was some brief crackling from his phone before he ended the call and switched it off.

Twenty minutes later Michael was in position, lying behind a huge Oak that had been uprooted in the storm that had battered the Somerset countryside when Michael and Rebecca had visited a few weeks earlier. As he looked through the binoculars, Michael was pleased that his assessment of the site had been correct. He could see the whole of the front of the house including most of the driveway and the gardens either side. The house was built with a main section and two symmetrical side wings. At the front, two cars had been parked on a gravel turning circle right next to the front door. They were expensive four-wheeled drive vehicles and Michael thought they were probably parked in marked spaces reserved for senior members of the household. As he looked at the front door, he could imagine the hallway, the locked gallery and the reception room the Pendletons had used during his visits. The rear of the house was partially obscured by the high roof, but Michael could just make out the corner of an orangery that looked to be joined on to the main part of the house at the back. Beyond that, the ground rose steeply before levelling off. He was in the ideal spot for observation, and Michael settled down to watch. It was 1.30 pm and there was still no sign of help.

It was 2pm before Michael saw any signs of life. An estate vehicle pulling a small trailer came up the drive and stopped near the gravel turning circle at the front of the house but slightly to one side. It was driven by a young man wearing dark clothes. He had cropped fair hair and there was something about his bearing that made him seem an unlikely gardener. The man got out of the vehicle and started to unload some branches and sticks. As he worked, Michael realized he was building a bonfire. It seemed a slightly strange place for a fire, and he wondered whether his prediction about the fate of the painting was about to become fact. As he pondered the reason for the fire, he heard a twig snap, and he turned his head to see a man standing right behind him. It was the same athletic man he had seen at Smithieson's, and his familiarity suggested he was also the burglar who had cracked Michael's rib. Worst of all, for the second time in less than 24 hours Michael was facing a gun, and this time it was an automatic weapon, and he was in no doubt it was loaded.

'Stay right where you are, Calvert,' the man growled and then made his instruction emphatic by giving Michael a dead leg with a hefty, booted kick to the side of his thigh. Michael breathed out trying to ignore the dull ache, and slightly relieved that his ribs hadn't been targeted again. He thought it was best to stay silent, and he didn't resist as his captor secured his hands behind his back with electrical ties and then searched his pockets. Michael lay very still and felt extremely vulnerable.

The man finished his search, and Michael heard the rasping sound of splitting Velcro as his assailant opened a pocket. A radio. He was reporting in.

'Alpha Three, this is Alpha Two, over. '

'Alpha Two go ahead. '

'Alpha Three, I am in Sector Four. Can you inform Alpha One that his visitor has arrived and I'm bringing him down now.'

'Alpha Two, that's copied. Wilco. Out.'

Down by the house, Michael saw the white face of the man building the fire look up to their position. That must be Alpha Three, Michael thought as he heard Velcro again. The man behind him replaced the radio, searched through Michael's pockets and then told him to get up. It was difficult to comply with bound hands, but encouraged by two further kicks, Michael eventually managed to stagger to his feet. He went down the path as directed, conscious of the automatic weapon that was trained on his back and considered the callsigns he had heard. If Alpha One was the General, then perhaps Alpha Two and Three were the full extent of the General's forces. Unless there was an Alpha Four. Or even Five. He would find out soon.

As they stumbled down the hill, Michael looked around hoping that his capture might provoke a helpful intervention from some hidden force in the bushes, but he could see nothing unusual, and the grounds were silent in the winter sunlight. A few minutes later, they emerged from the trees at the edge of a striped lawn, and they were met by the man who had been building the fire. He was younger, but had the same military bearing, and he clearly deferred to the man behind Michael. He joined the escort, and they marched Michael over the lawn and the gravel to the front door which opened to reveal General Francis Pendleton. He was standing by the doorway beaming with malevolence and expectation. The man behind Michael tossed the rucksack onto the wooden floor of the hallway, and he shoved Michael inside. He staggered and made an untidy arrival before the General. The hallway was just as he remembered, with Sir Roland and other relatives gazing down from their gilded frames high on the wall.

'Mr Calvert. Welcome. But you are early I think, and there was no need to take a circuitous route. The drive would have been fine.' The General paused for dramatic effect and replaced feigned amicability with angry scorn. 'I don't suppose you've heard of electronic surveillance, you pathetic has-been. If a fly tries to step over our perimeter, we know about it never mind a blundering fool like you.'

Michael groaned inwardly. He had never considered the possibility of things like movement sensors or thermal imaging. He really was an amateur challenging the professionals.

The General looked at the two men. 'Well, Hargreaves, does he have it?'

'No, Sir. I've checked his rucksack and searched him. There are no papers, but it looks like he came by car.' Hargreaves dangled the Fiat's car keys.

The General's face darkened at the possibility of defiance, and he turned to the younger man.

'Davidson, go and search the area around Sector Four and find out where he's hidden the car. Search the vehicle and be quick. We need to get on with this.' Davidson ran off with the car key, and moments later Michael heard a quad bike emerge from one of the outbuildings and race off to the west. His heart sank. They were looking for the Haberstock Letter, but they were going to find Flora's journal instead. He crumpled as he remembered that Sophie was depending on him. The General sensed Michael's despondency and decided an interrogation might bear fruit. He leaned over and brought his face close to Michael's.

'Where is it? Where have you hidden that letter? I told you what would happen if you deviated from my instructions. I warned you. Perhaps you need a reminder.' He turned to Hargreaves. 'Fetch the girl,' he ordered.

Michael had to play for time. He was not very good at bluff so perhaps the truth was best.

'Wait! There's no need for that. I'll tell you what I know.' The General nodded at Hargreaves who kept his ground. 'I know you won't like this, General,' Michael said using Pendleton's title in an effort to sound respectful, 'but I don't have the Haberstock Letter. In fact, until you demanded it from me, I thought you already had it. When I came here last time you will recall I was with a woman called Rebecca who I introduced as my research assistant. Well, after I had met my mother in Sweden the three of us retrieved the letter, but we never got the opportunity to read it because Rebecca stole it from my mother's hotel room and made off on a motorbike. Until your phone call, I assumed she was working for you. I think that everything she told me was a lie, so I don't know what she wants, where she is or who she's working for. I think it has something to do with the painting though. The Klimt hanging in there.' Michael's eyes pointed at the door of the locked gallery at the side of the hallway.

The General looked at him with the angry disbelief that Michael was expecting, but Michael also saw something else in the General's face. Something that was new and provided a morsal of hope. Michael saw doubt.

'What do you know about any of my paintings?' the General snapped, revealing the source of his concern. Michael's mind raced as he saw a possible way out of the situation.

'Quite a lot actually. I know that the painting is called Die Musik II. It was taken from its Jewish owners for Hitler's collection, but it was intercepted by a man called Karl Haberstock who sold it to your great uncle. A forged substitute was put into Hitler's store, but it was destroyed by the SS in 1945, so everyone thought the painting was lost when in fact it was only the forgery that was destroyed. I know this because I found some notes in Rebecca's room.' Then Michael added the thrust that he hoped would score a hit. 'Harming me or my daughter is pointless, General, and will just bring the police to your door. The story is already out there.'

Pendleton noted Michael's logic, but he was seething with frustration, and he ignored it. He was astonished that Michael knew so much. But was he telling the truth? How could he have uncovered so much without reading the Haberstock Letter? Who was the woman called Rebecca? There were too many imponderables. He was losing control of the situation, and it was time to start tidying up. The General issued his orders.

'Hargreaves, lock Calvert in the gallery with his daughter and then light the bonfire. I'll decide what to do with them later.'

Michael had bought some time, but only a little. As the General spoke, Michael noticed his eyes trace a path from the gallery door to a trolley that was parked alongside the staircase. He hadn't noticed it before, but he could now see that it carried a large painting already crated up for transportation. The picture was obscured by its wooden protective covering, but Michael knew it must contain the Klimt. All that wood, he thought thinking of the fire.

Pendleton handed a heavy key to Hargreaves who gestured with his gun to the gallery door. The key turned, and Michael was pushed inside. His daughter was sitting bound and gagged in a chair in the far corner. She looked pale but unharmed, and her eyes widened in relief at the sight of her father. Michael tried to send her a look of reassurance, but Hargreaves interrupted their silent exchange by knocking him to the floor. He bound Michael's ankles with more electrical ties and added a gag. The key turned, and Michael was left immobile and wondering how they would escape with their lives. He searched the room for a means of escape, but the windows were barred, and it looked like the door had been reinforced with steel on the inside. It was a stronghold for keeping out unwelcome intruders, and a convenient dungeon for keeping in desperate prisoners. They were trapped and unless help came soon their fate was entirely in the General's hands. Would he decide they were irrelevant and could be safely ignored, or did they need to be silenced?

As Michael wrestled with this unpalatable question, help did arrive and in a surprising form. A key rattled in the lock, the door swung open and in walked Emily Pendleton. She looked at Michael and Sophie and warned them to stay silent with a finger to her lips. She closed the door and locked it, went to a desk in the corner of the room next to Sophie and found a pair of scissors. She had been standing behind the staircase listening to Michael's exchange with her son, and she was appalled. As she sawed at the ties behind Michael's back, she said simply. 'This has gone far enough. I thought this was all about a family matter, I never dreamed the business was involved in such disgusting trade.' She tossed her head at the empty space on the gallery wall where the Klimt had once hung. 'There are things that need putting right but first we need to ensure your daughter's safety. My son has lost his reason. I will hide her while you call the police. Please be careful. I don't like the look of those two men.'

The ties behind Michael's back parted and a minute later, they were both free. Michael hugged his daughter who started to unload the anxiety and distress of her ordeal. Michael stopped her. He couldn't be certain that Emily was telling the truth, but she was releasing them, and she wanted to call the police and that was all reassuring.

'Not now, Sophie,' he said gently. 'There'll be time later, but I want you to go with Emily and hide. Hide well.'

'But what about you?' she protested.

'I'll be fine, please just do what you're told.'

She nodded, trusting her father's judgement. Emily unlocked the door, peered out and they entered the hall. She nudged Sophie and pointed down the corridor that led to the office that had been used by Sir Roland all those years ago.

'There's a way out down there, past the office and through the orangery. I'll take her out through there' she whispered.' She pointed at the reception room next to the gallery. 'The phone's in there.'

Michael's despair gave way to hope as he watched the two women starting to walk past the stairway towards the corridor and the safety that lay beyond. He noticed that the trolly had disappeared, and he turned to the sitting room door but never got the chance to open it as the General's shout intervened.

'Stop!' he bellowed. He was at the front door and this time he was holding a pistol. He had entered unobserved and had immediately appraised the situation. He was furious with his mother, and he waved the gun emphatically. 'Come back here,' he ordered. The two women joined Michael. 'You foolish woman,' he shouted at his mother. 'What are you doing? Where's your loyalty? Do you really think I'm going to let you unpick years of family heritage and destroy our business?'

She looked at him calmly. In the distance Michael heard Davidson returning on the quad bike as Emily addressed her son.

'Francis, listen to yourself. This is not the behaviour of a General. First of all, it's not my heritage, and I disown it completely. I knew that Pendleton International Art was not particular in its dealings but stolen Jewish art? That's disgusting.' Defiance and scornful anger entered her voice. 'You speak casually about family heritage but think of all those millions of poor people who were butchered by the Nazis. Whole families. Their heritage went up the chimneys in the camps, and the possessions that might have illustrated their history were shared out by the very thieves who took their lives so brutally. Their memory was totally extinguished. And you have lied to me, Francis. You, Maxwell and Roland. You all knew that painting wasn't a reproduction. It was the real thing. No wonder you've been so paranoid about the gallery. I want no part off this, and when it's over I want to set things right. It may cost us our reputations and livelihood but it's the correct thing to do. Put that gun down. Enough lives have been lost trying to conceal a lie, and it must stop. Let these people go.'

It was an impressive speech which reverberated with the truth, but Francis Pendleton was having none of it. His mother's intervention was unforeseen, but this was not over yet. If he could destroy the painting and any third-party evidence of Sir Roland's dealings, then any accusations would be pure conjecture. Even if his own mother went to the authorities, he would ensure she would go emptyhanded. He glared at her.

'You don't think I'm going stop because of some sentimental nonsense over events beyond our control. I don't think so, Mother.' Davidson appeared at the door, absorbed the scene before him and made his report.

'I found the car and searched it; I didn't find any letters, but I discovered this in the boot. I think it's some sort of diary.' The General gleamed with satisfaction. The servant girl's diary. So, it hadn't been destroyed in 1946 after all. He looked at Michael scornfully.

'Is this all you had? Did you really think I'd trade it for your daughter?' He dismissed the idea with a snort of derision. 'It can go on the fire with the painting.' He handed Flora's journal to Davidson and turned to his mother. 'You stay here,' he instructed her. 'No. not you two. You're coming with me,' he added, waving the pistol at Michael and Sophie to move them outside.

Michael looked at his daughter's terrified face, and he knew that she had recognized that they were also part of the physical evidence that the General had decided to remove. There was very little time left. A tear fell down her face and Michael felt a compelling need to freeze time and have a final exchange with his daughter. He was desperate to tell her of his love, explain his regret at their estrangement and apologise for his failure to protect her. But he knew they were not going to be granted such an opportunity, so he squeezed her arm, desperately hoping that she would understand the meaning behind his gesture. He also braced himself. He would not allow the General to end their lives so easily.

Outside, they were taken across the gravel to the blazing bonfire which summoned them forward like a beacon. Michael saw Hargreaves and Davidson standing side by side. They were facing him, both armed with automatic weapons and waiting patiently for the General's instructions. On the other side of the blaze, the trolly stood ready to commit its cargo to the flames. The crate containing the painting was still on it and Michael saw that it had been joined by Flora's diary.

The General nodded at the two men. 'Burn the painting and the diary and then bring the estate vehicle,' he ordered. He gestured at Michael and Sophie. 'We'll take them up to the old sawmill and deal with them there.' At this, Sophie's resolve broke, and the General turned in irritation to the sound of her sobbing and grabbed her arm.

It was at that moment that a small dot of red light suddenly appeared on Davidson's chest. There was a loud crack, and the red dot became the entrance hole for a high velocity round that passed through Davidson and into the garden beyond. Davidson dropped wordlessly. But it wasn't just one man, it was two. As his colleague fell, Hargreaves realized something was wrong and he even had chance to look down at a red dot on his own chest before a second loud crack sent him crashing to the ground too. The two men lay together in a growing pool of crimson. Michael had been physically and mentally preparing to defend his daughter, and when the two men were shot it triggered a further rush of adrenaline. He roared in sudden anger and dived towards the General and Sophie. But he never made it. The General saw him coming and fired at him. If the General hadn't been concerned about the unseen sniper, it would have been a more accurate shot, but Michael gasped in dull shock and pain as the 9mm bullet passed through his lower leg and sent him rolling away behind the trolley and the painting. The General considered a follow up shot, but he realized that he would be exposed to the sniper's laser gunsight. He was certain to be the next target, so he left Michael to groan in pain and held Sophie close to him as a shield while the red dot roamed over their enjoined bodies searching for a safe way in.

No further shots rang out, and the General backed slowly across the gravel to the front door chased relentlessly by the red dot for every step of the way. As they backed into the hallway, the General kicked the door closed and shoved Sophie roughly to the floor. He knew he'd lost, but he could still punish Michael for his meddling. That damn journalist he cursed. And Calvert's grandmother, he thought remembering Flora and her blasted diary. If he was going to die, he would take Sophie with him and deliver a lifetime of hurt and regret to the girl's father. General Pendleton couldn't see it, but his thinking was becoming unhinged as he struggled with the idea of defeat. He looked up at the Pendletons gazing down at him from the picture rail and imagined that he had their approval for what he intended to do next. He raised the gun to the terrified girl as she lay cowering and whimpering on the floor but stopped when his mother calmly intervened from somewhere behind him.

'No Francis, that is not the way. Come on. She's just a harmless girl. Have you lost all sense of honour and judgement?' He turned to face her. His mother was stood, slender and graceful looking at him with a mixture of quiet determination and something else that was new. Pity. Pity that he had fallen so far. His anger ebbed away slightly as the idea provoked some badly needed self-awareness. They both knew he was finished. His reputation would be shattered and all he faced was a lifetime of shame and incarceration. The only thing he still possessed was the manner of his death and he wouldn't donate that to Calvert and the rest of his pursuers. His mother sensed his capitulation, but a tear formed as she realized that Francis would never allow surrender to end in captivity. She understood this would be their final parting, but she couldn't bear to say goodbye, so she smiled sadly and simply said,

'Go, Francis. Go and find peace.'

Francis lowered the gun, nodded his understanding and replied calmly. 'Goodbye, Mother.' With that he turned and started to run down the corridor towards the orangery.

Emily came over to Sophie and held out a reassuring hand. 'Come on, dear, it's over now.' Sophie, looked blankly at her, and Emily realized she was in shock. Sophie would need weeks of care after this, but Emily could help her to make a start by taking her to her father. Sophie stood up and the two women went arm in arm to the door. Emily opened it and saw the two dead men, the blazing fire and the painting on its trolly. In the fading sunlight, it made an apocalyptic sight. For a moment, a red light played across Emily's chest, but it disappeared as Michael staggered to his feet from behind the painting and started waving wildly at some hidden presence in the bushes by the edge of the lawn.

'Dad!' Sophie released Emily's hand and rushed over to him as pain and blood loss took hold and he collapsed back into the pool of blood that was gathering at his feet. Sophie looked at his leg. 'Oh Dad! Are you okay?' He smiled back weakly. The bullet had missed the bone and major vessels as it passed through his calf, but the wound was nonetheless substantial. Michael was losing blood at an alarming rate, so she tore a strip off her tee-shirt and wrapped it around his leg to stem the flow. In the distance two men appeared from the trees with rifles slung over their shoulders. They were alert but they walked with an air that confirmed the drama was over. A Range Rover with tinted windows arrived and the men placed their weapons in the boot and calmly got inside the car to wait for the police. They knew that they would be held in custody for a while, but British officialdom would eventually ensure they were released. Two minutes later, a second identical Range Rover came down the drive and stopped near the fire. Michael looked over wondering who had arrived and was pleased to see Jocelyn get out followed moments later by Rebecca. The two women were concerned to find him lying in dark pool of blood.

'Oh Michael,' Jocelyn said as she knelt beside him. 'You should have waited.'

He smiled weakly. 'It's only a flesh wound,' he joked, and then he looked up at Rebecca. He was still angry with her, but he thought of his ex-wife, and he realized that it had to be different this time. It was time to purge the bitterness. He gazed at Rebecca's worried face and asked simply, 'Who are you? Who are you really?"

She was dreading this moment, and said, 'I'm truly sorry, Michael. I misled you over my part in all of this and I have much to explain if you'll let me. But before that, I want you to know that I love you and I will do anything to regain your forgiveness and trust. It's a long story but it begins with a simple fact. My family is the owner of the painting on that trolly. The one which this woman's family helped the Nazis to misappropriate.' She wagged an accusatory finger at Emily who was bracing herself for the tirade that was about to follow.

But Michael stopped Rebecca with his hand. "Rebecca, please wait. I'll listen to your explanation because I want to learn the truth and I'm still hoping that we can develop something meaningful between us. I wonder if you might do the same.' He gestured towards Emily. 'Rebecca, you've met Emily Pendleton before. She's the lady who wants to help you get your painting back.' Rebecca looked confused and then suddenly she understood Michael's point. She nodded at Emily and smiled as distant sirens grew louder. The two women had much to discuss.

As they waited for the police to arrive, Arthur Blackford was sitting on a tree stump on the high ground overlooking the rear of the house. He was rocking rhythmically, while mumbling to himself and making unintelligible threats. Since his encounter with David and Michael at the byre, his dementia had suddenly deteriorated as a series of new blood vessels had become blocked in the frontal lobe of his brain. This was not a new phenomenon; it had been going on for several years. But in the last twenty-four hours Arthur's powers of cognitive reasoning had declined markedly. There had also been a dangerous change of character too. He had lost all powers of judgement and his lifelong obsession to achieve justice for his father had become all consuming. After arriving at home from the byre on the previous night, he had retrieved some cartridges so that when he left again it was with a gun that was now properly loaded. He had driven to Barrington Hall and parked in an old quarry that was outside the area of the Pendletons' surveillance. It was pure chance that he avoided detection as he took up position above the rear of the house. Arthur had sat there for hours, his condition worsening by the minute as the cold and a lack of food took its toll, but eventually a movement caused Arthur's chanting to pause. Down below, General Pendleton had just emerged from the Orangery, and he was starting to walk up the hill. He was carrying a pistol, but he gave no indication that he was out for anything other than an evening stroll. In fact, Francis Pendleton was intent on taking his own life and he had a particular place in mind for ending it.

But his route to the chosen spot took him past Arthur. As the General approached, the old man stopped rocking and looked at him. Within Arthur's mind, a spark of recognition lost its way as it tried to navigate the old man's damaged neural pathways, and the message became corrupt. In his confusion, Arthur thought Francis Pendleton was Sir Roland. That idea provoked unrestrained rage as Arthur's obsession reasserted itself. He began rocking and chanting again but with increased urgency as his mind tried to rationalise the situation. The General vaguely recognised the old man, who was clearly deranged, and he tried to reason with him. But he spoke to Arthur like a child which seemed to infuriate the old man even more. Suddenly, the rocking and mumbling stopped and in an unexpected moment of apparent clarity, Arthur looked up at Francis, smiled, and said simply: 'This is for my father.' He then raised the shotgun and shot Francis Pendleton in the face.

In front of the hall, the first police cars had just appeared on the drive as Arthur's shot pierced the still evening air with a sound that suggested finality. Emily Pendleton understood its significance, and she lowered her head as a sob broke cover and tears of grief for her son began to fall. Realization eventually dawned on the others too, but they were all uplifted when Sophie left her father's protective embrace to sit next to Emily and put a comforting arm round her. Emily: The very woman whose son had come within a whisker of killing Sophie not even an hour earlier. Michael was so proud of his daughter that his own eyes turned watery.

The first police car pulled up and an astonished sergeant got out and struggled to take in the dystopian scene before him as he tried to describe it on the radio. Before long, more officers arrived, and they were all held in the ballroom and questioned separately. Michael's wounded leg had been treated in an ambulance as he was adamant that he wouldn't leave his daughter to go to hospital. He remembered the final shot, and suggested to a policeman that they should search the rear of the grounds too. Half an hour later, a slow procession came past the ballroom. A shrouded trolley moved Francis Pendleton on his final journey, followed by a policeman gently escorting Arthur, who was wrapped in a blanket. When the police had found them, Arthur was sitting next to Francis contentedly rocking and mumbling. The police ordered him to drop the shotgun which he did without argument, and they didn't bother with cuffs. Michael was glad they were treating the old man gently, as he watched them take Arthur away to spend the remainder of his life in a secure hospital.

The questioning went on for several hours, but eventually a man wearing a grey suit arrived and had a quiet conversation with the senior investigating officer who seemed grateful that the matter was being taken out of his hands. The suited man stood in the ballroom and informed them that he was from the Home Office, and they were all to be released including the armed men in the Range Rover. Michael suspected that the police investigation had been terminated by hidden hands in Whitehall and that the matter would stay quietly shelved while ownership of the painting was quietly settled, and any national embarrassment neatly side-stepped.

As the police started to pack away their interest, Michael started to feel dizzy, and he finally capitulated to the paramedics' demand that he received hospital treatment. As they loaded him into the ambulance, he realized that Flora's secret had finally been told. He had tossed a pebble into the sea of history, and the disturbance had exposed a series of dark events that, with Flora's help, the truth had overcome. The waters were already starting to settle, but the ripples had sufficient energy for one last surprise although it would be another two months before Michael encountered it.

Epilogue

February 2001

The number of people who gathered at Flora's grave on the second anniversary of her death was more than twice those present when she was first laid to rest. Her well-tended plot was in a quiet spot at the far end of the cemetery in Warrington, and it bore an unremarkable headstone that seemed at odds with Flora's remarkable life.

Michael leaned on a stick as he glanced around at the group of people standing with him in respectful silence. They had all been complete strangers, but Flora had brought them together not as a close-knit family but as a group of individuals with a shared heritage. That heritage had affected them in different ways, and in some cases, profoundly so.

The final events at Barrington Hall marked the end of Flora's mystery but the start of a new chapter for those that she had touched. In a way, it seemed that Flora's heritage had lain in the future not the past. Michael was glad that she had achieved a measure of peace in the latter part of her life, and he regretted that he had never met her. Three of her six children stood together nearby. Jocelyn had spent most of life resenting her mother, but her anger had been fuelled by assumptions rather than the facts.

Flora's diary had eventually filled in the gaps, and Michael was pleased that Jocelyn's hatred had given way to understanding. It was a poignant lesson, particularly for anyone considering an investigation of their family tree. Michael had read about an American company that was creating a computerised database containing the DNA of subscribers. The information would be supplemented by other sources like the official record of births, marriages and deaths that Michael had used, but also other information gleaned from parish records and newspapers. One day, the system would be fully automated, and it would provide an instant family tree including unexpected family secrets. But it couldn't provide any historical context. No computer could determine the reasoning or the feelings of distant relatives as they made their life decisions, and it would be left for their descendants to imagine their motives. Such conjecture could easily result in poor judgement and even distress as those searching the past created imaginary images of their ancestors that were built on sand.

Flora's second child, Andrew, was standing with Jocelyn. Michael had not yet spoken to the man who, like Jocelyn, had been evacuated during the war and later fostered. Michael looked forward to hearing about his life, and his presence at Flora's graveside indicated that he was interested to learn more too. Finally, he could see David Blackford. He had probably been affected the most by recent events because he had discovered a mother but then lost his father to the confines of a secure psychiatric hospital. David was now living alone but he didn't need to be lonely, Michael thought, looking at the assembled group.

Three of Flora's children were absent. Agnes was living concealed by the anonymity of adoption and would only emerge if she decided to follow Michael's path and chose to discover her past. And there were also the two girls, Marilyn and Carol Wainwright. Michael knew their full names and he could easily find them, but Flora had always wanted some peaceful stability in her life, and it seemed fitting to leave her final two children in ignorance of their mother's turbulent past. So, Michael had reluctantly filed their details leaving the two women unmolested by history unless chance or their curiosity brought them out into the open.

Michael thought about himself. His adoptive mother had hoped for a change in his outlook when she had sent him off on a voyage of self-discovery. The evidence of her successful intervention was at the rear of the group where his ex-wife, Isobel, stood with their daughter. They still spoke a little awkwardly, but it was without bitterness or reproach and Michael had invited Isobel, nonetheless. And that marked a new approach. Beside him, he felt Rebecca take his arm, and he smiled at her. Forgiveness had other advantages too. She had misled him, but the facts were healing, and as the poison of his old ways drained away, it was suddenly a simple matter to forgive Rebecca and to plan a shared future.

It would be a more positive life too, he thought, as he glanced at his daughter who was standing respectfully at the back. Sophie had recovered well from her ordeal, and Michael was enjoying renewing their relationship after several years of neglect. Sophie had developed a close relationship with Emily Pendleton who was also present. Emily had kept her word, and the legal arrangements were being made to transfer ownership of the painting to Rebecca's mother who owned the New York gallery that would house it.

Emily intended to wind up Pendleton International Art and create something more positive, and in an act of contrition she had approached Jocelyn and shyly sought her advice. Jocelyn was initially confused, but then realized that the two women were now related though their ties had been imposed in a dreadful manner. They had come up with an idea for an institute for the restitution of stolen art, and they were starting to make the necessary arrangements to found it. They had asked Michael to be Head of Investigations, and he had been delighted to accept. Michael had grown fond of Jocelyn and later that month he was returning to Sweden with her to meet the rest of her family.

Michael paused to marvel at the complexity of the relationships that his search had released, and how they seemed to multiply as they branched out into the future. He felt Rebecca relinquish his hand as the group started to disperse. Michael indicated that he wished to stay for a few moments longer, so she joined the others as they made their way down the slope and towards the exit. As they came to the gate, two women came the other way carrying fresh flowers, and both groups exchanged brief smiles as they passed by. The new arrivals continued up the slope towards the grave they were seeking and found a stranger leaning against a stick in quiet contemplation. They noticed the pile of fresh flowers and confusion spread across their faces. The older one stepped forward,

'Hello. May I ask who you are?'

Michael turned and looked into some intensely blue eyes. He paused and then held out his hand. 'Hello. My name is Michael Calvert. And I'm certain that you must be Marilyn and Carol.'

***

Historical Note.

Although this book is a work of fiction, some aspects of it are based on fact. During the 1930s, senior Nazi officials were actively seeking out Jewish artworks that they publicly described as "degenerate" but which they either kept for their own private collections or traded on the international market as a source of foreign currency. They formed a special unit for the collection of political material in the occupied countries for exploitation as propaganda in the "struggle against Jewry and Freemasonry". Goering extended the authority to include the confiscation of "ownerless" Jewish art collections and made this the primary mission which he exploited for his own personal gain. The unit included art experts, such as Haberstock and Hofer, and also historians. Sadly, many of the Jewish owners of these paintings were forced to give up their collections, and those that were unable to leave before the outbreak of war, later perished in the camps. It is true that some of Klimt's important works, like Die Musik II, were stored at the Schloss Immendorf, and that they were destroyed by the SS in the face of the advancing Russian Army in 1945.

The history of art restitution is somewhat chequered, and, even today, there are several important paintings of questionable provenance still hanging in the national art galleries of certain central European capital cities.

The Author and his Readers

I was born in Tanzania, but I have lived most of my life in the United Kingdom. At various times I have sold motor spares, served as an RAF fighter pilot and farmed the land.

To the reader, I offer my thanks for reading Dangerous Heritage. It is my first novel, so if you have enjoyed the story please help me to improve my writing skills by leaving a constructive review.

I shall take comfort from the fact that you have made it this far!

Printed in Great Britain
by Amazon